DEMON CLAIMED

SKYE MALONE

DEMON CLAIMED
Book Three of the Demon Guardians Series
by Skye Malone

Copyright 2020 - Skye Malone

Published by Wildflower Isle
P.O. Box 129, Savoy, IL 61874
www.wildflowerisle.com

ISBN-10: 1-940617-52-9
ISBN-13: 978-1-940617-52-7

Library of Congress Control Number: 2019906630

Cover design by Karri Klawiter
www.artbykarri.com

Proofreading by Monica Bogza
www.trustedaccomplice.com

Find out about all new releases:
Join Skye's mailing list at skyemalone.com/mailinglist!

1

KYLE

Much more of this, and the screams are going to give him a migraine.

But at least this time they don't last long.

The body thuds to the floor. Schooling his face into nonchalance, Kyle turns, tucking away his cell phone. From across the expanse of the old barn, Penny grins at him. That redheaded teenage psychopath is enjoying this. She enjoys all of it.

He figures she's probably making up for lost time.

"Done?" he asks, making certain his voice sounds polite rather than bored senseless with the never-ending carnage.

She treats him to a pouty look, but like the screams, it's also short-lived. "Oh, come on, silly." Her blue eyes shine. "You know you're loving this."

He doesn't argue. He's a strategist, not an idiot. Penelope "Penny" Campbell is an eighteen-year-old lunatic who burned her entire family alive and made cookies to eat while she enjoyed the event. Before she was turned into a Touched and then turned back by Cait only a few weeks ago, she'd spent years locked up in an institution. Her typical mental state could best be described as somewhere between a petulant toddler and Vlad the Impaler reborn, and if there's one thing he's understood after weeks of attempting to corral the bloodthirsty habits of this psychic Pollyanna from hell, it's that her temper and her favor are as mercurial as a yo-yo in a hurricane.

"Of course I'm loving this," he agrees. "But we need information, and I don't see how those people had any. We could be making progress elsewhere."

Penny sighs, swiping the bloody knife across the stained clothes of the corpse. It doesn't help much; there's blood everywhere. "I *told* you, my methods aren't always a straight line, and the visions come and go. I can't guarantee when I'll get one or what will make them happen."

"Then, perhaps we should change tactics."

Her patient expression dies in an instant, replaced by anger like that of a child who's been threatened with the loss of her favorite toy. "No."

Shit.

She turns away, looking down at the corpse of her latest victim. Some demon. A woman, if he remembers correctly, though it's been several hours since his people dragged her in, and Penny's been having fun with knives ever since. The demon hasn't been recognizable as much more than human-shaped for a while. He can't even recall if he heard what House she came from.

That is if anyone even bothered to tell him.

He keeps his face still, giving no hint of the myriad ways he's imagined taking knives to the redhead across from him over these past few weeks. This isn't what he'd pictured when she sauntered into his bedroom with a shotgun in the middle of the night, offering him the chance to rule the world. The teenage nutjob is more than a few crayons shy of a full box, but he still thought he could control her. Instead, she managed to charm half his allies within seconds of being introduced to them, and now they do pretty much anything she wants. The rest are scared of her, he's certain. But either way, she's damn near taken over in the short time since she showed up.

Now, she sends his people on clandestine missions to who knows where. She orders them to bring in House allies, neutrals, or any number of people without a trace of an explanation why. She even has a growing assortment of Touched now, collected from around the nation and turned by the incubi and succubi he'd worked his ass off to sway to his cause. The Touched haven't shown signs of any magic abilities like hers, though she insists they'll be useful regardless. The entire howling, chittering mess of them are now locked in various storage locations around town, a rabid menagerie of pets for a ginger psychopath.

He supposes it's progress—*some* manner of progress—though who the hell knows what kind. But not once has that redheaded bitch bothered to clear it with him. The idea never even seems to cross her mind. And it's not like he can go ask his underlings for the information; that would look pathetic. No, he has to play along like he has a clue of what she wants with this person or that location or anything at all.

Instead of being more in the dark than any of them.

Rage twitches over his face before he can wrestle it back under control. This isn't how it was supposed to go. He'd planned. He'd strategized. He'd fought and clawed and scraped his way from being the Legacy by-blow of some low-level waste of a succubus to being a spy for the

Mistress of House Volgert herself. For years, he'd worked in secret, putting the pieces in place for the coup that would let him take his rightful position as the leader of the demonic rabble, the first Legacy to rule a House in almost six hundred years, and thus, he is the *last* person to let some manipulative brat throw him off his game. But he'd burned nearly every bridge he had in order to get his hands on the annoying little bitch—and that was *before* she waltzed into his bedroom in the middle of the night and offered him the whole damn demon world on a platter— and pissing her off now would only result in her figuring out a way to go work for somebody else. He isn't a fool. He knows his control of her is tenuous, though it's still better than anyone else's. And the gods know that if he had his way, he would have gotten whatever visions he could out of her and then killed her annoying ass *ages* ago.

Assuming, of course, she hadn't already seen that coming.

She looks over her shoulder at him, and he buries any trace of expression as fast as he can. He never knows how much she sees, *what* she sees, or when she might make him pay for it. Any slip could cost him everything to a girl who is truly little more than a psychic ticking time bomb.

Her lip cocks in an impish smile. He's forgiven. Or she's decided to kill him. Magic tangles through his veins while he waits to learn which it'll be.

"You're frustrated," she says. "I understand. Really, I do. But you have to trust that this is for the good of *both* our plans. You'll have your chance at Lucretia. At all of them. When this is done, you'll rule any House you want. So don't worry, mm-kay? I have everything under cont—"

Penny gasps, and her eyes go wide while she staggers, one hand grasping at her throat. The other flies out, barely catching her when her knees buckle, sending her crashing to the wood-slat floor.

Kyle's eyebrow twitches up. *Well, this is interesting.*

"I...I see them," Penny chokes out. "Th-they're coming..."

His lip curls upward, his curiosity vanishing into anticipation. *Finally.* This is why he wanted to find her. This is why he put up with the lunacy and the sadism and the general annoyance of her presence. The visions. The thing that makes her the best damn weapon he could ever hope to get his hands on.

Penny's eyes snap up to meet his. Her pupils are large, too large. They nearly swallow the blue of her irises. And there's a look on her face like her words mean life or death. "The poison is working. The one that hid for years is found. The liar plays games, but I see them! I see them! It's all right there and...and...and..."

"And *what*?"

Her expression becomes more intense. Veins stand out on her forehead, and her eyes are so wide, he can see the white all around them. Short gasping noises escape her while she fights to get the words out. "The...convergence...comes."

Penny sags toward the floor, breathing hard. Her pupils shrink back to normal. The vision is gone.

He stares at her. "*Huh*?"

2

CAIT

"You *sure* about this?" I ask.

Sorcha adjusts her grip, bracing herself, and nods. "Yes."

"Oh, for gods' sakes," Bianca says without even glancing up from her cell phone. Pink gemstones encrust the case, a shade lighter than her Barbie-pink nails. Her blond hair shines, perfectly brushed and glistening under the glare of the warehouse lights. "Just do it already. It's not that hard."

Gritting my teeth, I ignore her. A breath enters my lungs.

A burst of purple lightning flashes across the room, heading for the auburn-haired werewolf. Sorcha dodges fast, bringing her makeshift shield of a rubber garbage can lid with her. Before I can even finish registering the thought, the lightning darts after her, tearing across the concrete room like it has a mind of its own.

The electricity strikes her shield, and she drops it with a yelp.

"Are you okay?" I call, worried.

Shaking her hands as if they sting, Sorcha nods while she surveys the smoking surface of the garbage can lid. "You're doing better. I was nearly going full speed that time."

"Yeah, it was brilliant," Bianca cuts in. "Except you didn't move at *all* while you were attacking, which means you're dead. The enemy shot you or whatever."

I wince. Moving. Right. Never mind that I'm using magical powers I didn't know I *possessed* a short while ago—magical powers that might run out at any time if I don't keep my strength up. I'm doing okay, given that I've spent the past few weeks surviving off of whatever energy I could get from hanging around the edges of the sparse crowds at Temptation. There aren't very many people to feed from yet at the nightclub, thanks to the "bombing" that was actually the magical blowback of Kyle breaking through their security several weeks ago. Regardless, feeding off the ambient sexual energy in the air around the dance floor isn't the same as what I'd get from sleeping with someone—a fact Bianca never hesitates to point out.

It's still overwhelming. I'm being trained by a succubus to attack a werewolf with magic. Some days, I wonder if I'm going to wake up and discover this has all been some insane dream.

I exhale. "Yeah. Right. Moving. Got it."

Bianca scoffs. I bite back a scowl.

"Go again?" Sorcha offers while she picks up the garbage can lid from the concrete floor.

I nod and then catch sight of the makeshift shield. Starbursts of soot blacken its center. I think I see some holes in it too. "Do we need another—"

An alarm starts beeping.

"Or not," Sorcha amends dryly.

I sigh while I draw out the phone and turn off the noise. Habit born of the past few weeks makes me check for messages, though I already suspect what I'll see. Nothing. No returned calls. No texts. Not even an email. My best friend, Ruby, has been radio-silent since she left town on the heels of us rescuing her from the Houses, and only the fact that the bodyguard Amar hired for her hasn't sent up a distress signal reassures me she might still be okay.

It's all I've got. It's not like she's answered a single one of my dozens of calls.

I shove the phone away, burying my disappointment as best I can, while Sorcha drops the garbage can lid and retrieves her bulky leather jacket from the corner. Even without the thing, the woman looks like a biker: all muscle and rough skin. Hell, she looks like she could snap someone in half, and that's without bringing into it the fact she's a werewolf.

I've never had a bodyguard before, but I know from the past few weeks, she's a damn good one.

Together, we walk to the sheet-metal slab that forms the door. Bianca is already there, rolling it aside as if she's done with us. Half a dozen bikers fall in around us the moment we leave the old warehouse—other members of Sorcha's mercenary pack, hired by Amar. I'm certain more bodyguards lurk nearby, probably put in place by Katsuro. The vampire leader of the Guardians is nothing if not thorough, it turns out, even if I haven't seen him in weeks. He took off a day after Penny's escape, leaving Blue and Leaf —the other two vampires I know—to watch over things here. They tell me he's attending to our safety, whatever the hell that means. But regardless, I've caught sight of more and more demons I recognize from his secret society as the weeks have gone by, watching me from the shadows at his orders.

I wish it weren't necessary—and that I could shake the ever-present anxiety that I'd hear them shout and all hell would break loose. It could be Penny. It could be a House. There was no way to predict which one of them would come after us—after *me*—first.

But I don't want to run. My dad is here. He's been sick since I was a kid, and bedridden for years with some wasting illness no doctor can identify, let alone fix. Moving him might kill him, and I'm not going to leave him here unprotected while I run for the hills. And that doesn't even start to address how hard it'd be to convince my stepmom or stepsisters to go.

Besides, Penny isn't perfect. She obviously can't see *everything,* or else we'd all already be dead. Meanwhile, Volgert and Linden have both gone totally quiet after their budding attempt at a war—a fact the others find disturbing and I just hope means the threat has passed. Yes, they could still come after me; that's why I have the bodyguards. That's why I've asked the Guardians to put a bunch of those people on watching my dad and my step-family. I apparently have a power they want: the ability to read whether people are lying or not, which would come in handy in their world of assassins and spies. But until I know for certain that they're still after me, I'd just as soon stay where I stand a chance of protecting my father.

And Amar.

My shoulders shift with discomfort, shrugging away the thought. I need to talk to him. I know that. And I will… eventually. But right now, he needs to rest. He's still recovering from the bullet that nearly took his life, after all. So it's not like this is the best time for an in-depth conversation about the fact he can kill people with barely more than a glance.

I'm being patient. It's not the same as avoiding him.

We reach the cars, and without a word, Bianca gets into hers and starts the engine. God knows why she's stuck around town. From all I've heard, she's got tons of evacuation plans in place for getting the hell out of Corvinson. She just hasn't followed through on any of them. I'm kind of glad, though. At least she's teaching me how to use these powers, even if she can be a pain in the ass.

I glance at Sorcha while Bianca drives away. "Tomorrow?"

She nods.

"You sure you're okay?" I press.

Her lip twitches. "Takes more than a jolt of magic to damage me, Cait."

I smile at the humor in her voice, relieved.

"You did good today. Remembering to move can be the hard part, kind of like doing two things at once. But the magic will become instinctive, and it won't take up so much concentration. Just give it time."

My smile turns grateful. "Thanks."

She nods again. I climb into my car while she heads for her bike to follow me.

The campus is already filling with students by the time we arrive. Most of the bikers have already broken off to find parking where they can. Like every day, Sorcha will stay close while the rest linger in the crowd to keep an eye on me. Over the past few weeks, the werewolves have endeavored to blend a bit more than they did at first, if only to keep the humans around us from raising an alarm at their continued presence. A few of them are wearing campus gear now, instead of their leather jackets, while others are toting backpacks.

I doubt the guises are really working, although at least no one has called campus security yet. But between their Viking-warrior size and their expressions like they chew rocks for fun, they're the kind of people who get noticed— if only so you can cross the road to avoid them.

But then, that's the point. Their presence is a warning, to demons anyway. They're here to make the Houses, or whoever else comes after me, wonder how many other bodyguards they *haven't* seen. They're here as a silent, ever-present threat to any of the countless monsters who could be lurking around me...even now.

I hate this.

My eyes skip across the other students in my lecture hall while the professor drones on about some principle of data management or another. It's difficult to concentrate; anyone in the room could be a demon. I mean, Amar and Bianca are, and they attend school here. How many more might be out there? How many more are just waiting for the chance to grab me, to hurt people I love? It's not like I can tell them apart from anyone else. No one can, except for humans who used to be Touched. I thought I might be able to get around that, considering this odd "gift" of mine.

But no. Unfortunately, my weird people-reading power doesn't work that way, though God knows why. My only guess is that, while lately I can usually tell when people are lying, demons aren't doing that. Not by having jobs and lives in the human world. They really *could* be bus drivers or business executives or whatever and simply happen to be demons as well. So until they actually lie about *being* human, I'm just as in the dark about whether the person in front of me is a demon as anyone else might be.

God, what a loophole.

I drag my attention back to the front of the class. At the base of the stadium-like seating, the professor is gesturing to the board with a laser pointer. There's a smudge of green ink on the sleeve of his pale blue button-down shirt. Sprigs of red hair stick out wildly around the bald spot forming on his head. His brown plastic-framed glasses sit atop his head, reflecting the overhead lights in brief flashes like they're sending signals to the mothership.

I wonder if he could be a demon too.

Burying a frown, I look back to my notes. Or where my notes would have been, had I taken any. If this keeps up, I might fail this class, considering how little I've paid attention recently.

I rub a hand over my eyes, cursing myself silently. I have to stay focused. Life will get back to normal eventually.

Unless it doesn't.

My hand clenches on my pen. It *will*. Or else I'll figure something out. Come up with a way to protect my dad and stepfamily somehow.

I just need a plan.

Nothing presents itself by the time class ends, same as it has been for weeks. I don't know how to do the magic that puts a Protection around anyone. Bianca laughed when I suggested she teach me to do it. The technique is complex. Do it wrong, and you'll end up addicting the person to your power and making them into a Touched. I had no idea it was that complicated when Amar did it for Ruby.

And without Amar to help me now…

I shove my things into my bag and rise to my feet. I'll figure something out. He still needs to rest.

"C-Caitlin Faire?"

I freeze, my attention snapping to the front of the lecture hall.

"May I—" The professor's laser pointer slips from his grasp. He fumbles after it while it clatters on the ground. "May I speak with you?"

"Um..." I glance over my shoulder to the lecture hall door, and relief hits me when I see Sorcha there. Several other bikers slip past the door behind her. They take up positions along the wall, and their eyes track the handful of students still making their way out of the room.

"I'm sorry," I call to the professor. "My friends and I have somewhere we need to be."

"Your..." He visibly struggles to pull his attention away from the bikers and back to me. "Th-this is important, Caitlin. It's about last week's assignment. It raised a number of red flags, and before I speak to the dean, I want your side of the story."

Alarm shoots through me. The dean? Why would he need to speak to—

I make myself draw another breath, trying to stay calm. I don't even know what he's accusing me of. "What do you mean?"

He flounders through his papers, finally retrieving one of them and then holding it up. I keep myself from moving closer. This could still be a trap. What *kind*, I don't have a clue, but that's not the point.

I look back to Sorcha. She starts down the stairs toward me, a wary expression on her face. Behind her, the other bikers fan out. A few students have stopped, their attention drawn by the professor's words, but when they see the muscular mercenaries coming toward them, they reconsider and make a beeline for the door.

"The assignment wasn't supposed to be collaborative." The professor tries for a stern look, though it's marred by the way his eyes keep twitching to Sorcha and the others. "And it was certainly not supposed to be an exact replica of a project *I* personally developed."

My mouth drops open. That can't be right. My abilities are telling me that *somehow* he's not lying, but…but still. "Professor McCleary, I didn't—"

"Caitlin, I understand my class can be difficult. I understand people can make mistakes. But what I want to know is how did you manage to find my—"

I don't wait for more. This has to be some kind of trick. Turning fast, I head up the steps toward Sorcha while the last of the other students disappear out the door.

"Young lady!" Professor McCleary snaps. "I *will* speak to the dean about—"

"Cait, stop!" Sorcha cries.

I slam to a halt while the air suddenly burns to life ahead of me, cracking and humming like I've nearly walked into an electrical field. I stumble back, barely avoiding tripping on the stairs.

"What is this?" Sorcha demands from a few steps above me. "Why have you—Stay where you are!"

The last is frantic, harsh, and totally directed at me. I'd started to move toward the weird feeling in the air.

I freeze, hardly daring to breathe.

"Do *not* come closer." Sorcha scans the lecture hall fast. It's only me, the werewolves, and the professor in here.

And he's staring at us like we've lost our minds.

"I asked you a question," Sorcha snaps at him.

He shakes his head. "What's *what*?"

"The barrier, you bastard!"

"Barrier?" His eyes dart around the room. "I-I don't—"

Behind him, another door opens. My whole body goes cold.

Alistair Linden walks in. Dressed in a charcoal suit with his gray hair shining under the bright lights, the old man looks like he could be here to deliver the lecture for the next class. Four others come with him, and people-reading power be damned, I know they have to be demons. It's in the way they look at me. In the smirking confidence with which they're eyeing the half-dozen were-wolves pacing the perimeter of whatever the hell is behind me.

The professor's relief is instantly apparent. "Mister Linden, oh thank—" He looks back at Sorcha and the others. "These people, they're—you told me I wouldn't have to deal with this sort of—"

"That'll be all, James," Alistair interrupts pleasantly. He doesn't take his eyes from me.

The professor falters. "You did all this?"

One of the demons gives him a brief look as if the answer is obvious. The professor nods like he's trying to regroup. "Oh. Um, okay. But they're—and she's—that's my *student,* and she's a—"

"We're well aware of what they are," Alistair replies.

Professor McCleary looks baffled. "But you *promised* you'd keep me away from—"

Alistair's lips tighten, and the professor cuts off, a panicked look flickering over his face. The demon closest to the old man motions sharply, and the professor scurries over, casting anxious glances back to us while he goes.

"My apologies," Alistair says, ignoring the pair while they disappear beyond the door. "James had a rather unpleasant introduction to demonkind before we brought him back from being Touched. It's left him rather jumpy."

"What do you want?" I demand.

He smiles. "It's a pleasure to see you again too, Cait. I trust the situation with your kidnapped friend was sorted out?"

I don't respond. He already knows the answer: how we damn near blew up Volgert's death match to save Ruby from being one of the Touched.

"And Amar?" Linden persists. "How is he faring these days? I heard he recently suffered a nasty accident."

My blood starts to boil.

"So much trouble you've been having lately," he continues. "Perhaps it's time we revisit the offer of my assistance?"

"Is *that* what this is?" I nod toward the weird feeling in the air without taking my eyes from him.

"Oh, that is simply a necessary measure, I'm afraid. Subtle as it is, your wolves would still have smelled the barrier oil if we'd put it nearer to the door, and then we never would have succeeded in getting you into this room. As it stands, I'm sure your other bodyguards have already been informed of this situation and are hurriedly attempting to contact your..." He chuckles. "...*interesting* friend."

My eyes narrow. Interesting friend?

"We do have quite a bit to discuss, Cait. Your place in this world, the fact that you as good as accepted my offer to join House Linden when your friend was in danger, and the rudeness of your break-in that resulted in the loss of my psychic and a substantial delay in my plans. I think we need to examine those things, wouldn't you agree?"

I cast a quick look at Sorcha. On the other side of the

invisible barrier, she's watching Alistair as if, the moment the defense drops, she's going to rip his throat out.

He doesn't even glance her way. "I hear you've learned the identity of your demonic parent, Josephine."

My eyes flash across the doors, the other bikers, and back to Alistair. I don't know what he's after, but I don't care. This feels like a game. Like he's killing time, waiting for something.

I don't want to be here when it comes. "How do I get past this, Sorcha?"

The woman's teeth grind, but I can tell from her expression, she's not sure.

"Your mother was an agent of House Volgert, correct?" Alistair continues as if I hadn't spoken. "Regretfully deceased these many years?" His smile reminds me of a jackal. "Or so I'm sure they told you."

My confusion returns. I try to hide it.

From his expression, I can tell instantly that I failed.

"You've been lied to, my dear. Your mother is alive. In rather dire straits, unfortunately, but very much alive."

I stare at him.

"What?" Sorcha demands from behind me.

I'm grateful. Her voice breaks my paralysis. "Bullshit."

Alistair's smile becomes amused. "Do you know what my talent is, Cait? Reading people. Not like you, of course. I don't have *that* magical gift. But I *am* over a thousand years old, and I've seen many people attempt to lie to me in that time." His eyebrow rises. "Rather like you are now. You're scared, not disbelieving, because you would also know if I was not telling you the truth."

My insides quake. He has to be lying. Nothing I can see or feel is telling me he is, but that's not the point. He just has to be.

Why?

I push the traitorous thought aside. Because he does, that's why. Because he leads a fucking *House,* and those bastards lie all the time.

Because I don't want to hear this.

"I'll admit," Alistair says. "For years, we believed the same story you've probably heard. That unknown assailants attacked your mother and beat her until there wasn't a bone in her body that hadn't been shattered. That they tossed the bloody pulp of her corpse to a pack of junkyard dogs, letting them rip their teeth into every scrap of her mutilated flesh, letting them feast on everything down to the marrow of her broken bones, all in the hope those animals would make certain no trace of her was ever found."

My stomach clenches, and I catch a flicker of a smile on his face. He knows exactly what his words are doing to me.

"But all that changed a few days ago. We intercepted a transmission from her to several of her old contacts. She's alive, and she needs assistance." He gives me a pointed look. "And you're going to help us be the ones who give that to her."

I stare, speechless.

The door behind me bangs open. I jump and look back.

Katsuro is there. I haven't seen him in weeks, and suddenly, he's—

I don't care. Not if it gets me out of here.

The vampire strides down the stairs. His angular face is like carved granite, and his expression is equally cold. His commanding presence seems to roll into the room like the inexorable power of a glacier across land, an ancient force of uncompromising power. He's covered in a full-length, billowing black coat with a hood that, if it were raised, looks like it would shield him entirely from the sun. Ram and Tank follow him. Both trolls are the size of heavyweight wrestlers and easily over six and a half feet tall.

At the sight of Katsuro, Alistair smiles, but it's not a faux-pleasant expression like before. It sends chills through me. He seems oddly satisfied—cold, but satisfied—like the vampire's presence confirms something.

Like it's what he's been waiting for.

"Well, hello, *Katsuro*."

The name sounds pointed. Maybe even like a joke. The vampire ignores the tone, stopping inches from the barrier behind me. "Let her out."

"I must say," Alistair continues, ignoring the command, "I was surprised to see you on the security footage several weeks back, breaking out my psychic and all. I'd almost become convinced you *were* dead these past few centuries. How did you survive Rome, old friend? I would have thought being nailed to a rooftop in broad daylight would kill even you."

"Let her out, and we will allow you to leave this place alive."

Alistair chuckles. "The tattered remnants of the Guardians, up against their destroyers." He makes an impressed noise. "That's bound to go well for you."

Katsuro motions sharply to Ram and Tank, who start toward the barrier.

"I wouldn't," Alistair cautions.

The trolls stop when Katsuro's hand twitches up.

"My witches were highly specific in creating this particular barrier recipe. Anyone tries to break through it and, well…" Alistair's brow shrugs illustratively.

"If you take Cait," Katsuro threatens, "we will hunt you down."

I look between them, alarmed. Like hell I'm going anywhere.

Of its own volition, purple mist starts rising from my hands.

Alistair's expression turns pitying—and more than a touch cruel. "Oh, Katsuro, now *why* do I doubt you'll be successful at that?"

The temperature of the room seems to plummet. Katsuro's dark eyes flash with utter hatred, and his lips peel back slightly, revealing the tips of fangs. The sight is terrifying. I didn't think the devil himself could upset the unflappable vampire.

My eyes slide to Alistair, shivers crawling down my spine when I realize the implication of that.

"How about this?" Alistair suggests. "You and Cait leave this place with me, and I swear she will be safe as houses—" He chuckles at his wordplay. "—while you and I discuss the *real* reason you're here." The old man gestures equitably. "Think on it, Katsuro. The only succubus you've swayed to your cause. The one for whom you've been searching all these centuries. Come with me now…or who knows what might happen to her?"

Sorcha snarls, her eyes flaring bright like backlit amber. The other werewolves start down the stairs toward us, their teeth bared and their necks cracking like their muscles and bones have suddenly become too stiff.

Alistair pays them no attention. "I'm offering you peace, old friend—with a bit of an incentive."

Katsuro watches him in silence for a moment. "Cait." He motions to the trolls again, his eyes never leaving Alistair. "Get back. Stay as far from him as you can, but get back."

"I promise you," Alistair warns. "Any attempt to pass

this defense will not go well for you. My people learned from your little attempt to claim my psychic. Don't sacrifice the few loyal fools you have left."

Katsuro doesn't respond. The trolls start forward. The air begins to crackle with blue-white lightning around them. Ram's and Tank's skin melts back like it was only an illusion, revealing shining metal that sparks when it comes in contact with the barrier.

I retreat, watching Alistair and the others equally while more mist winds around my arms. I don't know how much magic I've got left in me—it can't be a lot, not with how little energy I've been able to take in recently—but I'll be damned if this guy is going to get his hands on me.

Alistair shakes his head. "Very well, then."

The demon next to him moves fast. Silver flashes in his hand: a gun.

"Cait!" Sorcha shouts.

Something stings my neck. On instinct, my hand goes to the sensation.

My fingers find metal. A needle that burns when I draw it out. I look up to see Alistair smile.

And then the world tips like water pouring from a glass and goes dark before I hit the ground.

3

AMAR

THE WORST PART OF GETTING SHOT IS THE RECOVERY TIME.

The best is not being dead.

He sighs as he swings his legs over the side of the bed and climbs to his feet. It's only been a few weeks since a bullet tried to shred his insides. A few weeks of bed rest, of lurking around his apartment like a ghost, of generally avoiding the outside world. Even if he's going stir crazy, he knows he shouldn't be annoyed at the time it's taking to get back to full strength. If he weren't a demon, he'd probably be in the morgue.

His midsection aches when he pulls a t-shirt down over the white gauze still taped to his skin. According to the vampire doctor Leaf, he's healing up well. Another day or two, and even those bandages would be gone.

As would his excuse for avoiding Cait.

He scrubs his hand over his head and walks from the bedroom. It's what he's been doing—avoiding her—and he wants to claim it's for the best. He'd had no choice but to show her that deadly power inside him. Only luck and a few precious millimeters kept a bullet from doing more than grazing her cheek, and the people who shot at her had been aiming their guns to try again. His only choice was to kill them first. But the ability he'd inherited from his father is a horror show. Anyone with a brain would be petrified of it—and Cait is smart as hell. He wants to convince himself he's letting her have time to process, to deal, to decide what she wants to do.

Instead of simply lying to himself about it all.

He walks into the kitchen. The cabinet yields up cereal and a bowl, and the stainless-steel fridge contains a new half-gallon of milk, courtesy of the grocery delivery from yesterday. He puts breakfast together on autopilot, his mind elsewhere. With her. In the hallway of that abandoned building.

Watching her face change with horror.

He struggles to push the image aside. He'd known that would happen. Known it from the start. The people who are truly aware of what he can do are few and far between, and every single one of them wants to use him and is afraid of him, all at the same time. But Cait...She's basically human. Beyond the fear demons have for him lies the terror a human would feel at learning of an ability such as his. Of course she's stopped speaking to him.

Of course he's lost her.

You'll kill her, you know.

He closes his eyes, pausing midway through returning the milk to the refrigerator, and he makes himself keep breathing past the cold twist of fear gnawing at his gut. Penny could have meant anyone. Pronouns aren't exactly specific, after all. And while he never wants to be put in the position of having to take a life, regardless of whose it is, the psychic could have been referring to anybody.

Or she could have been referring to Cait.

He sets the carton back in the fridge and closes the door with all the careful control he's perfected for nearly a decade. Retrieving the bowl of cereal from the counter, he walks into the living room. The morning sun streams past the magic-guarded windows, touching the dove-gray furniture in ever-so-slightly muted beams of light. Nothing and no one will get inside here, not without his express permission. It would have been a good place to keep Cait safe.

Except she probably wants to be protected from him.

He sinks onto the hard cushions of the couch. He would never hurt her. Not on his life, not in a million years. The mere thought is torture, and yet so is the fear that the psychic might have seen a possibility that, by all rights, should only live in his nightmares. For weeks, his mind has spun in circles over it, endlessly torn by the truth that he could no more harm Cait than he could rip his lungs from his chest, and the fear that something, *somehow*, could go wrong.

But then, chances are, none of it will matter anyway. He saw Cait's face, saw her terror. She won't come near him again. Those short, priceless moments after he woke up from being shot aside, she's had time to think now, and she heard Penny's words, same as he did.

She'll stay away.

Hell, she has already, so that proves it. And as for talking to her…he knows it's over. It has to be. Whatever might have existed between them, whatever he hoped for, it's certainly ended now. These days and weeks of silence have shown that. Now, all that's left is to reassure her that he'll leave her alone, that she'll never see him again, and then go. Pay the wolves enough to make sure she'll always be safe…and then stay out of her life. It's the only thing he can still do for the woman who holds whatever is left of his heart.

If only he could get up the courage to face her and say it.

His cell phone rings, and he pauses, a spoon halfway to his mouth. Setting his breakfast back down, he digs the phone from his pocket, a tangled twist of relief and shame flaring in him when he sees it's Sorcha, not Cait. "Yeah?"

Her response is clipped. Shivers race through his skin at her words. *No.*

"When?" he demands.

The answer comes.

"Where are you?"

He's already moving when she responds, flicking a trace of magic at the defenses around his apartment and striding fast across the nearest line of shadow.

"We're sorry," Sorcha says the moment he appears. "We tried to stop him, but…"

Scanning the basement, he doesn't react to the apology. Most of the mercenaries he hired now lie on the cement floor, down in the depths of the computer science building. A few others crouch beside them, tending to wounds that would be fatal if the injured people weren't werewolves.

And that still might.

He glances at Sorcha. Bits of wood debris speckle her hair. Bloody scrapes mar her cheeks and forehead; a growing bruise darkens one side of her face. Compared to the others, she's barely injured.

"The trolls," she explains, seeming to read the look he gives her. "I managed to get behind them. They took the brunt of it."

He can't tell if the discomfited note in her voice is

embarrassment for needing the assistance or unease at someone else taking the blast. She doesn't say anything else, though, twitching her chin instead toward the other end of the basement. Past the support pillars and the storage for old desks and chairs, he spots the bulky form of the trolls in the shadows.

"How far could you track Cait?" he asks the werewolf.

"They shadow-crossed within moments of the explosion. The vampire's people couldn't follow it."

His teeth grind briefly. "Is she hurt?"

Sorcha pauses, and when she responds, it's bluntly honest—one of the traits he appreciates about the mercenary he hired. "Not when last I saw her."

"How many more of your people can come to help with this job?"

She hesitates. He waits, already suspecting he's not going to like the answer. The past several weeks have been hard on the mercenaries. They'd suffered heavy casualties at Volgert's set, the death match where Cait's friend Ruby had been held. Their leader, Ulric, was seriously injured in the ambush at Temptation. And then the three packs Bianca hired were almost wiped out in the attack on the factory where Penny was held.

"Linden and Volgert have hired nearly every other pack out there." Sorcha seems to weigh whether to continue. "Volgert even offered Ulric twice our normal fee to leave this job and work for them."

He ignores the statement, knowing she wouldn't mention it if they'd taken the deal. "How many of your people are left to hire?"

"None. There's just us."

That's what he'd been afraid of.

"You should know," Sorcha adds. "Alistair Linden told Cait that her mother was alive."

He gives the werewolf a skeptical look. That makes no sense, as a ploy or otherwise. Setting aside the fact House Volgert found Josephine's body, where would the woman have been for twenty years? Besides that, Cait would have been able to tell immediately that the statement wasn't true. What did Alistair gain by lying?

"And the vampire..." Sorcha continues. "...he and Linden have a history. Alistair knows they're Guardians." She jerks her chin toward the trolls. "Alistair set Cait up as bait to draw the vampire and his people in."

He pauses, meeting the werewolf's eyes. She ducks her head in a canine-like gesture, as if seeing the rage building in him.

Turning away, he tries smothering the reaction, but it's difficult. Alistair used Cait as *bait*. He and that damn vampire had *history*. Amar has learned precious little about these so-called *real* Guardians since Katsuro first admitted to being part of them—as opposed to part of the crazed cult most of the demon world calls "Guardians." Leaf was remarkably close-mouthed about it, and any other sources are drying up fast with the Houses around. Meanwhile, Katsuro had vanished shortly after freeing Penny—a fact that is disconcerting as hell.

But this...*this* would have been good to know.

"Is the vampire back in town?" he asks.

Sorcha nods.

"Get your people ready to go. Whoever's good to travel."

From the corner of his eye, he sees her grimace when she reads between the lines. Wolves despise shadow-crossing; the blur of sight and sound is like torture on their heightened senses. But she nods and returns to her pack while he continues toward the trolls.

Ram doesn't bother to look up when he approaches. Seated on the ground nearby, Tank does the same. Their skin looks like a thin tissue covering a metal sculpture. He can see scorch marks across the steel.

"Where's Katsuro?"

Ram snorts. "Where do you think? Looking for your *girlfriend*."

He ignores the attempted insult, a jab at the fact most incubi and succubi would sooner chew nails than care about someone romantically, let alone date. "And where is he doing that?"

The shadows to the right shift slightly before Ram can respond. Katsuro appears. A long black coat with a deep hood shelters his skin from the burning touch of sunlight that streams through a tiny barred window near the basement ceiling. "Ah, Amar. I hadn't thought you were well enough to travel."

"Where have you been?"

"This month or right now?"

Asshole.

He stifles the thought, keeping his face blank while he waits for the vampire to continue.

"Traveling," Katsuro finally acknowledges. "And now, searching for Cait. Neither has been particularly fruitful."

"What have you found?"

"They blocked their shadow-crossing path, and their human co-conspirator is missing. Her professor. From what your wolves tell me, it appears he used to be Touched. I have several people attempting to track him down now."

As leads go, that feels about as substantial as a spider's

web. And meanwhile, the clock is ticking.

But he needs to know what he's dealing with first—or at least hear the vampire's version of the truth, whatever that is. "What connection do you have to Alistair?"

Katsuro pauses.

"Do *not* say complicated." A few weeks back, that word seemed to be the vampire's favorite answer.

Katsuro shrugs. "It would be accurate."

His jaw tightens.

"We knew each other many years ago," Katsuro says. "He tried to kill me repeatedly and failed. Apparently, he hasn't given up that quest."

"Why does he want you dead?"

"Because I am a threat to his plans—plans that currently appear to involve Cait, which is why we need to find her quickly." Katsuro glances at the trolls. "The police have shut down the campus after the explosion in the lecture hall," he says to them. "They're scouring the grounds as well, searching for what they believe to be a bomber. Be careful when you leave."

Ram nods.

"Tell your wolves to come meet us once they are fit to move," Katsuro continues. "They can follow Ram and Tank and spare themselves the discomfort of other means of travel."

"Where are we going?"

"To a friend who may be able to find Cait's location. That is all I will say, for their sake and ours, until we are somewhere more secure." Katsuro steps closer to the line of shadow on the concrete floor. "The Guardians need you, Amar, and Cait does too. Will you help us?"

Like there was ever a question of the latter. But as for the former…

He doesn't want to say yes. Distrust is his default. It's what has kept him alive, almost as much as his nightmarish abilities.

But then, he needs these people and their resources—at least until Cait is safe.

He glances at the wolves. Sorcha nods, already having heard Katsuro's words.

"Fine," he agrees. "Let's go."

THEY APPEAR IN THE DIM STRETCH OF AN ALLEYWAY IN THE older section of downtown, and immediately, Katsuro heads for a door to the building on the right.

"Your friend is near this place?" Amar asks the vampire.

"Close, yes."

The vampire continues down the alleyway.

Amar checks around before moving to follow. At the end of the alley, cars zip past beneath the midmorning sunlight. On the roof ledges overhead, he can see no signs of security.

Somehow, he doubts that's actually the truth.

Restraining a frown, he walks after the vampire. Katsuro knocks briefly. Seconds creep past, and the door opens.

"Yes?" The teenage girl on the other side gives them a confused look, like she can't understand why they're here instead of wherever the front entrance might be. Amar looks beyond her. They appear to be standing by the side door of some kind of plant shop.

Katsuro lowers his hood. "We're here to speak with Nasreen."

The girl's eyes go wide. "Oh, Hisakawa-san! I'm so sorry, I didn't—" She drops whatever she'd been about to say and moves out of their path. "Come in, please."

"Thank you," Katsuro replies.

They step inside. Scents of dozens of flowers and plants fill the air along with the earthy smell of potting soil. Shelves line the walls, stretching from the floor to the ceiling over twenty feet above; their surfaces are covered in everything from ornamental pots to bottles of plant food. Thick vines with bright-green leaves climb the support pillars of the shelving while on tables around the shop, flowers bloom in every color imaginable. Three more women are there, and three men as well, their appearances ranging from teenage to gray-haired. All of them move intently among the tables while they tend to the exotic plants.

Amar's eyes narrow with suspicion, and he casts a brief look at the high ceiling. Burnished tin, ornate and yet uniform. No skylights. No source of illumination short of the windows at the front of the store.

Right.

"Katsuro," comes a warm, welcoming voice from some-where to the left.

A slender woman approaches them. She seems perhaps middle-aged from her bearing, but her appearance defies the impression. Her light olive skin is flawless as a young girl's. There isn't a trace of gray in her long black hair, and despite the fact she has the self-possession of an older woman, she moves with the fluidity of youth.

"That will be all," she says to the teenage girl, who bobs her head quickly and then hurries toward the tables of flowers. "You brought us a guest," the woman continues to Katsuro.

"Amar Okoro," the vampire acknowledges, nodding to him.

And for a moment, it's there, just as always. That flicker of recognition, of reevaluation, darts through her deep brown eyes.

She recovers swiftly. "Hello." She extends a hand to him. "I'm Nasreen."

He makes no move to take it.

Nasreen's smile grows. "I see you're aware of who we are."

He gestures briefly to the ceiling. "Witch or djinn?"

In answer, she blinks. Instantly, her eyes turn red as rubies.

Djinn, then.

"You'd be surprised how many humans don't notice that little lighting discrepancy," she says, "or, at least, do not question it."

"And you mark the ones who do," Katsuro adds dryly.

Nasreen shrugs, her eyes returning to a more human appearance. "Being naturally observant and confident are vital attributes, and one never knows from where the next student will come." She motions to the store behind her. "Shall we?"

Katsuro nods, and Amar follows him toward the rear of the shop, still eyeing the odd assortment of people. Students. Witches, most likely, given that djinn don't often require teachers—at least, not in the same way. But the rest of the school will be around here somewhere, since growing plants without almost any light is only one of the many tricks they learn.

In a shadowed corner, Nasreen pauses at a dark, wooden door. Her hand makes a brief gesture over the doorknob. The dull reflection of light on the brass knob seems to shift, as if the source that created it has moved. She pulls the door open and continues through the opening into the stairwell beyond. Brick walls surround narrow wooden steps. A small sconce flickers at chest height, lighting the path down. Nasreen leads the way, pausing only briefly to unlock the weathered door at the base of the stairs.

Amar's eyes slide swiftly across the space while he follows Katsuro and Nasreen inside. Despite the dank stairway they just left behind, the basement has more the feel of a business office. White walls. Desks—three of them—placed at even intervals along the right and all facing the door. A person sits at each, working attentively on a computer. Only the nearest of the people glances up briefly when Amar and the others come inside.

"I assume this visit is in regard to the girl?" Nasreen asks.

Amar's attention returns to her immediately.

"Yes," Katsuro says.

Nasreen's lips tighten.

"What is it?" Amar demands.

"Can he be trusted?" Nasreen asks of Katsuro, nodding in his direction. "Fully?"

"You brought him down here," Katsuro points out.

She appears unconvinced. "Indeed. His aura is..." She seems to search for a word, her gaze flicking over him. "Unusual, given what he is."

He doesn't react, but he's curious. She knows who he is, so what is *that* intended to imply?

The djinn doesn't elaborate. "I rely on your judgment," she consents, directing the words to the vampire. "As you do mine."

Katsuro bows his head briefly in acknowledgment.

Amar keeps himself from glancing between them despite his wariness at whatever just passed.

"The energy has increased," Nasreen continues as if the exchange had not happened. "Not only in the past day or week, but in the past hour. My analysts have been searching for any other event that could account for this rise, but as yet, it appears the attack at the university is the trigger."

"What energy?" he asks. "What does this have to do with Cait?"

Nasreen hesitates. "Everything. We are discussing the energy that gives you, me, and all of demonkind their power. Magic, as you may know, emanates into this world via streams of power called ley lines. Now, most humans don't notice it. Most humans don't believe ley lines or magic even *exist*. But their belief is irrelevant, and the magic continues to flow all the same." She takes a breath. "That is, until recently."

He remembers this. Katsuro alluded to it a few weeks back, though he'd never gone into detail.

And then he'd disappeared.

"For much of my lifetime and Katsuro's—" Nasreen acknowledges with a tilt of her head toward the vampire "—the power in the lines has remained stable to a significant degree. A small spike here or a slight dip there, perhaps. A few minor shifts caused by untrained humans who sought to harness that power. But nothing like what is happening now."

"What is that exactly?"

"Magic is collecting in places where, prior to this time, it simply flowed through. Other lines have been shifting location, though the alterations are so faint that no one short of witches and djinn could hope to detect them. But they are coalescing toward the larger lines, adding to the buildup, to the instability. And this—" Her lip twitches, something so much darker and colder than humor in the expression. "—this *convergence* is getting stronger."

He hears the way she says the word. The emphasis, as if convergence isn't simply another term for this.

"There were signs, of course, that something was changing. The Touched who have displayed powers like your kind. Other anomalies revealing that magic was behaving in ways we had never yet seen. To a great extent, we believe some of those developments were inadvertently caused by the Houses and may not connect to the convergence at all. They've meddled in human affairs for centuries, and though they did not take the time to consider the consequences of their actions, that meddling has had a profound impact upon this world. Add to that the fact demons now have little choice but to live in close proximity to humans, and now the convergence of magic in these ley lines, and you have a situation that has been growing progressively more volatile."

Nasreen gestures to the three people at the desks. "This is what my students and I have been tracking, and it has led us here. Corvinson. The site of the latest and arguably strongest convergence to date, and thus the one that concerns us the most."

"Why?" he asks.

She glances at Katsuro.

"Nearly a thousand years ago," Katsuro explains, "before the fall of the Guardians, there was a psychic. A succubus. She was the last we know of with that power until Penny, and *unlike* Penny, she was not insane. She foresaw a shift in the magic of the ley lines, including the convergence that took place at that time, and one that would follow at some point in the future. At that moment, she could not say when—or even *if*—it would happen for certain, but she foresaw signs that would accompany it as well: the Touched gaining powers, as Nasreen said, among other things. But that was not all."

"Get to the point."

Katsuro's mouth tightens. "We believe she saw Cait."

Amar's blood goes cold.

"When the convergence started to occur a thousand years ago," Nasreen says, "the psychic had a vision. She foretold that, the next time—*this* time—there would be signs of the convergence's coming. Certain people would appear, and among these would be powerful demons with abilities that surpass any previously seen. Some of these people, she said, would even be connected to this convergence in a way. Able to affect or control it in a fashion. Now, a little over twenty-five years ago when hints of the convergence occurred for the first time in a millennium, the Houses thought they had located a succubus who could be one such individual—though later events proved such speculation irrelevant."

"Cait's mother?"

"Seems like it should have been, yes?" Nasreen shakes her head. "But no, it was someone else. A young woman who subsequently died."

Amar doesn't comment, though he can see only too many ways the Houses probably had a hand in that.

And it only makes him want to find Cait more.

"After the young woman died," Nasreen continues, "the traces of the convergence faded. The convergence is highly unstable. It can appear and disappear at any time. For all we knew back then, that was the end of it. The magic drained from that area and became nearly undetectable anywhere else. But the Houses were undeterred. Their search continued in secret. They wanted to control the convergence and to discover more people who might be connected to it, all for the purpose of gaining power for themselves. They did not meet with much success, however, until this newest psychic arrived. After all, who better to help find the convergence *and* these special demons than someone who could foresee their existence, their locations, and any manner of other information at the same time?"

"What makes you think Cait figures into this?"

"Linden," Katsuro says.

Amar glances at the vampire.

"When he came to take Cait, Alistair called her the one for whom I've been searching, and he referenced what he considered the real reason I'm here."

"And that is?"

Katsuro gives him a dry look. "In truth, it's the same as I told you before: to stop the Houses and end their practice of destroying human lives by turning them into Touched. And yes—" He tilts his head briefly in admission. "—I also intend to prevent the Houses from exploiting the convergence for their own ends, because the damage they would do to humanity and the demon world is unthinkable. Last time was bad enough—the convergence a millennium ago led to the downfall of the Guardians and a war that cost thousands of lives. Alistair, I'm sure, is convinced there is more to my interest than that, but he has only lived this long by being incredibly suspicious by nature."

Amar doesn't comment.

"The fact Alistair called Cait the one I've been searching for leads me to believe he suspects she is one of these powerful demons, as does the fact that he moved to capture her only *after* he gained access to Penny's abilities for however brief a time." Katsuro looks at him pointedly. "Alistair knows something about Cait, and whatever that is, it has led him to act more openly than he has in years."

Amar exhales, his eyes flicking to the computers and the people behind them. "So what are you doing to get her back from him—and how does this figure in?" He twitches his head toward the desks.

Katsuro glances at Nasreen.

"We've been tracking the energy of this convergence, as I said," Nasreen supplies. "Several weeks ago, a sudden disruption in that energy accompanied the assault on the location where Linden had imprisoned this current psychic. Or, more specifically, it accompanied—as close as we can tell—the moment when she was freed. Now another disruption has coincided with Alistair's attack at the college."

"It's following Cait," Amar translates flatly.

Nasreen nods. "We believe so, yes. Now, the origin of these sudden disruptions in the energy of the convergence are difficult to isolate. Initially, we were only able to detect their existence, not their specific starting point. But as the weeks have passed and multiple instances of this disruptive effect have occurred, our detection methods have improved substantially, until now we hope we—"

"So you can find her." He tosses another look at the computers and the people there. "Then, why are you standing around—"

"No," Nasreen cuts in. "We've found the possible effect of her connection with the convergence—*maybe*. But it is also only a theory, and we—"

Impatience pushes at him. "What *have* you seen? Can we use it to start searching?"

Consternation flickers over Nasreen's face. "We believe the convergence may be interacting with her in some way. Perhaps *reacting* to her, or to danger around her—though to what end, we do not know. Indeed, even her connection to this is difficult to confirm with any certainty, as both her magic use and dangerous situations seem to coincide rather frequently. But..." Nasreen exhales. "Katsuro says she was knocked unconscious by a tranquilizer shortly before the explosion at the school. Once she wakes from the sedation, *if* she is able to defend herself and *if* we are right about this, then her effect on the convergence—"

A chime sounds from one of the desks. Amar glances over to see a gray-haired woman checking her cell phone, and for a brief moment, hope flares inside him. Maybe coincidence is working in their favor.

"Ram and the others have arrived," the woman reports to Nasreen. "They appear to have a pack of werewolves in their company."

Nasreen glances at Amar. "Yours, I assume?"

He keeps his face still, giving no sign of the disappointment stabbing at his chest. "Mercenaries I hired."

"Ah." She gestures to the door. "Shall we go meet them?"

Nasreen starts from the room.

Amar snags Katsuro's arm, stopping the vampire from following. "Did you know about this?" he demands in a low voice.

Katsuro looks from his hand to his face. Amar makes no move to release him. "Did I know about what?" the vampire replies coolly.

"That Cait might be connected to this? Did you know that before you had us meet you at the salvage yard that night?"

Katsuro pauses. "Not with any certainty."

Amar fights the impulse to clench his hand down tighter.

"I was far more certain she was Josephine's daughter. Everything else was only remote speculation." Katsuro's lips thin briefly. "I swear to you, I mean no harm to her. I only want to keep her safe from the Houses—Alistair's especially. On this, you have my word."

Amar eyes the vampire, wishing he had Cait's power to know whether the words are true.

"You may ask me again once Cait is safe," Katsuro offers as if reading his mind. "But I promise you, my answer will remain unchanged."

He weighs the reply, but there's no way to know whether to trust it for certain. He releases Katsuro.

"We will find her, Amar."

He doesn't respond. He knows there are no guarantees, and that for every second he's stood here, listening to this crazy story, Cait has been in Alistair's hands.

And there is no telling what's happening to her.

He strides toward the door.

Another chime sounds behind him. "S-sir?"

He glances over his shoulder to see a nervous kid with glasses rising from a desk and looking between the computer and Katsuro.

"We, um..." The kid checks his screen again. "The disruptions are back. They're faint and they're, um... they're *odd*, but..."

"What?" Katsuro snaps.

"I think she's awake."

4

CAIT

"—MAKE CERTAIN THE POLICE FIND NO TRACE, UNDERSTAND?"

"Yes, sir."

The words reach my ears like they're pushing their way through cotton, and a noise follows like a door closing. But I recognize the first voice, and at the sound, spikes of fury and adrenaline make my heart speed up and magic tingle under my skin. Memory plays back. Alistair. The lecture hall. The gun.

I struggle to open my eyes. Light burns hot and painful through the darkness, and I cringe away. But I need to get up. I need to get out of wherever the hell I—

"Hello, Cait. Sleep well?"

The light burns less this time. The white glare fractures into a confetti of colors and then coalesces into actual shapes.

Shapes like Alistair sitting on a metal folding chair, one leg crossed atop the other and a cup of coffee in his hand. Shapes like the narrow bed on which I'm lying, mint-green sheets beneath me. The room around me has a sterile look, with bare white walls that practically glow under the panel lighting in the ceiling. But there are no windows. No clocks. Nothing by which to tell how long I've been out. I could have been here for days for all I know.

I try to rise from the bed, but my limbs don't seem to be working right. My arms are heavy. My hands feel like they're made of clay. I succeed in scooting a few inches, but the effort leaves my heart galloping.

"The sedative will take some time to fully wear off. But meanwhile, I thought we could continue our little chat."

I look back at Alistair. "I'm not joining House Linden."

He chuckles like I've told a joke.

My heart starts pounding harder. "I don't—"

"I've been quite patient with you, Cait. I'm sure you can agree. Weeks to come to the correct decision, a hands-off approach…incredibly kind, wouldn't you say? Certainly, one can never be too careful when it comes to potential traps set by one's enemies, but even in that regard, I've given you more than enough time."

I flex my fingers, willing my arms and hands to wake up. "Listen, whatever is going on with you and—well, *anybody*—I'm not involved. I just want to stay neutral like Amar."

His expression turns pitying. "Do you really believe you've stayed neutral in all this?"

I'm silent.

"You *are* friends with Hisakawa Katsuro," Alistair points out.

A chill creeps through me.

"Has he told you why he sought you out? What he's after?"

"Stopping the sets. The Touched."

Alistair laughs. "Oh, of *course*. Well, that is true. He *does* want to stop the sets. He travels around under a false name meaning victorious son of the ancient river or some such nonsense, and his past is filled with so many centuries of deception and death that he should have his own section among the history books. Likewise, his plans are enough to destroy your world and mine, leaving no one but himself and his deluded acolytes standing. But, yes, he does wish to take the sets down as well."

I don't respond. The words can't be true. My power isn't cooperating and telling me that; maybe it's not working.

But the words still can't be true.

"Did it ever occur to you to wonder why he's here?" Alistair asks. "Why any of us are? Corvinson is a backwater town in a small buffer zone of neutral territory. It scarcely warrants the notice of *humans*, let alone the strongest forces in the demon world. Hardly the place a villain like Katsuro would choose to reveal himself after centuries of hiding, yes? And why is Lucretia so close? You think out of all the territories she controls around this planet, it is pure *chance* the leader of Volgert spends her time only a few hundred miles from here?"

I stay silent. His smile takes on a thoughtful edge, and he sets his coffee cup down on a small metal table nearby.

"A change is occurring," he says. "The Touched and their newfound abilities are only the beginning. The magical energy coursing through the ley lines of this world is building up and gathering in places that, before, it had mostly ignored. And the strongest of those places—and therefore arguably the most important—is currently here. The relatively unremarkable little town of Corvinson." His brow shrugs. "Now, that's interesting enough, to be sure. But added to that is *you*."

My skin crawls. I want to retreat, but there's nowhere to go.

"No matter how it keeps turning, no matter what happens, there you are. Seen in visions by my psychic. Sought out by a vampire I've hunted for the better part of a thousand years. Fiercely guarded by an incubus who is not only one of the strongest of his kind but who showed minimal interest in risking himself for *anyone* until you. Before you saved our Protected in that hospital, you scarcely appeared to *exist* in our world, and yet a few weeks later, here you are at the center of it." He shakes his head. "I'm a very old man, Cait, and I've learned that *coincidence* is merely what humans call the product of forces they do not understand."

My head moves back and forth of its own accord. "I…I just want to be left alone."

His eyes flick over me like he's reading something, and he chuckles softly. "Now we *both* know that is not going to happen."

Taking a deep breath, he pushes up from the chair. "Shortly before you attempted to steal her from me, my psychic developed a rather significant interest in you. You seemed to vex her somehow, a fact that didn't stop her from developing what could almost be called an obsession with your fate. She had a great deal to say about you—most of which, I'll admit, was utterly incomprehensible. But key parts were not, and those key parts are why I suspect Katsuro is after you, why I doubt Lucretia will stay long on the sidelines where you are concerned, and why *I* can no longer allow you to run free for either of them to grab." He smiles. "Willingly or otherwise, Cait, you *are* going to become a part of House Linden."

He crosses to the door and pulls it open. Two men and a woman walk into the room.

My hands push at the bed. I try to sit up, to do anything, but my muscles are as responsive as lead from the sedative. "What are you—"

"Has anyone ever told you about the interesting peculiarity that separates Legacies from their full-blood counterparts?" Alistair asks.

My blood goes cold. Oh God, no.

"You're half human. Now, normally, that human side of you is relatively dormant. The magic you intake from humans doesn't harm it and even helps keep your system in balance. But if you are fed enough mist by another one of your kind to *override* that balance, well..." He chuckles. "It can trigger your human side and turn you into a creature not unlike a Touched. But there is an added complexity in your case." He smiles. "You are not simply a Legacy. According to my psychic, you're not even like your mother—not fully. Perhaps you've already seen flashes of it, hints of a power that supersedes merely *reading* people. You're something more, Cait. Something rarer even than Josephine. But you aren't feeding enough —or so my psychic claimed—and thus, you haven't provided yourself with magical energy to fully catalyze the talent you have sleeping inside."

"No." My hands push harder at the bed, and my sweaty palms slip on the green sheets. "No, no, no..."

He continues on inexorably. "So we're going to change that. My succubus and incubi are going to pour enough magic into you to unlock everything that you are, and then they'll start training you to use that gift to the benefit of House Linden. Perhaps you'll stay sane through it. Most likely not. But either way, you're going to work for me."

His brow rises pointedly. "After all, my dear, you stole my weapon. I'm simply making certain you restock my arsenal."

He looks to the others. "Take all the time you need, but make sure it's done."

They nod.

Alistair glances back to me. "We'll find your mother, Cait, and you'll help us determine if she is who she claims. You'll also help us destroy Katsuro and the vestiges of the Guardians. But until then—" He smiles. "—enjoy your meal."

He pulls the door closed behind him.

The three demons walk toward me. My eyes lock on them while my palms shove at the sheets and my heels dig into the bed in a desperate attempt to get me away. Tingling builds up beneath my skin. "Listen," I try. "You don't have to—"

One of them reaches toward me. A pulse of energy rushes away from my body, slamming into them.

They rock backward. The air around them crackles with lights like the ghosts of firecrackers, and the demons wince. A brief flash of hope flares inside me.

But nothing else happens. They straighten again. Start toward me again.

"Nice try," the nearest demon growls.

They reach down, grabbing my wrists and pinning me. Another pulse of energy leaves me, barely strong enough to make the air sparkle.

Then the mist envelopes me.

5

AMAR

THE GRAY WORLD OF SHADOW-CROSSING FALLS BEHIND AMAR, delivering him to an alleyway cast in sharp shadow by the angle of the bright sun. Immediately, Katsuro retreats deeper into the shade, despite the black coat and deep hood still covering him. Sorcha and her werewolf companions stand stock-still, their eyes locked on the concrete as if they're waiting for the ground to stop moving.

"Where?" Amar demands of Nasreen's student, a skinny young witch named Martin, who'd accompanied them from the plant shop.

The kid fumbles his cell phone from his pocket and then dials a number. Nasreen claimed the boy was one of her best students, regardless of the fact he looks like he'd need a fake ID to convince someone he was even a teenager. His mop of messy brown hair stands up in odd places, and his large glasses glare in the sunlight, obscuring his eyes in a disconcerting way. An oversized khaki raincoat covers him, making him look like a child playing spy. "A-ahead. Yeah…ahead."

Amar buries a scowl. The stammering uncertainty in the boy's voice isn't exactly reassuring.

And *ahead* is vague as hell.

He scans the buildings in front of them, his view limited by the walls of the alleyway but sufficient to let him know where they are. The River District, two miles from downtown and three miles upriver from Terchett Wharf. Gentrified in the past decade, the place is a collection of aging factories and old office buildings that have been retrofitted to contain chic businesses in their husks. He'd had no idea Linden owned property in this area— though, knowing the Houses, they could have bought a location as recently as this morning.

His scowl tries to return. The place is also filled with humans who could be hurt if this goes badly.

Humans who could get in the way.

Martin starts out of the alley, his hand still pressing the cell phone to his ear. "They think from the overlaid map of the city that—wait…what?" He stops for a heartbeat and then bolts forward, ignoring the traffic that skids to a stop when he charges into the road without looking. "Something's happening!" he shouts over his shoulder.

Amar curses silently and races after the kid. Cars honk at them, their drivers shouting angrily from inside the vehicles. On the sidewalks, people stop and stare. He knows they must look like a strange group—the mercenaries with their murderous-yet-nauseated expressions, Katsuro engulfed by his protective black coat, Martin scampering ahead like he's leading some bizarre scavenger hunt—but the humans aren't the ones who leave Amar uneasy.

There are a thousand windows around them. A thousand places for Linden's defensive forces to hide. Back in the old days, when his father was alive, the man told him of how he'd worked with snipers who could kill someone in broad daylight and make their death look like an accident, at least in the short term. A properly timed shot, a victim who stumbles into traffic ahead of an oncoming bus or car…

"This way." Martin veers down a side street.

Amar shoves the thoughts aside and continues after the skinny kid. The turn is followed by another, and another, and the minutes tick past. Anxiety builds like a hot ball in his chest, growing stronger with every second lost. His imagination works to slip beyond his control and torment him with visions of what the Houses could do. Already too much time has gone by. There's no reason to think the Houses wouldn't have also figured out that this disturbance and Cait seem connected. Volgert or who knows who else could be out here looking for her, tracking her the same way as Martin and Nasreen. And that wasn't even the worst of it. With near-infinite resources at their disposal, Alistair and his damned agents could—

"Are we close?" Katsuro asks, his voice hard.

Amar glances at the vampire while Martin comes to a stop. Despite the cool autumn weather, heat ripples from Katsuro's dark coat, like a shimmer rising from a blacktop road on a summer day.

"Uh, yeah," Martin supplies. "I-I think. The effect on the convergence is stronger—" He cuts off, alarm on his face. "Wait, what? A-are you sure?" A heartbeat passes. He lowers the phone from his ear. "It's gone."

For a heartbeat, Amar stares at the kid. It doesn't mean anything. Cait could have passed out again.

Why would Cait have passed out?

Magic ripples under his skin like ice-cold water. He

draws a slow breath, controlling the power, and then turns to Sorcha. The werewolf is watching him.

"Find her," he orders.

Sorcha nods and takes off, the other werewolves stalking down the road after her and scanning their surroundings like they're daring the city to continue hiding Cait.

He strides after them, trying to shove down the knowledge of how unlikely it is they'll be able to detect Cait's scent now, given the fact the wolves have probably been trying to pick up a trail this entire time. Linden would have used shadow-crossing to bring Cait to their destination. There wouldn't be a trail to follow.

Maybe.

He moves faster. The buildings here are taller, newer, and offer even more places to hide. Worse, they overlook the river only a few blocks away and the sprawl of West Corvinson beyond. The water's proximity means he's running out of city, running out of places to search, and finding the nearest bridge to cross the water will take too damn long.

A growl from one of the mercenaries draws his attention. He looks over in time to see three of the werewolves start running.

"Those men on their cell phones," Sorcha says, her voice thick with a barely suppressed growl. She jerks her chin toward a pair of guys walking on the sidewalk ahead. "They smell of her."

He runs toward them. The werewolves grab the men, jostling their phones from their hands. As Amar arrives, they shove the guys against the nearest wall.

"Hey, hold on," one of the men protests. "What the—"

"Where is she?" Amar demands.

The guy blinks and glances around like he's searching for someone to call the cops for help. "What? Who?"

"The girl," Katsuro says. "Cait. The one your people kidnapped this morning."

His voice is sharp. Wisps of smoke drift up from his coat.

"W-we didn't kidnap any—"

"Now!" Katsuro barks.

The guys stare at him.

And one of the men snickers. The other glances at his chuckling companion. His confused expression lasts only a heartbeat longer before it slips from his face, replaced with a nervous sort of amusement.

"Where did you take her?" Amar snaps at the laughing guy.

"Wouldn't you like to know?"

Ice swirls in his core, offering a quick solution to his rage. He holds it back—it's not the answer here—and he steps closer to the men. Except for the two mercenaries pinning the guys to the wall, the other werewolves melt away, wary deference in their gaze.

"Where?" he repeats in a low voice.

The first guy adopts a look of tense bravado. "Nowhere. She's dead."

Amar doesn't move. From the corner of his eye, he can see the other man start trembling, watching his companion. "You lie."

The guy doesn't respond.

Without taking his eyes from the man, Amar turns his head toward Sorcha. "Can you follow their scent back the way they came?"

"Yes."

Amar lifts a brow at the first guy. "Well, then. I don't

suppose we need you." His expression becomes cold again. "Convince me otherwise."

"You won't find her," the second guy blurts out. "We shadow-crossed to get here. You—"

"Shut up!" the first man hisses.

Amar turns toward Martin this time. His own abilities could trace the path to within a few dozen feet, but a strong witch could get them even closer. "How precisely can you track shadow-crossing?"

The kid's shoulders twitch in an anxious shrug. "I, uh, I can get you within a couple inches of where they left."

"It doesn't matter," the first guy snaps. "She's dead. I told you. We threw her body in the river."

Amar studies the guy for a heartbeat before sliding his attention to the second man. And it clicks, their expressions. Their taunts. The fact they were simply walking along the street, easy to find. "They're buying time." He looks to Sorcha. "Go. Now."

The woman takes off, several of the other mercenaries on her heels. Martin throws a frantic glance between them all and then chases after her while Amar turns to Katsuro.

"Head back," he orders the vampire. "Bring these two with you. Have your people question them."

"Gladly."

Katsuro motions to the werewolves holding the guys. They haul the men into an alleyway.

Amar races after Sorcha and the others. In the distance, he can hear sirens howling; someone must have called the cops after all. But the police won't be able to catch up with them. Blocks disappear behind him while he chases the mercenaries along a serpentine path, weaving through the city toward the river. Fifty yards from the water, the werewolves veer sharply into an alley and then skid to a halt halfway down the narrow stretch.

"It ends here," Sorcha says, her gaze darting around at the walls. "Right here."

He motions Martin toward the space where she's pointing. Breathing hard from the run, the kid scampers closer, digging in the pockets of his oversized coat as he goes. A cobbled-together collection of objects emerges with his shaking hands: crystals, small vials of colored liquid, a spool of thread, a matchstick, a rock pierced by a hole. Swiftly, he sorts the items out on the concrete and checks the entrance of the alley nervously.

"Hurry," Sorcha growls.

The boy nods. He whispers something to the objects. Electricity crackles among the assortment. Light shimmers for a heartbeat, flares brightly, and then disappears, leaving the items lying just as they had been.

But a shimmer remains in the air, hanging on the border of the shadows and sunlight in the alleyway.

It's enough.

The alley falls behind Amar. A cement stairwell takes its place.

Sorcha appears at his side. The seasick cast to her face doesn't stop her from bolting up the stairs immediately.

He runs after her. They scale three floors before she darts through an exit. A corridor with pale blue walls and soot-colored tile greets them. She races onward, past a series of gray doors and around the corner. He finds her stopped halfway down the next hall.

And the look on her face sends his heart plummeting into his stomach.

No.

Ice and darkness swirling through him, he walks closer. The door is open.

The room is empty.

His eyes flick around. White walls. Clean floor. A small metal table and a folding chair face a vacant space on the opposite end of the room, as if whatever they'd been positioned beside has been removed.

"She was here," Sorcha says.

He glances at the werewolf. She winces like she can see the question he can't bring himself to ask. The expression sends ice flooding through his body all over again.

"Some blood," she confesses. "Hers."

He's going to kill them.

Without a word, he spins away from the room and strides back down the hall, searching for Martin. The kid is hurrying from the stairwell, several mercenaries accompanying him.

"Amar!" Sorcha calls.

He ignores her. "Find how they left this place," he snaps at Martin. "Where they took her. Do it now."

Martin blinks at him.

"Amar," Sorcha repeats, coming up beside him. "There wasn't much. Some, but—" She grimaces as if she knows how hollow the words sound. "If they'd killed her, there would've been more."

He looks away. That's not the point. They *hurt her*.

With a sharp gesture, he directs Martin back toward the room. The kid darts past and drops to the tile when he reaches it, digging the implements for his spell out of his pockets even faster than before.

Energy crackles around the assorted objects in response to Martin's frantic whisper. Light rises from within the circle, misty and translucent.

And then it surges brighter, flaring in a blinding display and buzzing like a live wire. A loud pop like a tripped circuit follows. Yelping, Martin scrambles backward.

The light dies. Smoke rises from the blackened objects.

Martin stumbles to his feet, putting more distance between himself and the remnants of his spell. "I-I'm sorry," he stammers. "They blocked their path. A-a lot. I can't..." He trails off with a desperately apologetic expression.

For a moment, Amar doesn't speak. They could be anywhere. On the other side of town. Heading out of the state.

Out of the country.

"Those men," Sorcha says. "The ones who smelled of her."

The message between the short lines breaks his paralysis. He turns fast, striding for the nearest line of light and shadow in the room. Linden's men are his best resource right now, and they *will* talk. They'll tell him where to find her.

He refuses to consider the alternative.

6

CAIT

I FEEL LIKE I'M FLYING. FALLING. LIKE MY MIND IS TUGGED this way and that by ever-shifting gravity, all of it pierced by a whistling like wind howling in my ears.

The white light vanishes again.

My screams die. The metal-frame bed catches me, but it can't stop the room from spinning. The walls keep fading in and out. I'm not sure they're still in the right places. Maybe someone needs to nail them down.

A person moves to my left, but my eyes don't want to turn toward them. Something bad happens when I look toward them. I wish I could remember what.

I wish they'd bring the light back.

Garbled noises reach my ears. "...can't take much more...be a vegetable."

"...said to make sure..."

Silence. Bright light. Whistling that turns to screaming that drains to silence.

And for a time, there's only darkness.

My eyes open to a gray-and-buttercream blur that

doesn't move. I lie still. Something hurts, but it's far away. I don't think it matters right now.

The ache disagrees, growing worse. I grimace and look toward the pain.

Blood sullies the mint-green bedsheet below my hands. Half-moon marks score my palms. Dried blood crusts them too, in little paths that lead from the wounds to the sheets.

Huh. That's not good.

My eyes lift. The gray-and-buttercream blur resolves into a room barely illuminated by dimmed panels overhead and the twilit sky I can see through a small window on the wall behind my head. I don't recognize this place, but I don't like it. I'm not certain why.

I miss the misty light. I want it back.

A hungry, desperate shudder wracks my body at the thought. I roll over and push myself away from the bed, wincing when my injured palms ache at the pressure. My muscles creak in protest like they've rusted into place, and when I reach my feet, it's all I can do to stay standing. My arms hug my middle, and my feet lurch forward, my shoes squeaking on the cream-colored tile. The gray walls swirl, and unsteady gravity threatens to tip me over while I stumble toward the door.

But I think I need to get out of here. It mattered for some reason, not being here. It was important.

I wish I could remember why.

My feet lurch faster across the tile. My hands fumble forward and find the cold metal doorknob, but the thing won't turn. A frantic cry leaves me, choked and wild; I barely recognize the sound. My eyes twitch up to the narrow window of safety glass in the door. A hallway waits outside, its walls buttercream-yellow in color like the dimmed lights above me.

But I can't see anything else. No people, but no other doors or ways out either.

I'm trapped.

I yank harder on the doorknob. I can't be here, though. I have to—

Someone appears at the window in the door. I jump back with a yelp.

The world swirls, but it's not like before. Colors this time, smearing together like thick paint. A sound follows, like someone shrieking. Someone crying.

I snap back to the cold gray room. The noise is gone. The colors too. My heart races, and my body shakes like I'm going to fall apart.

A clicking sound comes from the door. My feet stumble back of their own accord.

The door opens. A moment passes before a man peers cautiously into the room.

I brace myself just in time. Colors flare across my vision again. They tangle around him like an electrical charge, twisting toward shapes and then disintegrating before I can make sense of their forms. They surge up in front of him, blurring his body in a mad kaleidoscope of smeared pigments and light. Screams and cries bombard me like punches. It's all I can do not to scream too.

"Caitlin?" His voice comes across the distance like a mosquito buzzing amid the chaos. I latch onto the sound all the same.

The colors start to fade. The screams do too.

I'm crouched on the floor, my hands clasping my ears, and when I look up, I find the guy staring at me. Threads of a thousand shades threaten to surge out from him.

Images still flash at the corners of my vision. But they're not as strong as before, almost like afterimages from an explosion that's already passed.

And I...I know him. At least...I think. Red-haired and balding, he's dressed in khakis and a pale blue button-down shirt. I'd swear he's familiar, but I'm not sure it's in a good way. "Cait?"

My brow twitches down. Cait? What's a Cait?

It doesn't matter. He's coming closer now, and my eyes dart to the open doorway. I should run. I just need to get my feet to respond.

"Can you understand me?" He reaches a hand toward me like he's afraid I'll bite. "Can you speak?"

I look back at him. Huh?

He glances at the door. "Listen, I overheard some of these...*things* talking. They say you have powerful connections. Is that right?"

My eyes narrow.

"We can help each other," he urges. "Do you understand? Mister Linden betrayed me. He *promised* I'd be safe. He made me a deal. But now the police are looking for me, wanting to question me about the explosion that old bastard caused in my classroom, and if those cops find me —" He cuts off, checking the door again. "So I'll make you a deal instead. I'll get you out of here, and you'll convince your friends to offer me protection in exchange for my services. Sound good?"

Getting out of here sounds good, yeah. But as for the rest, I have no idea what he's talking about.

I nod anyway.

He echoes the motion. "O-okay. Great. Then, um—" He checks around and then returns his attention to me. "Let's just—" His hand takes my elbow.

It's a mistake.

Images and sounds roar into my mind like a freight train. I can't breathe at the force of them. A brown-haired girl. She's beneath me. Crying. Screaming. Fighting with no chance of winning while I tug her clothes away because I know she wants it. They all do. I saw the way she smiled in class, the shy way she blushed when I said I liked her work. But there's an office now, and she's there too, lying on the floor.

Her wrists are cut. Blood surrounds her.

More images follow, more and more, because she wasn't the first. She was simply the only one who died. Who *he* found dead. But then another woman came, a creature, a thing with such power…and she knew what he'd done. She tracked him down and pinned him to the ground and poured so much pleasure and ecstasy into him that everything else went away. He begged and cried, and oh, how he craved it, but then she threw him into a blood-soaked pit to fight with his bare hands for even a taste, rewarding him when he clawed and bit and ripped and—

I slam into a wall and the images shatter. I'm in the hallway. The room is gone. The guy too, and for that I'm so grateful. But what I saw…what he *did*…

Nausea claws its way up my throat, and I don't stand a chance in hell of stopping it. My stomach heaves. Whatever I have left in me ends up on the floor.

Shivers wrack my body. My fingers dig into the wall to hold me steady. With the back of my other hand, I swipe my mouth while I look around. I have no idea where I am, but there's an exit sign at the end of the rightmost hall.

That's good enough. Oh my *God*, I've got to get out of this place.

I shamble toward it as quickly as I can. The push bar

for the door sounds unbearably loud in the quiet hall. I stumble past the opening and into another room. A loading bay of some kind. Acrid smells of exhaust and oil burn my nose. But there's a door on the other end of the space, and a window in it too. I think I see a tree beyond the glass.

The sight sends a surge of adrenaline rushing through me. Urging my heavy legs to move faster, I stumble across the room.

"Hey!"

I throw a panicked glance over my shoulder.

Another mistake.

A woman and two men are there, but I barely have the chance to register that fact. Instantly, images crash into me. An old man giving orders. A guy dying in the throes of an orgasm. A young woman foaming at the mouth, driven to madness. A man howling while another man rips into him like a rabid dog. Other people now. Fighting and bleeding and dying again and again, and someone is screaming. Someone won't stop screaming.

Make it stop, make it stop, make it *STOP!*

The images rush away from me, driven back the way they came like mist confronted by a hurricane.

And they hit something.

The nightmare vanishes. My vision clears. And the three people crumple to the ground. Their eyes go wide, and their mouths do too. They lurch like they're choking in an effort to breathe. Staring at nothing, the men seem horror-struck and confused, as if they can't understand what's in front of their eyes. The woman retreats, crawling crab-like across the floor. Short, panicked noises leave her, and her eyes dart around as if monsters are coming from the walls.

"Wha—Cait?"

I look up. It's the guy. The one from the other room. The one I *know* that I know somehow, even without seeing what he'd done.

And this time, I'm ready.

The images race away before they fully reach me. I hear nothing more than the whisper of a scream, see a ghost of a bloody fight, and then he's staggering backward. Hitting the wall. Shrieking and flailing like hell itself has opened up in front of him.

In a heartbeat, I'm the only one in the room left standing.

My eyes skip over them. My body feels hollow from more than how I lost the contents of my stomach in the hallway. Everything hurts. I miss the misty light, and I want it back so badly I could cry. But somewhere inside, there's satisfaction too—for that girl he hurt and all the others, if nothing else. There's a sense that maybe I did something right.

Now I just have to get out of here.

An alarm starts up somewhere deeper in the building. I look toward the sound, my heart pounding.

As fast as my shaking limbs can carry me, I run for the door.

7

AMAR

He's never lived through a longer day than this one.

And it's not over.

Shoving to his feet, he leaves the chair where he's sat for the past five-minute eternity and resumes pacing the length of Nasreen's basement office. He wants to be out there, searching. He has been for most of the day, and only came back here because Martin suggested they try additional spells in a place where they wouldn't be disturbed.

But still there's nothing.

He turns, starting back across the basement, but memory pulls him up short as it has every time he's crossed this room. Cait, weeks ago, pacing the office at Temptation in desperate need to be doing *something* while they hunted for Ruby. That intense, worried look on her face. The way he'd wanted to hold her in an attempt to take the fear away.

The way he hadn't.

His fingers curl into a fist in an effort to stay in control. They'll find her. Save her.

He'll hold her again.

Willing himself to believe the thought, he returns to the chair. "Anything?" he calls to Martin.

The boy makes a distracted motion. Crouched on the floor near the center of the room, he doesn't take his eyes from the jumbled collection of objects and herbs arranged before him.

Amar scowls. He doesn't need to be here. He should be out, searching.

And that, too, reminds him of Cait.

He sits down on the wooden chair, closing his eyes and anxiously throwing a few silent prayers up to the demon gods he doesn't even believe in.

But he'll take any help he can get right now.

Bianca is out there, assisting with the search. Brett and Rafael are as well. They're reaching out to every connection they have, though the local ones are few and far between these days. Demons have left Corvinson in droves. No one wants to be where Linden and Volgert seem inclined to start another war.

But Bianca and the others *are* searching. The only reason he's *not* stems from Martin's idea that his familiarity with Cait might help narrow down a target for the spell.

And Bianca's *expression* at that suggestion…

He pushes the thought away. He'll deal with that once Cait is out of danger.

The basement door opens. Katsuro walks in, Sorcha on his heels.

Amar shoots up out of the chair. "Did they say anything else?"

Katsuro hesitates. "Not exactly. The demons we brought in know Alistair intended to keep her in the city, which makes sense if he suspects she is connected to the convergence here, but they don't have any specifics beyond that. They were supposed to wait for a call to tell them where to go, but even though my people went back and retrieved the phones..." He shakes his head. "Nothing."

"Someone saw us take those guys."

"Or else Linden believed we'd kill them, so they never planned to call in the first place."

Amar bites back a curse, looking away. "What about the building where Linden first had her? Is there anything else you—"

Brilliant light like a tiny supernova erupts in the center of the room. He turns away sharply, lifting a hand on instinct to block his eyes while Martin cries out in alarm. Chiming alerts from the computers trip over one another in rapid succession, interspersed with shouts from the students. The light dies as quickly as it came, and when it's gone, he looks over to find a smoking ring of ash where the implements of Martin's spell had been.

For a moment, the kid doesn't move. His face and glasses are blackened by soot, and his expression is frozen with shock. Lifting a shaking hand, he takes his glasses and wipes them on his shirt, though it does nothing but smear the coating. "Spike...spike in the..."

"Spike in the convergence," another student finishes from her post by a computer. "Big one. Um..." She seems to run out of ability to explain.

Katsuro strides toward her. "What happened? Where is it located?"

The girl shakes her head, her mouth moving like she can't find the words.

"Is Cait all right?" Amar asks.

The girl looks up, uncertainty and fear in her eyes as if she doesn't want to respond. Shivers course through him at the sight.

Katsuro glances between them. "Is it still happening? The spike. Is it still there?"

Blinking fast, the girl returns her attention to her screen. "I-I'm not sure. Maybe. Our instruments are—"

"What was that?" Nasreen demands, rushing into the room.

"Power surge," the girl answers. "The convergence just…" She makes an exploding gesture with her hands.

Nasreen shares a quick look with Katsuro. Immediately, the vampire reaches for his cell phone. Nasreen hurries to the girl's desk. "Okay. Attempt to isolate the—"

Alerts ring out from the computers again.

"What is it?" Katsuro asks, covering the phone with one hand.

The girl looks stunned. "Another one. I don't…" She abandons whatever she'd been about to say and begins rapidly typing commands into the computer, her eyes darting up to Amar with every few heartbeats. The sight makes him want to race across the nearest line of shadow, lack of destination be damned. Cait's at the heart of whatever just occurred. He can tell from the expressions of everyone around him, even if no one has confirmed it yet.

They know it's true.

"Martin!" Nasreen calls.

Seated on the ground, the boy is still staring at the remnants of his spell, but at the sound of his name, he flinches. "Y-yeah?"

"Did you get a location?"

"Uh…" Distractedly, Martin attempts to put on his glasses, only to frown when he realizes they're still smeared with soot. "West Corvinson, maybe. It was—" He exhales like he can't find the words.

Amar looks to Sorcha.

"Don't!" Nasreen snaps before they can move. "You'll be searching for hours if you go now." She walks over to Martin quickly and sinks into a crouch at his side. "Focus, Martin." She puts a hand on the boy's shoulder. "We need whatever you can give us."

The kid swallows hard and puts his sooty glasses back on. "Yeah, okay. Um…yes. Right. It came from West Corvinson. There were fluctuations in that area of town just…just like a *minute* before…"

Nasreen's eyes flick away from the boy, landing on Amar for a moment as if to make certain he's still there. "Okay," she persists, returning her attention to Martin. "Then, I need you to find whatever afterimages of that signal are left. Can you do that?"

The kid nods like her words are bolstering him. "Yeah. Yeah, I think I…" He scoots closer to the charred remnants of his spell. Holding his hands above the mess, he closes his eyes and starts whispering quick, nearly inaudible words.

Over the ash and the burned objects, the smoke begins shifting position, drifting as if a breeze has started up in the room.

"How are the sensors?" Nasreen asks her other students.

Sorcha leans closer to Amar, speaking in a low voice. "My people spotted several known Volgert agents in West Corvinson a few minutes ago." Her amber eyes meet his solemnly.

The urge to leave is overwhelming.

"Nasreen!" Martin cries.

The woman hurries over, takes one look at his spell and then turns to her other students. "You picking this up?"

Her attention on the screen, the girl nods. "Yeah. Yeah, I've got that."

Nasreen looks to Amar and Sorcha. "You need to be outside to shadow-cross. Defenses here are too strong."

"Where are they?" Katsuro interjects.

"Close to Belson Street and Fourteenth. Be careful."

They run for the stairs.

⁓

RAIN BEGINS TO SOAK HIM WITHIN MOMENTS OF ARRIVING, BUT Amar ignores it. The moisture will only help the wolves, making scents stronger to their canine senses. And they'll need that. An office complex surrounds them, and every one of the tan buildings appears precisely the same. The streets are dark and nearly featureless. He can't see a single person besides Katsuro and the mercenaries around him.

"Anything?" he asks Sorcha.

She glances briefly at the other werewolves and then shakes her head. "No. There's—" As one, the bikers stop walking.

He hears it a moment later. An alarm ringing. The sound is faint and carried on the breeze that twists between the buildings. He can't track down the source.

"Where?" he asks.

One of the werewolves jerks his chin at a blocky ten-story structure on the other side of the street. The windows are reflective, giving nothing away. No one can be seen at ground level either. But for the whisper of alarms, there's nothing to set the place apart from anything around it.

Keeping an eye to the rest of the complex, he jogs after the wolves across the street.

Glass double doors are the only visible entrance on this side of the building. They reveal the drab interior of the darkened foyer—an empty front desk, several potted plants, a hall with a red exit sign glowing at the end—but the room is unoccupied. The lock on the metal door handle gives immediately to Katsuro's quick tug, and nothing else follows. The alarms are louder here, emanating from beyond the double doors at the end of the hallway.

Sharp, percussive sounds cut through the alarm's blare.

Gunfire.

Amar runs for the hall, and in only a moment, the others catch up. At the end of the corridor, Sorcha skids to a stop and motions for them all to stay behind her while she nudges one of the double doors open.

Bullets shred chips of wood from the edge of the door near her head. She flinches back.

Shouts carry from beyond the opening. The air buzzes with the electric charge of magic. Gritting his teeth, Amar resists the urge to let his own power out. Striking blindly could hit Cait too.

More gunfire follows, growing farther away.

Sorcha releases a breath and inches the door open wider, scanning the hall swiftly before slipping through the gap. Amar follows, and the others do too.

Two corridors greet them, one running straight ahead, and the other branching off on either side. The walls are a bland shade of muted yellow, except for the leftmost, which is speckled with blood and peppered with holes where bullets have torn through.

The door at the end of the hallway ahead bursts open.

People rush through, only to skid to a halt at the sight of them.

And immediately, the newcomers start to growl.

Amar lunges aside, knowing what's coming.

The shift is nearly instantaneous and then come the snarls. The yelps. He shoves to his feet, rushing to put more distance between himself and the growling-werewolf melee.

Katsuro appears beside him. "This way." The vampire races toward the turn of the corridor.

"What is it?" Amar calls, chasing after him.

"Strange noises."

Katsuro doesn't say anything more. They round the corner and keep running, passing open doorways and empty rooms devoid of even the most basic office furniture.

More gunfire rings out ahead.

That Volgert bastard, Kyle, bursts past a door at the end of the hallway. At his back, two men hold a third guy between them. The prisoner looks sedated. His balding head lolls against the shoulder of one of his captors, and his eyes are closed behind his glasses. A red pendant is looped haphazardly around his neck. He hasn't completely passed out, though; choked, desperate sounds leave him, and he twitches and spasms like he's having a seizure.

At the sight of them, Kyle slams to a stop. "Back!" he orders his people.

Katsuro crosses the distance to them in a heartbeat. His hand wraps around Kyle's throat, and he drives the bastard against the wall.

The two men holding the prisoner freeze, looking from Amar to the vampire and back as if they can't figure out who to be more afraid of. Threads of lightning crackle around Amar's hands, vibrant blue. The men recoil.

"Where's Cait?" Katsuro demands.

Surprise flickers in Kyle's eyes. Confusion too, though it's gone only a moment later. But the prisoner starts shrieking and thrashing at the sound of her name like they've put him face-to-face with a nightmare.

"Fuck you," Kyle spits. Silver flashes in his hand.

Katsuro releases him fast, dodging back to avoid the blade, but the knife still catches his side. A pained grunt leaves the vampire.

Clutching his throat, Kyle flips the knife in his free hand and then hurls it through the air. Amar drops to a crouch quickly; the knife sails past. Blue lightning arcs from his hand at Kyle.

The guy's defenses shred before it. Sparks fly, and Kyle staggers, barely keeping his feet. He stumbles forward, throwing himself at the shadows of an open office doorway. The air ripples, and he's gone.

Instantly, Amar sends a second blast at Kyle's companions, tossing one of them to the ground. The other guy grabs their prisoner. Using the shrieking man as a shield, he races after Kyle and disappears.

Amar lets the lightning die. "You okay?" he calls to Katsuro.

The vampire makes an angry noise. "Fine. I've dealt with worse." He straightens, a pained look on his face. "He wasn't here for Cait."

"Yeah." And it's irrelevant. Kyle didn't have her. That doesn't mean she's not in the building somewhere.

Pushing to his feet, Amar walks toward the guy on the ground. He's unconscious.

Dammit.

His attention shifts to the end of the hall. Strange noises, Katsuro said.

He heads for the door.

A loading bay greets him, with the far door standing open to the increasingly rainy night. Industrial lights glare down on the concrete floor. The reek of shit and bile fills the air, undercut by oil and gasoline. But that isn't all.

He walks forward, barely breathing, tightly holding the power inside him in check lest what he fears comes true and he loses control. A trio of bodies lies ahead of him, curled in on themselves. He can't tell who they are. Can't see for sure. Several more people lie nearby, clearly having been shot, and given the gunfire he just heard, he can assume Kyle was behind that.

A choked noise comes from the corpses up ahead. His attention snaps toward the sound. One of the bodies is moving.

Cautiously, Amar paces toward the trio, circling wide. Their faces come into view. Cait's not there.

But he can't understand what he's seeing.

Alarm rolls through him in a slow wave, the feeling growing stronger by the second. Two men and one woman lie on the concrete. Tiny gasps leave the woman, interspersed with the same choked noises as Kyle's prisoner. Like the two other men on the ground nearby, the woman has contorted herself into a fetal position. Like the others, her face is locked in a rictus of absolute terror. Her hands are curled like claws; her arms and legs spasm like she's being shocked. Her eyes are open. They're red-stained from the blood vessels that have burst inside them. More blood coats her cheeks, drying after pouring down like twin rivers from her eyes.

A frightened whimper leaves the woman. Her red gaze

is locked on the ceiling like abominations from hell are descending toward her. She lurches once, twice, and then her body seems to give up, sagging boneless to the ground.

Her eyes roll back in her head, staring upward at nothing.

Amar doesn't move, drawing slow breaths, steadying himself. He grew up with an assassin. He knows more horrifying ways for people to die than he ever wants to remember. But in all that time, in all his *life*, he's never seen anything like whatever killed the three people in front of him now.

"What is this?" he demands of Katsuro. "What happened here?"

The vampire appears flabbergasted. "I..." He shakes his head, not taking his eyes from the bodies. "I don't know."

"Did Cait do this?"

For a moment, the other man doesn't respond. The shock drains from his face, though, settling into something infinitely more disturbing.

Dread.

Katsuro looks over at him. "Call your wolves. We need to find Cait *now*."

8

CAIT

I'M COLD. I'M WET.

And I'm totally lost.

My heart pounds while I race through yet another unknown alleyway. I don't know how long I've been running. The streets blur around me, lost in sheets of icy rain and glaring street lamps. I've steered clear of every major road, every intersection, every place where I hear people's voices.

Because when I come near them…

I choke down another breath, my throat burning, and swipe my drenched hair from my eyes. I tried to keep the visions away from me, tried to hide that first time I came around a corner and saw a person up ahead. I want to hope I didn't hurt them. That I didn't do to them *whatever* it is I did to the people in that building that made them so scared.

But I can't be sure, and I can't stop to find out, so I stay hidden.

And I keep running.

The downpour gets stronger. I'm in a different part of the city now. An industrial district, or maybe what used to be. Signs glow on the walls, neon and vibrant but infrequent. Dark swaths of nothing divide the few bright beacons. I run past them too quickly to read any names.

But my body is growing heavier. My feet stumble more often. My shoes are soaked from endless puddles, ones I can no longer find the energy to avoid.

My running slows. Stops. I come to a halt in the middle of an alley, just beyond the glare of a blue neon sign.

Bewilderment drifts through me while I stare at the glowing blue lights. *Joe's*, the sign reads. I don't recognize it, don't feel like I even should. The neon sign reminds me of another place, though, and that place was important. *Really* important. Scary too, but in a weird way where the memory of it feels sort of safe as well.

It doesn't make any sense.

The clatter of a door opening jolts my thoughts. I turn away quickly, trying to avoid seeing whoever is coming outside while I retreat into the shadows.

My body is so tired.

I stumble. My feet refuse to cooperate with the ground, and then the ground catches me instead. Pain shoots through my palms and my wrists, becoming my entire focus for the one moment I need to use to escape.

"Hey!"

The owner of the voice sounds concerned. Footsteps hurry toward me. I gulp down a breath, my eyes darting toward the sound out of fear. I see the shadowy form of a guy before I tear my attention away.

Too late. A man in an office, gesturing for me to leave. People at their desks, smirking or skirting their eyes away. Security guards, escorting me out while shame burns in my chest. A house now. Pain that would be tears if I could find them. A woman outside, refusing to speak to me, refusing to answer my pleas to stay. That we can still make things work between us. Deaf to my cries, she packs a sobbing boy and girl into a minivan and drives off.

Reality snaps back.

"Hey, are you okay?"

I shriek when he reaches toward me. He freezes.

"I'm not going to hurt you," he protests.

I'm shivering so hard I can't breathe. My body feels like someone replaced my blood with concrete. Rain plasters my sodden shirt and jeans to my skin; they're like lead weights holding me down. I need to move though, because I'm not the only one who might get hurt here.

My head shakes. I can't form the words I need to tell him to go away.

"My God, you're soaked. Listen, I'm going to get you inside. You'll freeze to death if you stay like this."

I flinch when I catch sight of his hand reaching toward me again. He stops, and for a heartbeat, he doesn't move at all.

A breath escapes him. "Okay."

I hear fabric rustling. Warily, I inch my eyes toward the sound.

He's half-silhouetted by the light from the blue sign, but that doesn't stop colors and images from crackling around the edges of his form. Staying clear of me, he shrugs off his coat and then extends it toward me. I tense.

"Take it," he urges flatly. "You need it more than I do."

My confusion grows. Cautiously, I reach out. My fingers wrap around fabric still warm from his body.

He nods. In the dim light, I see his gaze flick over me, over the wet clothes plastered to my body.

Something weird joins the colors crackling around him. Something foggy wisps away from his skin.

And enters mine.

I gasp. A sparkle of energy thrills through my veins like a shiver that doesn't feel cold at all, and abruptly, I remember. I need this. It's not like the white light, like the mist that made me fly even while I was on the bed at that other horrible place. It's food, whatever it is. Sustenance. Balance. It's *important*.

The guy tears his eyes from me, shaking his head almost like he's frustrated with himself, before he pushes to his feet. He walks away, taking the mist with him.

"Wait!"

I blink at the sound of my own voice, rough and cracked like it's raw. But he stops all the same, looking back. "Please?" I rasp.

He hesitates and then walks toward me. Silently, I beg the visions not to return.

"What?" he asks.

I can't figure out what to say. "Don't go?"

He pauses again before sinking down into a crouch. The mist comes with him, brushing across my skin, and suddenly, it's all I can do to keep breathing.

Memories tumble through my mind like rocks cascading down a hill. Katsuro. The lecture hall. Sorcha. Training. Bianca. Amar.

Oh my God, *Amar*…

Pain joins the mess inside me, stabbing my chest like longing and sadness and fear all rolled into one. But… demons. That's what we are. And there's a war coming… and a psych—

"We should probably get inside."

I choke on a breath, my focus returning to the guy in

front of me. He appears edgy, and he glances behind him as if he's torn between staying or leaving me here.

"I-I'm sorry," I manage quickly. I slip his coat around my shoulders. "Thank you."

He doesn't respond. The mist is still there, though. It's getting stronger with every swiftly aborted glance he gives to my body. It feels like life itself pouring into my veins.

But it's not enough. I can feel that too. The demons… what Alistair had them do to me…my mind still hurts, still feels broken, like part of me is stranded atop a steep slope that used to be a level plain. They tipped my whole life out of balance, and if I'm not careful, I'll lose myself to what they did again.

A new, sharper agony stabs at me. I know what it'll take to fix it, though. I remember what Bianca said. What Amar can't help me with.

No matter how much I wish he could.

The pain grows, and with a rough breath, I attempt to push past it. I have to do this. The darkness is still there, and the hunger too, lurking at the edge of my mind.

I can't let it have me.

Swallowing hard, I look up at the guy again. I do my best to ignore the crackling colors around him—with every new brush of mist, they're becoming more controllable anyhow—and I make myself reach toward him. I make myself smile.

"My name's Cait," I tell him. "What's yours?"

9

KYLE

HE'S STARTING TO FORGET ALL THE REASONS HE WANTS THAT Legacy bastard dead, if only as a result of the sheer quantity, but potentially giving him scars is *definitely* on the list.

"Careful!" He glares at the demon binding up his shoulder.

The woman freezes, fear in her eyes. "Sorry, sir."

He exhales sharply, disgusted with her, and returns his attention to the television across the room while she resumes her work. The news is on, though there's no sign the humans noticed anything of their assault on the Linden facility. The oblivious morons were all too busy with some massive kitchen fire at an Indian restaurant on campus. But it's just as well. He wouldn't want human interference with finding that bastard anyway.

Kyle scowls. He'd been distracted; that's why his defenses hadn't held against Amar's attack. That Legacy ass was lucky.

Next time, though…

"Aw, you found him!"

Penny bounces into the room. She's plaited her hair into pigtails since last he saw her an hour ago, back before she wheedled him into going with an attack team to some secret Linden location to retrieve the vegetable currently twitching and drooling on the floor. Never mind that she didn't bother to detail *why* they were going or told him *anything* of what she'd seen in her latest vision. And she certainly didn't tell him that *Cait* would be there, let alone Amar.

No, she'd simply smiled and batted her eyes at his people and cajoled them all into apparently risking their lives, all while she stayed here in safety, playing with her damn hair.

She looks like an idiot.

He fights back a snarl. "Amar Okoro was there."

The brat doesn't respond, her attention on the old guy on the floor. Sedated enough to slow the toxin Penny claimed is poisoning him, the balding man doesn't seem to notice anyone's presence.

"His vampire buddy thought Cait was at that place."

She prods the guy with her foot, smudging a bit more dirt on his already filthy blue button-down shirt. "Wakey-wakey."

"*Penny.*" It's hard to keep the anger from his voice.

She looks up. "What?"

"Why the *hell* didn't you…" He draws a breath, trying to gather his patience. It's a losing battle. "Dammit, we could have grabbed her. Cait's useful."

A peevish noise leaves the girl.

"Why didn't you say she was going to be there?"

"It didn't matter."

His brow climbs. "It didn't *matter*? Penny, she—"

"*I said she doesn't matter!*"

The shriek rings through the room. He stops, hearing something strange in her tone.

He'd swear it's fear.

"What have you seen about her?" he asks carefully.

The girl doesn't respond.

"Is she *dangerous*?"

Her face twitches with an anxious tic.

His alarm grows. "Penny, answer me. Is there something—"

"No."

"But then, why—"

"I said no!" Angrily, she flips one of her pigtails over her shoulder like the hairstyle suddenly infuriates her. "I don't see everything, okay? I'm not like...*perfect*. And that...that stupid girl just..."

He gapes at her. *Excuse me?* "'That girl' what?"

She exhales sharply. "There's a convergence, okay? One of the demons we brought in, they told me about it."

Convergence. She'd said that, back when she had a vision at the barn, though he hadn't been able to get anything else out of her about it. She'd claimed not to know what it meant.

Obviously, that had changed. "What is it?"

Her mouth twists sourly. "A magical *thing* that's in my way. This place, this town, is where it's happening, and *Cait*—" Penny spits the name like a curse. "—is tied right into it. She has to be, because it's screwing with my abilities and means I can't always see her. Or things around her. Or any of it. Not like I can with other people. With her, I just get glimpses. Moments. Flashes. And the stronger it gets, the less I see of her, and..." He can practically hear Penny's teeth grinding. "It doesn't matter. I know what we need to do about it." Penny pulls one of her plaited pigtails back and absently strokes the end like it's a lucky rabbit's foot. "I have the Touched stored away. Hundreds now, from all over the place. They're what's important. I've seen enough."

He stares at the girl, reeling. The *Touched* are what matter here? The rabid horde she's had his demons creating for weeks and they…but Penny can't…she doesn't always see…

Holy shit, *this* would have been good to know.

"You're wasting time," she snipes. "That tranquilizer I told you to give him is going to wear off."

Releasing the end of her pigtail, Penny flounces over to the guy on the ground. She clasps her hands behind her back and bends over, studying the man. "Hi, Mister. You doing okay?"

It's a ridiculous question. Blood has started leaking from the man's eyes.

"I just have one little thing I want to know. Can you help me with that?"

She leans her ear toward him like she's listening for an answer. A pleading expression on his face, the man mewls something. It sounds like "help me."

"Oh, of *course* we will. You'll be peachy, I swear." She smiles. "So okay, here's my question: do you think these pigtails work for me?"

The man gapes at her. His head wobbles in a desperate nod.

"Great." She turns away, leaving the guy begging inarticulately behind her.

Kyle waits, but nothing else comes. "That's it?"

"Uh-huh."

"But…what now?"

Penny shrugs. "Nothing. I just wanted to know."

He chokes on an incredulous scoff. "You just...What the hell did we go get him for?"

"So we'd have him, and Alistair wouldn't."

It's impossible to hang onto his patience this time. "He's a human! He's not *even* one of those damned Touched you've got hidden around town! Who gives a shit if we—"

"He's important."

"*How?*"

Penny gives him a patient look. He wants to strangle her for it. "Because he is."

Magic races through his veins, begging him to kill her.

"Oh, come on," she sighs. "Don't you trust me?"

His teeth grate against each other.

She smiles. "The future's not a straight line, Kyle. You know that, right? You can't just jump ahead. Everything is a mess of probabilities, like puzzle pieces that keep shifting their shape. You have to put them into place very carefully if you want to get the right result. But you do that by finding the fulcrums. The levers. The teeny-tiny moments that shift everything else. A late bus, an early flight, an overlooked person who disappears at just the right time." She tilts her head toward the guy on the floor, grinning. "See, silly, we don't need to worry about *Cait*. She doesn't matter. She *won't* matter. But killing Alistair, killing *Lucretia*—"

Her grin broadens, and something about it bothers him. She knows he'd like that. Knows he wants to do it himself. But there's a weird look in her eye. "One little moment," she says. "One little person. And a few more little puzzle pieces fall neatly into place."

He glances at the man on the ground. The guy is making gagging noises now. His bloodied face makes him look like a monster from a horror movie. With a last, frantic gasp, the man lurches up and then sags to the floor and doesn't move again.

"So we took him so he'd be missing," Kyle says flatly.

Penny nods.

"And how does that translate into killing Alistair and Lucretia?"

"Oh, don't worry about Lucretia. I have that all under control. And as for Alistair...he saw you on the surveillance video for his facility, and his people told him that you work for Volgert. He changes his plans now, out of concern that this human might give you information about him." Penny smiles. "And that puts him right where we need him to be."

I O

———

CAIT

Cool air brushes my back and dries my sweat into a layer of salt on my skin. Thin carpet, barely more than rough fabric over concrete, rests below my bare feet. Soft sounds of breathing come from behind me, where the guy from the alleyway sleeps beneath a tangle of sheets. Mark is his name. I wonder if he'll remember mine, come morning.

My eyes close briefly, and then I rise from the bed, careful not to disturb him. My clothes lie strewn around the tiny studio apartment. I find them by the glow coming through the window from the street lamp outside. In silence, I get dressed and slip out the door. Bare light bulbs burn in the narrow hallway. I can hear the muted sounds of an argument beyond one dark wooden door, the drone of a television infomercial behind another.

And then I'm back outside in the rainy night.

It's nothing like before.

Hugging my arms to my middle, I hurry through the

darkness. I left Mark's coat in his apartment. It wasn't really mine to keep.

And I probably won't ever see him again, anyway.

I shiver. I didn't hurt him; of that much, I'm fairly certain. The force of his desire had nearly overwhelmed me when he first started inside me, and the flood of energy I got from him was unlike anything I've ever felt. Through it all, the visions had still been there too, teasing at the corners of my eyes, trying to draw me in. But I didn't lose control of them—or myself.

Mark would be all right.

I'm not so sure about me.

My stomach twists, and I hug my arms closer. I'll be fine. I'm still me, and I didn't drain him to death.

Tonight could have been so much worse.

The blue neon of Temptation's sign glows brilliantly in the darkness, reflecting on the rain-slicked sidewalk and the windows of the businesses across the street. We'd taken Mark's car to his apartment, ending up only a few blocks from the club—something in which I'm sure there's irony, even if I can't quite find it. But at this hour, even Temptation is long since closed, though a few drunks still linger on the curbside.

I look away from them fast, and the burst of images that follows is mercifully short. I don't try to fight it, don't push it back. I don't need to scare them like I did Alistair's people. I let the images and sounds wash past me without looking too close, and in only a few moments, it's over. The drunks don't react, as if they haven't noticed anything at all. Nothing around me has changed. I release a shuddering breath and keep moving until I reach the door leading to the rear of the club.

Nothing changes after I knock. I glance either way

down the alley, wary of the shadows and the drunks alike, but no one approaches me. On the wall, the twisted magical symbol marking the place as safe for demons glows, same as ever, though humans would only see graffiti. Late-night Ubers slip past on the street, and around me, the rain is the only sound.

The door opens.

"Holy shit," Rafael blurts.

I start to look toward him and catch myself quickly. "Hey."

"Hey." He sounds shocked. "Uh, come on in."

I brace myself and inch my eyes over just enough to see his arm motioning for me to enter the club. But nothing else happens.

My brow furrows.

"You okay?" he asks.

Regrouping, I nod and step inside.

"You're soaked," he says. "Hang on."

The air stirs to my left. I glance toward the feeling, but Rafael is gone. Movement in the hallway on the other side of the club catches my eye. The bartender-turned-ghost emerges from the narrow corridor with a blanket in his arms.

I tense, yanking my focus away.

No visions follow.

I pause, confused.

"Here," he says.

Carefully, I look toward him again. No images bombard me. No colors dance around him like crackling electricity.

He spots my expression. "What?"

I swallow hard, working to find my voice. "Nothing." I

take the blanket and wrap it around my shoulders. "Thank you."

"Are you okay?"

A breathless sound leaves me. I don't know how to answer that. "Is anyone else here?"

He shakes his head. "They're out looking for you."

I hesitate. "Amar too?"

"Yeah."

I pull the blanket tighter around me. I'm not sure what to say.

"Let me get you something to drink, eh?" Rafael suggests. He motions toward the corridor leading to the bar.

I trail after him when he moves that way. When we reach the seating area, he flickers out of sight, and a heartbeat later, lights come on over the bar. He's standing by the door to the kitchen on the other side of the room.

Avoiding his eyes, I walk to one of the barstools and sit down. He gets out a glass.

"We've got to stop meeting like this," he jokes half-heartedly.

Keeping my attention on the glossy bar, I manage something resembling a smile. He turns to the array of bottles. I glance at him.

Still no colors, no images. Nothing.

He turns back toward me. I dart my eyes away while he sets down a shimmering drink of something gold-colored.

"Gimme a second?" he asks.

I start to nod, but he's already gone. Picking up the glass, I look around. The booths by the wall are lost in shadow, and the hall leading to the dance floor is a black abyss. Nothing stirs in the silence.

It's sort of creepy.

I shift my shoulders uncomfortably and take a small drink. The liquid has a woodsy, honeyed taste, and it burns my throat and nose. I grimace at the sensation, but after a few moments, warmth spreads through me like I suppose Rafael intended. Bracing myself, I take another sip.

The door to the kitchen opens.

I jump at the sudden noise. My drink sloshes toward the edge of the glass, coming close to spilling.

Rafael freezes, wincing. "Sorry." He twitches his head toward the kitchen door. "I was trying not to startle—"

"It's fine." I let out a breath and set down the glass. "Not your fault."

He hesitates and then steps past the door, leaving it swinging behind him. "I called the others. They should be here—"

Beyond the hallway, I hear another door open.

"Soon," he finishes.

Footsteps thud in the hall. Lots of them, and the noise sends a surge of panic rushing through me. I exhale sharply, trying to brace myself, and glance toward them—

Death and blood and sex and pain and screaming and fire and carnage, and it has to stop, make it stop, make it stop, make it stop—

I will not frighten them!

The visions melt into darkness.

"Don't touch her!"

"Stay back."

"What the *hell*?"

My eyes open. I'm on the ground, my hands over my face. My head throbs, from the visions or something I hit on the way down, I'm not sure. Through the web of my fingers, I can see the posts of the barstools and a broken glass with my drink spilled around it.

A ragged breath escapes me. I ease my hands down from my face. I can hear the others; they seem all right. I didn't push this back on them and do *whatever* the hell it was I did to terrify those demons where Alistair held me.

It's a relief.

"Cait?"

I hesitate at the sound of Amar's voice. "I'm okay," I tell him, keeping my eyes on the floor.

Silence follows.

Cautiously, I turn toward him. Colors crackle around him. I swallow hard and concentrate, working to see past them, see through them, without doing any damage or really letting any of the images register on me.

The colors fade until they're only a faint shimmer of light. I don't see any details.

I let out a breath, relieved. I don't want to learn things about him without his permission. I don't want to do that to him. Or to myself.

"What was—" Amar starts.

I shake my head. "It's…nothing. It's just—"

"What did Linden do to you?" Katsuro interrupts, his voice carefully even.

I brace myself and glance up at him.

I instantly regret it.

He looks like an overloaded electrical substation met a rainbow from hell. I jerk my eyes away, but not quickly enough. There's too much to see through, too much to even let me breathe. Suddenly, I'm on my knees on the sandy bank of a wide river. A dead young woman is in my arms. She's been beaten until I can only barely see remnants of the once-beautiful girl I knew. Grief crushes me, but I can't cry. I want to scream, but even that sound won't come. Behind me, my beloved village burns, coating the river with ashes while flames paint orange light and gray smoke across the starry sky.

Reality returns in a rush.

I'm clutching my head with my hands. Amar is reaching toward me.

"Don't!" I scuttle backward and bump into the bar.

He freezes.

My heart races. I don't know where to look. What to do. "Sorry, I just…" I gulp in a breath, locking my eyes on the floor. "Please. *Please* don't touch me."

Amar doesn't move.

I draw in another breath. Gritting my teeth, I inch my eyes back up again, finding Katsuro.

Fire and corpses and slaughter…

The colors crackle and dance, and slowly, ever-so-slowly, they fade.

Shuddering, I skirt my eyes around the rest of the room, watching the electrical color storm become only shimmering hints of light around Sorcha, the other werewolves…

I swallow hard. "Sorry," I say again.

"What's going on, Cait?" Amar asks carefully.

I search for the words.

"Is it a danger to us?" Katsuro asks before I can speak. That same tone is in his voice; the flat, neutral one that says I might be a trap now.

And I'm not certain he's wrong. I'm not certain of anything.

Including whether or not I should trust him.

Another breath escapes me. I steady myself on the wall of the bar and climb awkwardly to my feet. Amar takes a step back, giving me space, but he watches me like, the moment I look as if I might collapse again, he's going to grab me no matter what.

It's comforting and painful and terrifying, all at the same time.

"Not if I control it," I manage. My words are met with silence.

"What did they do to you, Cait?" Amar asks, his voice tight. I can hear the worry threading through his tone.

I don't know how to respond. *If* I should respond. It's not about Amar, not really. It's just that I don't have a clue what to say.

My eyes twitch back up toward Katsuro. "Why do you know Alistair?"

I see him tense. It's tiny—a hint of a shift in posture—but it's there. Tingling spreads through me in response, so much stronger than I've ever felt before. It makes my heart race, just trying to hold the magic in.

"Because, as I told you, nearly a thousand years ago, I was one of the leaders of the demon world." Katsuro pauses. "And so was he."

I can't hide my surprise.

"There were thirteen of us who led the Guardians back then. The Guardian Council, we were called, or the Thirteen for short. And, along with countless other Guardians who worked on our behalf, our sole purpose was to keep the peace between the races. But then Alistair betrayed us. In the years leading up to the downfall of the Guardians, he was evicted from the ranks of the Thirteen for his ruthless and often sadistic ambitions, but that was not enough to stop him. He gathered allies and started a war that resulted in thousands of demon and human deaths. And once the Guardians had fallen and many of my friends were murdered, he and his fellow conspirators founded the Houses as their method for creating *peace* in our world."

"What *is* he?" I ask.

Humor flickers over Katsuro's face. "Human, actually. At least, he used to be."

My surprise returns.

"We did have humans among our number, as back then relations between our world and theirs were much better. More equal. More respectful. Alistair was once the foremost advocate for humankind among the demons. But over time, he became unsatisfied. I suspect he made deals, perhaps exchanged favors with witches and djinn and all manner of demons to extend his life, and now he's something else entirely." Katsuro shakes his head. "I honestly have no idea how he continues to remain alive."

I shiver.

"I don't know what he told you about me, Cait, but I swear to you, I mean you no harm. None of my people do. We didn't yesterday, or any day before that, and we don't now."

I watch him warily, not sure what to believe. Nothing I see tells me he's lying, yet Alistair hadn't seemed like he was, either.

But Alistair is a monster.

I glance at the others. I can't tell if Katsuro is telling the truth, no, but I watched Alistair try to use Ruby as leverage to get me into his House. I saw that jackal-smile on his face while he waited for Katsuro to arrive at the lecture hall. In the memories of those demons, I'd witnessed Alistair order them to kill people time and again for his own ends.

But Katsuro saved my life. Amar's life. His people

helped us find Ruby in the first place, not because of a deal we'd made, but because it saved her too.

This isn't about magical powers. It's about facts, plain and simple.

"Okay," I agree.

Katsuro gives me a grateful nod. "Can you tell us what he did to you?"

I tremble. I don't really want to.

Not in the least because I'm not even sure.

"What happened to those people at Linden's property, Cait?" Amar asks. "How'd they die?"

Alarm shoots through me. I look to him in confusion.

And just for a second, it's there. The power slips from my grasp in a twist of light, a flash, and I see them. The demons. They're dead. Curled up and contorted on the ground. Blood has poured from their eyes, drying on their cheeks. The woman's body lurches, gasping, spasming, until she dies too. Oh my *God*, I—

I stumble back, reality snapping into place.

Amar reaches out fast to hold me steady.

I choke. "Don't—"

He catches my arm.

A tall, dark-skinned man with a jagged scar down his cheek, slamming my mother and stepfather against the kitchen wall without touching them. My little sister screaming in terror. The threat, the *promise*, that if I don't leave with him at that very moment, he'll skin them alive and make me watch as they die. More memories now. The man slapping me, punching me, kicking and beating me until I bleed. The man killing people in front of me, torturing them and forcing me to witness every second of their agony.

The man at my feet, dead.

I rip myself away from Amar. He's staring at me. There's confusion in his eyes, not shock, not fear. I can tell in an instant he has no idea what I've seen.

My mouth moves, soundless. I killed those people. Oh my God, I *killed* those people. And Amar…he…

I want to sob. "Don't touch me. Please. Please don't—"

The confusion in his eyes grows stronger, and something else is there too. Hurt. Regret. He thinks this is about him. "Cait," he starts.

My head shakes. I can't risk this. I don't want this.

I bolt from the club.

⚬

I DON'T MAKE IT TEN FEET DOWN THE SIDEWALK BEFORE I HEAR the door open again behind me. I choke on a desperate cry, wanting to shout at the person behind me to go away. They don't know what they're risking. What I could do if I don't keep this under control.

And I don't want to see anything else.

My God, what that bastard *did* to Amar…

"Cait, stop."

Shudders race through me at Katsuro's voice. I keep going.

"Cait!"

My feet obey. The rest of me just wants to scream.

"Don't turn around," he says.

Like I was going to.

Tears burn my eyes. I want to vanish. Shadow-cross into oblivion, even if I still can't figure that magic out.

"Is it sight or touch that causes this?" Katsuro asks.

I swallow hard. "Both."

He's silent for a moment. "Can you control it? Right now, can you control it?"

A shaky breath leaves me.

"Can you *try*?"

I manage a nod.

He's quiet again. I hear his shoes scrape on the concrete. It's for my benefit, I know. One thing I've learned over the past few weeks: vampires don't make a sound unless they want to.

"There's an alley to your left," he says from just behind me. "Walk down there, as far as you're comfortable. We should get off the street."

My eyes close briefly. Right.

I head into the alley. Beyond the glow of the street-lights, the narrow passage is a black abyss. I can't see how far it extends or what might be in my way.

"Four more paces, and then there's a large crate to your right. You can sit down if you want."

I nod. I walk forward, reaching out until my hand finds the wooden crate. I lower myself down.

Silence follows.

"Katsuro?"

"What did he do, Cait?"

My head turns toward the sound of his voice, but I don't try to see him in the darkness. I don't want to; it's easier this way. But there's an odd note in his voice, almost pained somehow, like he's hurting for me too.

I wrap my arms around my middle. "He had these demons. A succubus and two incubi. And they…with the mist, they…" I shake my head, not wanting to go on. I can remember it, what they did. How it felt.

How much I wanted them to continue, no matter the cost.

"Alistair said I wasn't like my mother. Not exactly. Penny saw I had some other power and if I fed enough, it would come out…so that's what he had them do."

"What power?"

"I see things. Memories, I think. Bad ones. And if I'm not careful, or if I try, I can push them back and…" I can't continue.

"Is that what happened to those demons?"

I shiver. "I didn't know I killed them. I only saw it when—"

"When you looked at Amar."

It's not a question. I answer anyway. "Yeah."

He's quiet for a moment. "Don't blame yourself for what happened there, Cait. You did what you had to do."

I swallow hard. I wish I could believe him. I wish it could make this feel better, knowing that I'd had no choice. Knowing that it'd been them or me.

Seconds slip by, broken only by the ambient noise of traffic somewhere deeper in the city.

"Katsuro?"

"Yes?"

"Who was the girl? The one who died on the riverbank by your village?"

He doesn't answer. The alley is so soundless, I'm not even sure he's still standing there.

"I-I'm sorry," I stammer. "I shouldn't have—"

"My sister."

I hear gravel scrape. The crate rocks slightly when he sits down next to me. I shift farther away to avoid touching him. "Was she your, um…only family?"

"No."

I look away, not sure how to ask about what happened, what I'd seen.

The gut-wrenching sorrow I'd felt.

It's not my business, but I can still feel that horror in me. The pain he'd experienced, the loss, and I have nowhere to put it inside.

"I had seven brothers and sisters," he continues quietly.

"What happened to them?"

"They died."

I shift on the crate, embarrassed, uncomfortable. Of course they did. He's a thousand years old. Everyone he knew was probably—

"What would it help you to know, Cait?" he asks softly.

"I…I don't…" I shake my head, not even sure if he can see it. "I'm sorry. I shouldn't have asked."

"Did Alistair tell you things about me?"

I bite my lip. "He said your name wasn't Katsuro."

"Ah."

Silence settles between us. Somewhere in the distance, a woman laughs, the sound fading as she walks away.

I hear fabric rustle, and the crate moves as if he's leaned back a bit. "It isn't. That name is merely an alias I adopted over the past few centuries, since leaving my home in Japan. When I was still human, I was a restless young man, and reckless too, and for a very short while, I was a sailor. Escorting Buddhist monks to the mainland, that sort of thing. But on one voyage out, a storm hit and the ship sank. I managed to swim to an island that, fortunately or not, was home to a reclusive vampire hiding from his own kind. Rather than kill me, he had pity on me and saved my life…after a fashion."

I shiver.

"A newly turned vampire is not all that different from a Touched in some respects, though fortunately, in our case, the effects can be overcome. It took me five years to break free of his thrall and get home. But when they saw me, my family thought I was a ghost. I hadn't aged a day. I was pale, *too* pale, and I couldn't go out in the sun without receiving horrible burns." He pauses. "It was difficult, but as time went by, their fear diminished. They came to see me as a protector. A watchful spirit. The family defender."

He doesn't speak for a moment. "I'd been a member of the Guardian Council only a short while when Alistair staged his coup. The others...I don't think they saw it coming. Or if they did, they were too late to stop it. Six of us survived the initial attack. Four of us were still alive a year after it happened. But in the meantime..." I feel him shift slightly on the crate. "Alistair tracked down our families. My youngest sister—the one I suspect you saw in my memory—was killed outright. Perhaps she fought too much to be captured; she always was the fiercest of us. But for the rest, he saved a special kind of hell. They were turned into Touched."

A breath leaves me.

"I tore the world apart to find them, chasing while Alistair and his people secreted them from place to place. But every time I *did* find them, I was too late. My mother, my sisters, and brothers...they all died in the pit. And my father...that kind, gentle man who loved his family more than life itself, had become their killer."

My stomach quivers. I can't even imagine—No, I can, a little bit. I'd seen my best friend, rabid and insane. It still haunts me.

But to know your *father* had...

"Stories reached me," Katsuro continues softly. "Stories of how his keepers would throw him in the pit with his children and cheer while, in a rabid craze, he tore his family to shreds. And as the years wore on, the popularity of that spectacle only grew. More people were turned into Touched. More pit matches were opened, for betting or vengeance or who knows what else. My family was the start, you see. The beginning of the sick entertainment of watching people die. Before them, making someone into a Touched was typically an accident, and the incubus or succubus who did it was often disciplined for the mistake. To be made into a Touched *deliberately* was seen as a heinous punishment, inflicted upon criminals only in *extremely* rare cases. But after Alistair…" He scoffs, cold and ancient anger in the sound.

"Did you ever find your father?"

Katsuro is silent for so long, I'm not certain he's going to answer me. "I did. He lasted four years in that hell before I discovered where he was being kept. Before I broke him out."

"What happened?"

"The incubus I'd hired couldn't bring him back. No one could. In the end, I was desperate. I tried to turn him." Katsuro goes quiet for a moment. "He didn't survive."

"I'm sorry."

He makes a small noise of acknowledgment. Seconds creep past, filled with old ghosts.

"I will help you, Cait," he says. "In any way I can. My past, my history…it's not pleasant, but it's open to you if it will be of assistance."

I exhale roughly. "But if I can't control this—"

"You'll learn."

I'm speechless at his faith in me. I can't see a reason why he has it.

"You're unique, Cait, and not just because of this ability," he says like he can hear my thoughts. "You care for others. You *fight* for others. I heard from my people about how you went after your friend, and I've seen your determination for myself. There is tremendous power in you—power from who you are and from your link to the convergence alike—and while that power is yours to use how you see fit, I would still count myself a great fool if I didn't do all I could to help you."

I'm not sure how to respond. "Thank you."

"Of course."

I sit in silence for a moment. "Where have you been these past few weeks?"

"Traveling."

I wait, hoping he'll say more.

"The convergence is massive," he continues finally. "It seems concentrated here, but magic all over is changing. There are indications of that fact everywhere. And even the concentration here might shift and go elsewhere." He pauses. "The last convergence was disastrous. The war came of it. So many people died. I've been trying to track down every sign and portent I can, to get ahead of this before it harms us all."

I rub my hands on my arms, suddenly chilled. "Alistair said something about that too. The convergence."

"And you want to know more of what it is," he fills in.

I feel like I'm standing at the edge of a cliff, being asked if I want to jump. But I need to know. "Yeah."

And he tells me.

❧

I WALK BACK TOWARD THE CLUB HALF AN HOUR LATER, feeling like the world has become unstable beneath my feet. I can't detect anything of this convergence around me. Except for the magic I've gained by sleeping with Mark thrumming through my veins, I don't feel anything different at all.

But maybe that's part of it. It's not like I have anything to compare the sensation to.

Sorcha finds me before I make it to the door. One moment, the sidewalk seems empty, and the next, she's stepping out into the glow of the streetlight. I know she didn't shadow-cross; she's just that hard to see.

"Thank you for keeping watch," Katsuro says.

Her eyes cut toward him, but after a heartbeat, she gives a slight nod. "The others are waiting inside." She pauses. "The Chastains as well."

Alarm hits me. Bianca and Brett are here? I mean, yeah, it's Brett's club, but—

I register her careful lack of expression. She was giving me a heads-up, I realize.

"Thank you," I say.

She nods again.

With a nervous glance at Katsuro, I brace myself and walk inside.

"—get the hell out of here already!"

I close my eyes briefly, *so* grateful for Sorcha's warning.

"I'm telling you, Amar," Bianca continues. "We spent the whole damn day tearing this town apart looking for her, and now she waltzes in the door like—"

She catches sight of me. Contempt, distrust, and maybe even fear chase across her face so fast, they last nothing more than a few heartbeats. On the opposite end of the room, Ram leans against a wall, his arms crossed. I can't see any colors or images around the enormous troll, though I have no idea why. But he's watching Bianca with a small smile on his face like he finds her entertaining.

"Why did Linden let her go?" Bianca demands of Amar before I can say a word.

"I told you," Amar replies. "They didn't. She escaped."

"You don't know that. I heard what you found at that building. Cait barely had enough power in her to dent a *trash can*. You expect me to believe she—"

"I'm right here, you know."

Bianca glares at me furiously.

"You okay?" Amar asks me, his voice carefully level.

"Yeah."

Bianca makes an angry sound. "This is bullshit, Amar."

He doesn't respond. Ram snorts quietly in amusement, and Bianca throws the troll a glare for good measure. Ram's grin broadens.

"So where the hell were you, then?" Bianca rounds on me. "The wolves lost your scent halfway across town from that place, and since I *know* you still can't damn well shadow-cross on your own—"

"I got a ride."

"Really?" The contempt in her expression is cutting. "You disappeared for *hours*."

I hesitate. "Yeah."

I don't look at Amar, at anyone but her, and I hope desperately she doesn't put the pieces together. That none of them do. Right here, right in front of everyone, is the last place I want to talk about the *other* thing that happened tonight.

"You were discussing leaving?" Katsuro comments from behind me.

I could hug him. The contempt in Bianca's expression deepens while she pulls her attention from me to the vampire.

"I agree you should," he adds. "And Cait should as well."

My relief dims immediately. "No, I'm not—"

"Alistair succeeded in capturing you once," Katsuro interrupts. "We cannot allow him a second opportunity." He looks to the others. "I've already arranged a location. A small town in Missouri that is home to several of Nasreen's former students. From there, we can—"

"I'm *not* going," I cut in emphatically.

"Cait," Amar begins. "He has a point."

"You have a previously unheard-of ability," Katsuro says. "Along with an apparent connection to the convergence—a connection for which we have no answers. Even if Alistair is unaware of this, which I *sincerely* doubt, we cannot risk that he will remain so. He *will* come after you again."

My heart pounds at the words. "I don't care. My dad is sick. He might die if we move him. I'm not leaving my family unprotected."

"The Houses may not be aware of them," Katsuro suggests.

"*Yet.*"

The vampire's face tightens. "Humans are incredibly difficult to defend, Cait, especially if they know nothing of demonkind. As it stands, they are in far less danger if you leave than—"

"No!" I glare at him. "Volgert used Ruby to get to me. You really want to argue like they might not do it again?"

Katsuro's eyebrow twitches up.

"I won't leave my dad."

"And if we try to get him moved safely?" Amar asks quietly.

"How?" I look at him.

"We tell your family there's a new treatment center. They want him as a test case, free of charge."

I stare at him. It's…It's not a bad plan. It might even work, at least for my dad and stepmom. "What if the demons try to grab them? I know Bianca said the Protection magic was difficult, but…could you put that on them too? It'd be my dad, my stepmom, and two stepsisters."

Amar glances at Bianca. "You willing to help with this?"

She scoffs, but after a moment, she gives an irritated shrug. "Yeah, fine. Whatever."

I turn back to Katsuro.

"Excellent," the vampire says. "Then we'll get your family out of town, and you go as well. Agreed?"

I hesitate. It's not that simple. Not anymore.

Frustration tinges the vampire's expression.

"Alistair said my mother was alive," I tell him.

Katsuro's irritation falters. "When?"

"Before your arrival at the lecture hall," Sorcha says.

"He said she was in trouble," I add. "That she was trying to reach her old contacts for help. He plans to go after her."

Katsuro glances at Ram.

"I'll have someone look into it," Ram states without the vampire saying a word.

Katsuro lifts an eyebrow at me in silent question.

"I can tell if she is who she says she is," I argue.

"We bring her in first," he counters. "And we get you out of town immediately after."

I scowl. I know Amar is watching me. The others too. I feel vaguely cornered, but at the same time, they have a point. Again.

A breath leaves me. They're going to help me protect

my family. Even the shitty parts of it. That's worth something.

"Okay," I agree.

He nods.

I glance at Amar and Bianca. "The twins share an apartment near campus. Arlene and Dad are over on Beecher Street. Can we start there first?"

Amar nods. "Yeah."

Bianca is already striding for the club's back door. Amar motions for Sorcha to follow and waits for me to join him.

My stomach churning with anxiety, I hurry after them.

11

CAIT

We appear in the shadows near the house, beside Arlene's prized rose bushes and out of sight of the road. A glow from the neighbor's back porch lamp provides just enough light to see by and to give us a place to shadow-cross. Amar lets my hand go the moment we reach the yard, and I can't help but be grateful. I've been holding my breath the entire time, fighting to keep from seeing even a *flicker* of memory from him.

"This way." I slip past the bushes and head for the back door, digging my keys from my pocket as I go. Sorcha returned them to me before we left; apparently, Alistair's people left my backpack when they took me, and with it, my keys and wallet and phone. With a nervous glance at the windows, still thankfully dark, I unlock the door. I know it would have been easier to arrive inside the house —surely there's a line of shadow somewhere in the living room—but I worried Arlene might be awake. It's unlikely, given that it's only an hour or so until dawn, but still.

The last thing I need is my stepmother seeing me appear out of nowhere.

Everything seems quiet when I ease the back door open. Shadows cluster in the kitchen, obscuring all but the vague shapes of a refrigerator, stove, and the pristine countertops. Past the entryway to the living room, a hint of light passes through a gap in the curtains, touching on the sofa and coffee table alike. I motion for the others to follow while I weave past the furniture toward the stairs. From the calm way they're walking after me, I get the impression they can see a lot better than I can in this darkness.

"Last door at the end of the hall is Dad's," I whisper when I reach the stairs. I can feel the nervous sweat on my palm when I grasp the cool wood of the banister. "Arlene is in the bedroom to the right. Just...be careful not to wake her."

They don't respond. Carpet dulls my careful footsteps while I creep up the staircase. At the end of the hallway, Dad's door is open a crack. I sneak down to it, eyeing Arlene's door while I pass.

It stays closed.

Cautiously, I push Dad's door wide. Faint light from outside spills past the curtains on the far end of the room, thinning the darkness and turning his green comforter into an emerald-tinted shadow. His face is turned away from us, making it hard to be certain he's asleep, and for the first time in my life, I find myself hoping he's still on his medications since the drugs normally knock him out at night. Better to get rest for healing and all that, even if the doctors have never been entirely sure what's wrong.

He doesn't stir when I step farther inside and hold the door for the others. Amar pauses at the entryway, glancing between the rooms with a considering expression on his face, and then he jerks his chin toward my father. "Make it strong as you can," he whispers to Bianca.

A small grimace crosses her face, but she nods and slips past us into the room. I track her, anxiety twisting tighter in my stomach. Dad's doing better than he has in years, yeah; a few weeks back, when life felt more sane, he and I were even able to have a conversation for longer than a couple of minutes. But exposing him to magic still worries me. It could hurt him if Bianca isn't careful.

It could hurt him no matter what.

I trail after her, watching for the first sign something has gone wrong. The girl extends her palm over his sleeping form, a focused expression on her face. I hug my arms to my middle, not taking my eyes from him.

"Cait." Amar's whisper makes me jump. I brace myself against my own powers and then look over my shoulder to find he's followed me into the room. Sorcha stands by the wall behind us, watching everything with amber eyes that reflect every hint of light with a greenish sheen.

Wolf's eyes.

"Your dad'll be okay," Amar says to me softly. "Promise."

I nod and try to look like I believe the words.

He watches me a heartbeat longer, as if weighing my response, before he nods in return. He moves toward Arlene's door.

It opens before he gets there.

"What the—" Arlene appears at the doorway, her startled face turning white above her paisley nightgown.

An invisible wall slams into me, knocking me backward. I hit the side of Dad's bed and tumble to the carpet. I hear a growl, a shriek, and something shatters nearby.

Glass shards from a vase on Dad's dresser rain down on me.

What the *hell*?

Gasping, I look over to see Sorcha pinning Arlene to the wall by her throat. Pink lightning tangles up Bianca's arms. Her eyes are locked on my stepmother.

My stepmother, who has wisps of virulent green mist emanating from her hands.

I stare. That's magic. She's using *magic*.

Oh my *God*, my stepmother has—

"Arlene?"

My dad's voice shatters my paralysis. I scramble to my feet.

He's trying to push himself up in the bed, a groggy look on his face. Panic rushes up in me, and from the corner of my eye, I see Amar motion quickly. Sorcha releases my stepmom while the magic vanishes from around Bianca's hands.

It disappears almost as swiftly from Arlene's.

"What…what's going on here?" Dad asks, sounding confused.

Arlene's eyes dart over us like lightning, and then her every expression is enveloped by a sugar-sweet mask I know all too well.

"Cait's friends got lost looking for the bathroom, dear," she tells my dad. "No worries. I'll show them out."

"Cait's friends? But why are they—"

"It's fine," Arlene insists. "I promise. Go back to sleep."

Still appearing confused, Dad eases himself down onto the mattress. Arlene waves a hand for us to leave, backing away from Sorcha while she does so.

Amar glances at my dad and then motions for me to

go. He keeps himself between my stepmother and me while we head for the door.

"But, Arlene, I don't—" Dad starts.

"Everything is fine, darling." I can hear an edge in Arlene's sweet tone this time. "I have it all under control."

She pulls the door closed behind us. In the shadows of the hallway, Bianca leads the way while I back toward the stairs. Amar and Sorcha do the same, not letting my stepmother out of their sight all the way down to the first floor.

Arlene switches on a lamp when we reach the living room. The dim, buttery light doesn't fully dispel the shadows clustering at the edges of the room. It makes the place feel like a cave with furniture.

From a corner, Arlene watches us. Her hands are clasped in front of her so tightly that her knuckles are white. She's shaking too. I can see the fabric of her paisley nightgown quivering.

I can't take my eyes from her.

"What the hell is this?" Bianca demands. "Your stepmom's a succubus?"

I want to laugh at the words, except they're not remotely funny. Arlene tormented me for years. She made my life a living hell. She swore I'd turn out just like my birth mother, who abandoned me on their doorstep after I was born.

And she was *this* the whole time. A demon. A succubus who feeds off the—

Oh my God, I want to throw up.

"Did you *hurt* him?" I barely recognize my own voice. "Did you *do* this? Make Dad sick? Did you feed off him and—"

Amar steps in front of me. I realize I'd started stalking

toward her, my voice growing louder and louder with every word.

Arlene's mouth twitches toward the disgusted expression I've seen all my life. Electricity surges through me. Purple mist swirls up around my fists.

Her eyes dart from my face to the magic. The contemptuous expression fades, transforming into the maliciously petty look I know too. The one that says she isn't getting her way, so she'll find some other tactic for causing pain. "What? You think it was easy, repressing two demonic powers in this house?"

I stare at her.

"You think I didn't want to drop you in the river the second I laid eyes on you? I knew what you were when you turned up on our doorstep. That note? That timing? You think I don't know how demons operate?" She scoffs. "Bad enough your father drew attention by sleeping with that bitch. He had to go and get her knocked up with a Legacy brat like *you* too."

I'm shaking so hard I can't breathe.

"Drew attention?" Bianca repeats.

Arlene's eyes cut to her.

"What do you mean 'repressing *two* demonic powers'?" Amar asks.

"Wait, you're repressing your own?" Bianca sounds incredulous. "Why the hell would you do that?"

Arlene's lips thin.

Lightning joins the mist on my hands. "Answer them. Tell them why."

Tell me.

My body aches with the urge to unleash the power I can feel inside my veins. I want to slam her into the wall. I want to throw every memory, every painful moment from my childhood back in her face until she bleeds. Already, I can see the colors around her, weirdly muted and ghostly, yes, but hinting at her past and the answers to all my questions, and it would be easy. *So* easy…

Amar shifts position in front of me like he's ready to hold me back from lunging at her while Sorcha shifts position nearby as if to make sure that she's the one who reaches Arlene first. A sharp breath enters my lungs, painful. It tastes like blood.

"Who are you hiding from?" Amar's voice is carefully level.

A flicker of contempt returns to Arlene's face. "Like I'm going to—"

"Cait has a power that could kill you," Amar interrupts in the same meticulously calm tone. "As do I. But she is barely in control of it, and right now, you are risking your life by goading her."

Arlene's eyes twitch to me, skipping up and down my body like she's trying to see evidence of my ability.

"Answer my question," Amar finishes.

Arlene is silent for a moment. "I want a deal."

Bianca makes a rude noise. "What do you think this is? Television? We're not the police, moron."

Arlene glares at her. "You want what I know; I want to be protected by whatever House you belong to. I want out of this town."

"Information first," Amar replies.

Arlene shakes her head. "I'm not—"

Sorcha growls. The sound is low, menacing, and it filters through the room like a commentary on the continued length of Arlene's life. My stepmother cuts off, watching the werewolf with fear creeping into her expression.

"Who are you hiding from?" Amar repeats.

Arlene's fingers attempt to strangle each other. "Everyone."

"Why?"

Her eyes scurry across us like she's waiting for one of us to lunge at her throat. "Because of what they think I can do." She trembles. "What do you know about ley lines? Convergences?"

The words are about the last things I expected her to say.

"We know enough," Amar responds after a heartbeat.

"Yeah, well, the Houses think I can control it."

I stare at her, reeling. "*What?*"

"We all have talents. Mine is deadening magic."

"Like a troll," Bianca says, half-questioning.

"Tell a joke, you little bitch," Arlene snipes back. "I dare you."

Bianca's brow climbs, her expression more amused than surprised.

"How did that help them with a convergence?" Amar asks.

Arlene drags her attention from Bianca. "They wanted me to control it. Funnel it wherever they said. Linden, Volgert, all of them tried to be the one who kept *me* under control, so I left. Twenty-five years ago, I left."

Amar pauses. "You were the one they thought was the conduit," he says like he's filling in some blank. "They believe you're dead."

"And I want to keep it that way."

Amar doesn't respond.

"Listen," Arlene spits. "I had everything perfect, you understand? I set up a life, married a human, got the picket fence in a territory that's been neutral for damn near a century. Witches sold me magic to repress my hunger, and I had fallback plans for when that wasn't enough. Everything would've been fine, except that *she* showed up." She thrusts her chin toward me.

"Why did that matter?" I try to stop my voice from shaking.

Arlene gives me a dark look.

"Answer her," Amar orders. "Carefully."

Her mouth twists. "Because," Arlene says, her tone edging toward honeyed, "keeping you from developing as a succubus and keeping my hunger under control at the same time wasn't exactly easy. Sure, there were always going to be side effects to my plan, but they would've been manageable. Your daddy probably wouldn't even have noticed, barring a few extra sick days and all. But you changed that. You put a strain on the spells I had, and if I'd tried to buy the kind of magic it would've taken to cover you and me *both*, the energy output *alone* would've drawn attention and defeated the whole purpose. Plus, you were the spawn of some demon bitch who would have come to claim you, meaning I had to take care of that too. You—"

"Wait, what?" Bianca interrupts.

Arlene glares at her.

"You had something to do with Josephine's disappearance," Amar supplies, not quite asking.

I can read the answer in Arlene's face. "You tried to kill her," I say. "You—"

"I *did* kill her."

I go cold. I watch while the cruel enjoyment of seeing me in pain creeps back into her eyes in spite of everyone around us. She likes to hurt me. She always has. She's been smart enough to act with self-preservation when my father is around, but when there's nobody to jeopardize his image of her—

"You think I was going to leave some demon out there to come find you?" Arlene asks. "Find *me*? Please. It wasn't even like it was that hard, considering the Houses are always fighting over some damn thing or another. People get killed in those squabbles all the time. And your mommy was pretty pathetic too, bargaining for her life when she realized she couldn't overcome what I can do. She offered up all sorts of connections and resources—though a fat lot of good those connections have done me now that the Houses decided to start a war here. I need a place to go, a way to move that lug upstairs, but damn near everyone's abandoned this backwater waste of a town. I can't get in touch with most of my own contacts for a safe way out of this place, let alone hers."

A breathless sound leaves me. Alistair said Josephine had been reaching out to her old connections. Said she'd resurfaced after all these years, in dire straits and need of assistance.

I feel like the ground is rocking beneath my feet. My hand grips the back of a nearby easy chair, keeping me steady.

"So why not kill Cait too?" Bianca offers up casually.

I look over at her, alarmed, but there's nothing casual about her expression. Something else, actually. Disgust, but not for me. More like Arlene is the most despicable thing she's ever seen.

"I mean," Bianca continues. "*I* have standards, but if you were willing to do all that to protect yourself…"

"A sick husband *and* a dead brat?" Arlene retorts. "Don't you think that would have raised a couple questions?" She scoffs, glaring at me. "God knows I would have, but from the moment you showed up, that useless lump upstairs was determined to keep you. He called that very day, getting the wheels in motion to adopt you, and next thing I knew, we had caseworkers breathing down our necks, making sure we were a fit mommy and daddy for your squalling little self. It was disgusting. And by the time we'd passed all their tests and jumped through all their hoops, he'd started to get sick." She makes a contemptuous noise. "So I didn't have a choice. I had to let the damage you caused flow out from *practically* the second you came in the door. It took a while for the effects to build up, of course, and I did my best to keep it from the twins because I need them healthy. Their health reflects on me in other people's eyes. But your father's doesn't, so I just had to hang on until you left and hope the magical overload would eventually wear off—not to mention that you'd *stay* gone and keep it from starting up again."

My chest quivers, and I feel like I've been punched in the gut. She'd basically shoved me out the door when I went to college. I hadn't argued, obviously; I'd wanted to get away from her too. But this whole time…

"Twins?"

Bianca's question breaks through my paralysis. "My… my stepsisters," I manage.

"Wait, but then that would make them—"

Arlene snorts. "Funny what you can buy on the black market. Human ova are nothing, and the right doctor will artificially inseminate them for a song."

I struggle to keep my jaw from dropping.

She raises an eyebrow at me. "What? I wasn't going to risk *you* being our only child. You don't even look like me."

I turn away. I can't help myself. It's that or lose control.

Every time I think she can't get more horrible…

I pace farther into the living room, my eyes skipping over the décor. The sterile sofa and chairs, the spotless end tables, the precisely placed family photos—with the twins Kelly and Bethany front and center, of course. They really do look like Arlene. Somehow, I'd always assumed that was genetics.

"Of course," Arlene points out. "Now that you *have* been gone for a while, look how much better your dad has finally started to become."

A shudder runs through me. My skin tingles with the urge to let go of my power and just…*fix* something.

"If you all set me up somewhere," Arlene persists. "Who knows how much healthier he might—"

The steps creak. I look back.

My dad is standing on the stairs. One of his hands clutches the banister while the other braces him on the wall, and both are white with the effort of keeping him upright after all these years of being bedridden. His eyes are locked on Arlene.

Blood drains from Arlene's face. "Honey—"

"Get out." His voice is rough. Furious. I've never heard that tone from him before.

Arlene blinks rapidly, a sugary expression struggling onto her face. "You aren't supposed to be out of bed, sweet—"

"*Get out!*"

She tries for a smile. "You're confused, darling. The medicines, they're making you—"

"I said get the hell out of my house!" He takes a step down the stairway, his hands scooting along the banister and wall, and my breath catches with the fear that he'll fall. But he just glares at Arlene. "And don't you *dare* come near my daughters. Not any of them, not *ever*, do you hear me?"

Arlene stares at him. For a moment, she doesn't even seem to breathe, and then every trace of saccharine falls from her face, transforming into rage.

Sorcha is already moving. She collides with Arlene, sending my stepmother's attack wide. The magic hits the wall beside the stairway, scattering into a small fountain of green sparks that leave a scorch mark on the wallpaper. Snarling, Sorcha grabs Arlene and shoves her toward the door.

My eyes fly to my dad. He's gaping at Sorcha and Arlene, his face utterly pale.

Arlene staggers to her feet. Green mist sputters from her hands, thinner and fainter than before, and suddenly the truth hits me. She's weak. I can see it in the way she's shaking, in the bloodless cast to her skin. She probably hasn't fed in years, and the power she's expended in attacking all of us...

Magic flares to life around Bianca's hands. "Try it, bitch."

Sorcha lets out a low growl like she's seconding the threat, a deadly promise in the sound.

Arlene looks between us. "We had a bargain. I—"

A harsh noise escapes me. Purple lightning surges up to engulf my forearms, snapping and crackling, and I know that if I let it go—if I let *any* of my abilities go—I'm going to kill her.

I'm not sure I care. She tried to hurt my father. She's *been* hurting him for years.

"Go," Amar orders Arlene. "Now."

Arlene trembles so hard her hair shakes. She hesitates for another heartbeat and then fumbles for the lock.

She leaves the door gaping open when she runs outside.

A gasp escapes me, rough and raw. Sorcha strides to the doorway. She scans the indigo predawn shadows of the neighborhood for a long moment before closing the door.

The mist and lightning fade from around my hands.

Amar comes closer. He's careful not to touch me. "Breathe," he whispers.

I attempt to do what he says. Shuddering breaths enter me, like my muscles can't quite make my lungs work. My eyes skip up, finding Sorcha, Bianca.

My father.

He's frozen on the stairs. He's staring at me, just me, and I can't read anything in his blue eyes.

Words fail me. My mouth moves for a moment before the first thing that pops into my head emerges. "Hey, Dad."

❧

HALF AN HOUR LATER, WE'RE WALKING DOWN A SIDEWALK ON our way to meet someone named Nasreen. Amar supports my father, the better to keep my dad and me both safe from what I can do. Katsuro is with us, wrapped in a voluminous black coat that shields him from the first rays of sunrise, and Ram accompanies us as well. The two of them showed up in a large SUV only minutes after Amar called them from the house, and to their credit, they've taken my father's dumbstruck reaction to the words *vampire* and *troll* in stride. Dad's still watching them, though. He's watching all of us, and it's clear he can't quite wrap his head around what he's been told.

Not that I blame him.

I take another steadying breath when we arrive at an alleyway and Katsuro turns. Dad looks to me, questions clear in his eyes.

"It's fine," I say. "I promise."

I hope I'm right.

We follow the vampire around the corner. It's narrow, this alley, but weirdly familiar. I cast a quick glance back to the street, confused, before it hits me.

Katsuro. This is the place he took me after the parking garage and the attack on Temptation, back when his people saved me from Kyle a few weeks before. The alley that was close to safety, he'd said. But I'd insisted we return to Temptation before I'd learned what was actually here.

Anxiety thrums through me. I stay with the others, continuing on until Katsuro reaches a metal door halfway down the alley. I wait while he knocks.

And I cringe when the door opens.

A slender woman stands there. She wears a simple shirt of silky blue fabric and a long skirt with a mosaic pattern a shade darker. Her light olive skin is framed by long coal-black hair, but colors and images whirl around her like a maelstrom, and I can't breathe for the seconds it takes them to fade. The intensity of it reminds me of Katsuro. I'm starting to wonder if it means someone is far older than they appear.

"Welcome." The woman steps aside, gesturing for us to enter. "My name is Nasreen."

I manage a smile while I watch Amar help Dad inside. I know Amar is keeping a close eye on him, but he's still weak. I've spent most of the trip here worrying he'll collapse.

"Katsuro informed me of your situation," Nasreen continues. "I assure you, you will all be quite safe here."

"The twins?" I ask. "Dad called them, but—"

"I have already sent several of my people out to meet them and bring them here," Nasreen assures me.

I hesitate.

"Nasreen trains witches," Katsuro fills in as if he sees my next question. "Her students will be well equipped to handle anything that comes their way."

"Witches," Dad repeats, his voice hoarse. "So does that mean she's a—you're a—"

Nasreen smiles, her large, dark brown eyes flashing red as gemstones for a heartbeat. "Oh no, I'm a djinn. We're something else entirely."

He stares at her. I try not to do the same.

"This way, please." Nasreen starts toward the back of the shop. "I own the floors above this store; the entire building, in point of fact. Several of my students live above us. I've arranged for you all to stay in an apartment between two of my pupils, both of whom will take turns checking on you for as long as you choose to stay here." She glances at my dad when she reaches a door in the back corner of the shop, her eyes kind. "Whatever was done to you, we'll make sure you recover just fine."

I can feel Dad watching me. I attempt to smile as well, though I can't bring myself to meet his gaze. I hurry up the steps when Nasreen opens the door.

On the third floor, she leads us from the stairway into a narrow hallway with dark brown doors along either side. A window at the end lets in the pink-gold glow of sunrise.

I can't believe it's only been a few hours since I got away from Linden. Since Mark. Since everything.

It feels like a lifetime.

Nasreen stops halfway down the corridor. She unlocks a door on the left and then hands the brass-colored key to my father. "You're free to go if you choose, of course. I'd recommend staying, though, at least until we can be certain you'll be safe."

Dad's fingers wrap around the key. He seems as if he can't figure out what to say.

She smiles again and pushes the door open. A well-furnished apartment meets my gaze. A living room lies directly ahead, while open doors on either side of the space lead into bedrooms with queen-size beds under neutral-patterned comforters. The décor all around us is made up of muted shades of greens and browns. In the small kitchen to our left, a kettle waits on the stove with several boxes for tea on the counter nearby.

"Please make yourselves comfortable," Nasreen offers. "Katsuro and I have a few additional arrangements to put in place, but we should have more information about relocation plans soon."

I manage a nod. Nasreen and Katsuro walk back down the hall. Amar helps my dad over to the couch and then steps aside to allow me space to sit as well. I murmur my thanks while I lower myself onto the brown cushions. The smell of cinnamon and sage rises from the throw pillows beside me, adding to the earthy feeling of the room.

Amar returns to the door where Bianca is waiting. My eyes track him.

"Caitie," my dad says.

I tense. Over by the doorway, Bianca is talking to Amar in a low voice. I can't hear a word of what they're saying.

From the corner of my eye, I see my dad reach for my hand. I flinch away. "Yeah?"

He doesn't respond for a heartbeat. "Are you okay?"

"Yeah."

I don't need my supposed superpower to tell he doesn't believe me.

"These people…" he prompts.

"They're okay."

He's silent.

"I know it's a lot. All this…" I struggle to regroup. "But they're good. Different…but good."

He nods, glancing toward Amar and Bianca. "And the people who are after you…"

I freeze.

"I've seen the way these folks are staying close to you, honey, and how jumpy you are too. You're in trouble, aren't you?"

I don't know what to say. His brow rises, waiting.

"Yeah," I admit in a small voice.

He takes a slow breath. "Is it because of Arlene?"

I shake my head. "No, it's just—" I cut off, not sure how to explain. "There are some others. De—" I push the word out. "Demons, mostly. But it's not a big—"

"Caitlin." He's not buying my claim for a second.

I rephrase. "I'll be fine."

He studies me. I try not to fidget under the scrutiny.

"But you're doing okay otherwise?" He says it like he's making sure, like it's all that matters to him. A breath presses from my chest, pained with how much I know he cares.

"Yeah. Much as I can."

"And these folks, they'll take care of you?"

I hesitate, wanting to point out that I can take care of myself. But I can't say that. It means explaining what I can do…what I've *done*…

And something in his expression stops me too. Guilt,

maybe. He's never been able to look out for me the way I know he wanted to, and with his wife turning out to be a demon…

I manage a smile. "Yeah."

He nods again, more firmly, and it hurts to see. I look away.

Amar is watching us askance, even while he says something to Bianca. She scowls, clearly displeased.

I hear my dad let out a breath. I glance back. "Why don't you try to get some sleep, eh?"

He seems to consider arguing, but fatigue wins out, and he murmurs in agreement. I get up and look over in time to see Amar heading for us again.

"Mister Faire." Amar reaches down, offering to take my father's hand. "May I, sir?"

Dad pauses. "Your name's Amar, right?"

Amar nods.

"Thank you for helping my daughter, Amar."

I bite my lip, uncomfortable, but Amar just nods again.

Dad gives him a smile, though I can see how it's strained by exhaustion. Amar supports him while he rises to his feet. Gently, he leads my dad into the other room. I trail after them, glancing to the door while I go. Bianca is there. She watches us, her attention staying on me a heartbeat longer than the others. I can't read the look in her eyes.

Without a word, she turns and leaves the apartment.

Shifting my shoulders, I continue to the bedroom door. Amar is helping my dad to the bedside.

"We'll be outside if you need anything," he offers while Dad sits down.

Dad hesitates, checking toward me again, before he nods.

Amar walks back. I retreat a few steps, giving him space while he closes the door.

And then it's just the two of us.

"Thank you for..." I don't know where to begin. I gesture to the bedroom. "And just, you know..."

"Of course."

That brings an end to everything I can figure out how to say. The silence stretches, filled with every creak of the building and noise from the street outside, but utterly devoid of anything resembling conversation.

"You've gotten stronger," Amar says quietly. "Your magic, I mean."

My stomach drops out. Oh God...

"You fed from someone."

It's not a question, because clearly, he knows the answer. But what he thinks of that—hell, what *I* think of that—is a total unknown. And I can't bring myself to talk about it. I'm too exhausted. I've *been* too exhausted for days. My whole life has come down to surviving the next moment, the next crisis. I've got nothing left to process this.

"I-I should really check about the twins. Make sure they're—"

"Are you okay?" Amar interrupts.

I falter.

"Cait, that's all I want to know. If you're all right?"

I manage to drag my eyes back to him.

"*Are* you all right?" he repeats.

My shoulder twitches. "I guess."

His eyes flick over my face like he's reading whether or not to believe me. I look away.

"Did this person hurt you?" An edge comes into his voice. "Was it someone Alistair—"

I shake my head fast. "No, no, Alistair didn't…" I can't finish the sentence.

"Cait."

"It's fine. I just…"

"What?"

A grimace twists my face. "I don't know."

He's quiet. My stomach explores how to turn itself into a pretzel. My attention darts to the hallway, to the door of my father's room, to anything that might be an escape from this non-conversation.

"We are what we are."

Confused, I glance up at him before I can stop myself.

"This doesn't change anything for me."

I'm silent. He doesn't seem to be lying.

But I'm not sure how that could be the truth. I know he's probably been with others, even in the time since we slept together. It's been weeks, after all, and I only made it through that time by hanging around the edges of crowds at Temptation. It's difficult to think about. Difficult to wrap my feelings and emotions around that fact without pain, but then it's not like he has much of a choice.

Neither did I.

But it still sucks.

"I know that we don't get what others have," he says quietly. "The choice to only share a bed with each other. I've known for most of my life I would never have that with anyone. But that's not the point for me, because also I didn't think for one *second* that I'd get what I have with you." His fingers move toward mine, pausing several inches away. "Someone to…to care about…like I care about you."

His dark eyes flick up to meet my own. Air presses from my chest at the intensity I find there.

"This *doesn't* change anything for me," he says again. "Please don't think that it ever will."

And I'm supposed to be the one with the people-reading power.

I draw in a rough breath, at a loss for what to say. I look down, wanting to take his hand, frightened that I can't.

That feeding on others isn't, ultimately, what will tear us apart.

"Katsuro told me what you're seeing," Amar says quietly. "When I called him from your dad's house, he explained it."

His fingers move closer to mine, only to stop when I pull back.

"And so now," he continues. "If I touch you…"

Tears burn in my eyes. It's so ridiculously ironic. All this time, I've been struggling to know how to talk to him, how to *begin* to engage the fact he has a power that can kill people with a glance.

And now I do too.

"What did you see when I touched you in the bar?" he asks.

I struggle for words. I'm scared I'll upset him if I tell him this. That no matter what he just said, if I tell him the truth, he'll try to leave, pull away.

Something.

"Cait?"

"Your dad."

Amar is silent. The pressure builds. I have to look up.

He just seems sad. "I'm sorry you had to see that."

The words are absurd. "That's not—" I sputter. "Amar, what he did to you—"

"Was over a long time ago."

My mouth moves. I don't know what to say.

"I'm sorry you saw it, though."

I shift my shoulders slightly. It wasn't all I saw. His father's body had…"How did he die?" I can't hold back the question.

Amar pauses.

"I saw…he was on the ground and—"

"I didn't kill him." Amar seems to consider his words. "But I didn't stop him from being killed."

I wait.

"Linden sent assassins. I saw them coming. He didn't."

I let out a shaky breath. "Is that why he—Alistair, I mean—why he doesn't bother you or—"

"Yeah. I think so, anyway. Alistair knows I could have killed the people he sent. Lucretia doesn't, but she has her own reasons for leaving me alone. And because those two do, and because no one trusts each other not to have some ulterior motive, the other Houses leave me alone as well, so…"

I nod.

The silence creeps back again.

"Cait, I—"

"I'm sorry," I blurt out.

He pauses.

"For these past few weeks," I explain. "For avoiding you and—"

"No," he starts before I finish. "I shouldn't have been avoiding—wait, what?"

"What?"

I stare at him. He stares at me.

"You were avoiding me?" I ask.

He's silent.

"Why?"

For a heartbeat, he seems to search for a way to respond. "Penny."

"But…I don't understand. She's not—"

"It's what she said, before you brought her back. Do you remember?"

I hesitate, the memory falling into place. *You'll kill her, you know.*

He thinks she meant me.

"Yeah." My voice is small. I'm not sure what else to say.

He nods like I've confirmed something else entirely.

"But I don't believe her," I add, a touch desperately.

His eyes find mine again.

"I don't," I repeat.

"Why not?"

The words hurt. I don't really have an answer to them. Not a good one made of magic or verifiable proof, anyway.

I only have him. Me. Us before fear got the better of me and made me question what I know.

"Because I trust you," I reply quietly.

Something pained moves through his expression. He lifts a hand slowly, cautiously, watching me the whole time, and he stops only inches from my cheek. "I terrified you. I never…" He struggles for words. "I hate that. I…"

"Seems we're even now," I whisper.

The pain on his face grows. "I would never hurt you with what I can do. I *swear* to you. I would die before I let this power touch you."

I tremble. My fingers reach up, and I don't even breathe. Carefully, I slip my hand atop his and bring his palm over to cup my cheek.

Relief flickers across his face. Gently, he slides his other arm around me, his careful movements making clear he'll pull away the moment I look like I'm struggling.

But I'm okay.

I close my eyes and let out a breath, resting my head against his chest while he holds me. Colors flare across the edges of my vision, hinting at the past, but I ignore them. They're stronger around demons than humans; I'm figuring that out. But if I try, I can keep from seeing them too.

"I'm not going to hurt you, either," I whisper.

I feel him nod. "I trust you."

Tears sting my eyes. His hand strokes my hair, the sensation so soothing, and slowly, the whole world fades away. There's only his strong arms around me, his warm chest against my cheek. There's only the gentle rise and fall of his breaths, and the tension seeping from my muscles, and the peace settling over me.

There's only us.

Someone clears their throat over by the front door. I draw a quick breath, opening my eyes.

Katsuro is standing there, two people behind him who I can only assume are Nasreen's students. "My apologies," Katsuro says.

Amar makes no move to release me, and I can feel a statement in the gesture, like he's making something clear to the vampire, although I don't know what. Protectiveness, perhaps. Or that he doesn't give a damn anymore if the vampire knows he cares about me.

Or maybe it's just too late to pretend we're only acquaintances.

"What do you need?" Amar asks levelly.

"We're nearly prepared to go."

Air escapes me. What? Already? "But my dad—"

Tension shows on Katsuro's face, making me cut off. "We'll get him and your stepsisters out of here too, but it would be better if you stayed separate from them for a while—for their sake and yours, in case the Houses come after you." His mouth tightens. "Or in case your stepmother lets them know any details that could help them find you."

"But I can help protect him if—"

"Not when it's you the Houses are after." Katsuro's face is solemn. "You don't want your family caught in the crossfire, Cait."

I shrink inside, chilled by the memory of what happened to his family.

"We'll keep them safe," he says. "I promise you. We simply need your help getting a few things in place before we leave." Katsuro motions to the two people with him. "They will stay to help watch over your father."

Amar nods. "We'll be downstairs in a minute."

Katsuro bows his head briefly. He doesn't make a sound when he disappears back down the hall. The students remain by the open doorway.

I look at my dad's room. How can I be leaving already? I just got here, and he won't—

Amar reaches up, brushing back a strand of my hair. "It'll be all right," he promises. "But we do need to get you out of here. You're the one the Houses will be after. Your family will be safer if you're away from them."

The words hurt like the twist of a knife in my chest. I'm a danger to Dad. A danger to him and my stepsisters in a way that I never even knew I could be.

And suddenly, a new thought hits me.

This is the same choice Amar made all those years ago. The choice to shield his family from the demon world in the only way he could. By staying away from them. By making sure anyone coming after him wouldn't look their way. Even with his dad dead, he never went back except once, when he put a Protection on them. And then he just…left.

I never thought I could make that choice too.

"Come on," he says gently.

I nod distantly and walk with him when he starts toward the door. It's not forever, I remind myself. It's only…only for a while.

Even if I don't know how long that's going to be.

1 2

KYLE

Of all the places he'd intended to spend the morning, a cheap diner stinking from years of grease and burnt food was definitely not on the list.

"You're sure about this?" he asks.

A slurping noise answers him. Across the table, Penny looks up from her strawberry milkshake. Pigtails still hang down behind her, now adorned with pink polka dot ribbons that clash with her red hair. The demented eighteen-year-old has added a frilly pink dress too, though where the hell she got it is anyone's guess. Another favor from one of his people, Kyle is sure, not that she bothered to clear it with him. The only reason he's here is to make sure he maintains some semblance of authority over the damn coup he started, even if the effort hasn't done him any good lately. She hasn't told him much about why they're here, and she hasn't explained what she brought with her either. A pink backpack painted with white butterflies sits on the chair next to her. He has no clue what's inside.

"Huh?" She blinks at him in confusion.

"I asked if you're sure about this? This person you say we need to meet before going to get you-know-who—"

She releases her straw and giggles like she can't believe his words. "That's a silly question, don't you think? 'Am I sure?' This *is* me we're talking about." Her pigtails swing when she looks past him, scanning the diner. "Have you seen the waitress?"

He eyes her balefully. "No." He turns back to the window. Despite its plastic-and-grease interior, the diner has the audacity to charge an arm and a leg for their milkshakes.

Penny is on her third. He knows. He's kept count, seeing as how she and the waitress both seem to think that he—Penny's "big brother"—is going to pay for them.

For gods' sakes, it's not like he even looks that much older than the girl, barring the fact she's dressed like a goddamn child.

His teeth grind. On the road outside, cars roll down the street in fits and starts, rushing ahead or coming to reluctant stops depending upon the whims of the stoplight at the corner. A cluster of vehicles occupies every spot in the sliver of parking lot in front of the diner. The breakfast crowd is in full swing.

But there's no sign of their target.

"You done already, honey?"

He scowls at the sound of the waitress's cheery voice.

"I'll have another one," Penny replies promptly. "Chocolate this time."

The waitress pauses. "Now, sweetie, you might want to save some room for—"

Kyle straightens quickly in his chair, barely noticing how the waitress cuts off at his sudden movement. Down the street, a woman has just gotten off a city bus. Her attention scurries around like she's trying to watch for an attack from every angle while her tension screams she's trying—and failing—to look inconspicuous at the same time.

But that's not what matters. She matches the description Penny gave, from her disheveled auburn hair to a ragged, too-large trench coat that looks like it probably belonged to a homeless guy. Beneath the stained coat, she's wearing a pair of cheap pink flip-flops and what are *clearly* pajamas.

"She's here," he says to Penny. Quickly, he fishes out his wallet and yanks out several bills. He pushes them at the waitress. "Leave."

The waitress blinks at him.

"*Now.*"

She huffs and takes the money. He ignores her muttered insult while she walks away. The woman is coming inside now. She's scanning the diner like she's looking for someone.

"Mom!" Penny hops up from her chair and bounces toward the woman, her pigtails swinging wildly. She stops squarely in the midst of the other restaurant tables, ignoring the way the people around her stare. "We saved you a seat over here!"

Penny waves a hand for the woman to follow. Warily, the woman walks toward the girl, still eyeing the diner like she's expecting a trap. Staying just out of reach, Penny retreats till she reaches the table, grinning all the while.

"Sit, sit." Penny gestures at the cheap plastic chairs. "You want a milkshake? He's paying."

Kyle fights back a glower.

The woman's attention skirts to him before returning to Penny. "Who are you?" she asks, her voice low.

"*Sit.*" Penny points insistently to the chair beside him. He scoots farther away, not wanting to get too close to the woman or her repulsive coat. The stench of rank sweat, garbage, and what could only be roadkill hangs around it like a cloud, assaulting his nose.

The woman eases into the chair.

"Perfect. So yes, introductions. Easy. I'm Penny. This is Kyle."

He restrains the urge to curse for how she introduces him—both of them—so casually. And with their real names too.

Idiot.

"And you're Arlene, right?"

The woman stares at her.

"Oh, don't worry." Penny grins. "We're not your enemies. We're just here to stop you from making a huge mistake."

He didn't think it was possible, but the woman looks even more edgy than before. "Mistake?" Arlene asks.

"*Huge,*" Penny repeats. "Like, *epic.* You were here to meet your contacts at Volgert, right? Or, I mean, *somebody's* contacts. I don't think they were really yours. They don't believe you. Or they won't. Or, rather, they wouldn't have. The future's so funny, don't you think? The verb tenses *alone.*" Penny huffs dramatically. "But anyway, the Volgert guys would get really mad, and then you'd have to kill them, and it would have gotten *totally* messy. Or, well..." She giggles like she's told a joke.

Arlene stares at her. Kyle glances around quickly, hoping that despite the general noise of the restaurant, nobody overheard. He'd swear sometimes the girl has no survival skills, except that he knows that's probably not it. She'd simply see the threat coming.

"So what do *you* want?" the woman asks.

"Your help. See, we can offer you a deal. You want to get out of town, run for the hills, all that. But we can offer you something better."

"What?"

Penny grins. "Power. Protection. Other things that start with P, I'm sure. Plus revenge. *Lots* of that."

Arlene pauses. "Revenge?" Her tone is cagey, but Kyle can hear the interest in it.

"Absolutely. I mean, you're a succubus. A beautiful, powerful demon, right? You should have men, women, *anybody* just eating out of your hand. But here you are, in your pajamas and that *nasty* coat, planning to bargain for help from those sillies in House Volgert. There has to be someone you want to make pay for that, yeah? Maybe more than one someone."

Arlene's gaze flicks from Penny to Kyle and back again. "In exchange for what?"

He wishes he knew.

"You have a talent, yeah? Something that makes you special? Well, we'd like you to use that for us."

The woman's expression goes totally blank in the space of a heartbeat. "I don't know what you're talking about."

Penny smiles. "We're not with the Houses, Arlene. Not even close. We're going to take them apart into itty-bitty pieces and make their leaders cry. And you'd like to be a part of that, wouldn't you? I *know* you would. So that's what we're offering. You help us, and together we'll destroy the Houses and take over the world. Sound fun?"

Arlene scrutinizes them both like she's working to

figure out how they're going to bite her. "How?" she challenges finally.

"Simple. You've heard of the convergence, right? Well, we just need you to—" Penny cuts off suddenly, looking past them both to the diner entrance. "Whoops, hold that thought."

Kyle turns in his seat. Half a dozen men have walked into the restaurant, all of them enormous. They have builds like they're solid muscle under their crisp black suits, and they're scanning the interior of the diner as if they're searching for somebody to shred.

His heart plummets. He recognizes a few of them. Volgert. And more importantly, that means they'll probably recognize him too. He's managed to keep Lucretia from knowing about his defection so far. He's even succeeded in recruiting more of her people to his cause—though lately, they've all ended up answering to Penny within hours of joining him. But this...

He turns back quickly. "Penny, we—"

She's jumped up on her chair.

And she has a gun.

"Hey, guys!" she shouts.

The men look toward her, but it's already too late.

She fires. Her hands buck with the force of the gun, but she doesn't stumble or drop the weapon.

Or miss.

Kyle watches with mounting shock. Screaming, the other people in the restaurant hit the deck, cower behind their tables, or scurry for the door. Penny doesn't spare them a glance. The Volgert guys scatter, but that doesn't matter either. Every shot hits them. She doesn't even seem to be searching for them, just firing with the absolute confidence that she knows exactly where they're going to be. Nobody else may as well be in the diner at all.

The last Volgert guy falls. He's not dead, though. Penny only clipped his shoulder; her first shot that even came close to being a miss.

But it doesn't appear to bother her. The girl simply hops down from her chair. Keeping the gun out, she slings her pink butterfly backpack up onto her shoulders and then skips across the room, her pigtails swinging, until she reaches the Volgert henchman.

Arlene stares at her. Morbid fascination propels Kyle from his seat. This is…He knew she was nuts, but shooting up a busy restaurant in broad daylight?

Shit.

He checks for security cameras while he follows the girl. There's only one. It hangs behind the front counter, pointed at the register. He doesn't think it could have spotted them, but he's not certain.

"Hey." Penny bends over where the guy is lying on the ground, pain clear on his face.

Kyle ducks away, watching the Volgert henchman askance and hoping the man won't look at him too closely. Humans are one thing, but a lackey of Lucretia's is quite another. Penny might still kill the man, but just in case…

"Hey!" Penny nudges the Volgert guy with her foot.

The man glowers up at her.

Penny grins. "Tell Lucretia that Alistair Linden says hi."

The man's eyes widen with enraged alarm.

Penny steps back. "Well?" She motions with the gun when the man doesn't move. "Go on. Go tell her."

For another heartbeat, the man glares up at her before

his eyes dart around to the other Volgert people lying dead on the ground.

Penny makes an expectant sound.

Gritting his teeth against the pain, the guy shoves himself up with his good arm. He clutches his wounded shoulder and never quite takes his eyes from Penny while he runs from the restaurant.

Penny whirls away from the entrance. "Time to go, brother dear." Without waiting for his response, she starts toward the swinging kitchen door of the diner.

Kyle looks to Arlene. The woman is staring at Penny… and at him.

"You coming, Mom?" Penny calls. "More unfriendly people are on their way, not to mention the cops who'll be here in four minutes and fifteen seconds. I promise it'll be *much* more fun if you're with us."

Arlene's mouth moves, her words inaudible. He can guess what she says, though. Penny brings out the urge to swear in him damn near constantly. But after another moment, Arlene seems to conclude following is her best option. She hurries after the girl toward the kitchen door.

Kyle mutters a curse and does the same.

In the kitchen, one of the cooks starts toward them with an urgent expression. "Little girl, are you—"

Penny swings the gun up, and the man slams to a halt, his feet skidding on the tile and his eyes going wide. But Penny doesn't fire. Trotting past, she keeps the gun aimed at the man while she heads toward another door near the rear exit of the diner.

"Just one more thing," she calls cheerily.

Kyle glances into the room after her. A cramped office lies past the doorway, with barely enough space for the bedraggled and mismatched furniture inside. Along the opposite wall, a tiny desk is wedged between two dented file cabinets. A monitor sits atop the wooden surface, views from the security camera playing in black and white across its screen while, under the desk, a cheap computer tower blinks green lights at the crowded little room.

Without hesitation, Penny levels her gun at the computer tower below the desk and fires several shots in rapid succession.

Plastic and metal fragments fly. The monitor goes black instantly. Penny bends her head to the side, studying the mess that used to be a computer and then fires another carefully placed shot for good measure.

She turns away, a satisfied expression on her face. He doesn't know what to say. He steps aside while she strides out of the office and toward the back door.

"What do you think, Mom?" she calls. "Big brother?" She flashes another grin over her shoulder. "Ready to go make Alistair regret he was ever born?"

She disappears out the door, giggling all the way.

✦

"Who *are* you?" Arlene demands.

Her glare includes Kyle in the question, but he ignores it while he scans the alley behind the diner. It's barely wide enough for a garbage truck and is currently only occupied by one dumpster. The morning light casts plenty of shadows from the leftmost building, though. It leaves him jumpy.

Penny flashes her a brief smile. "Oh, come on." She slips her backpack from her shoulders. Reaching inside, she draws out another magazine for the gun. "I told you already."

Arlene's face darkens. "Listen, I don't care what you're after. The last thing I need are two crazy—"

"*We are not crazy!*" Penny screeches, her eyes wild.

The woman stays silent. Kyle's estimation of her intelligence creeps up a notch.

Penny reloads the gun and then rises to her feet. Her grin returns. "Okay, then."

A moment passes, but the girl doesn't move.

Kyle glances around. "Um...Penny?" he prompts, eyeing the empty alleyway. The shadows.

Realization hits him.

Instantly, the shadows deliver on their potential. Half a dozen people appear in the alley, the darkness and light shifting like the group has been there the whole time, only he didn't notice them. After nearly a lifetime around magic, the impression left by shadow-crossing doesn't faze him a bit. The guns they're holding, on the other hand...

The demons stop, several of them looking to him like he's the threat in the situation. But the nearest one retreats frantically. "Oh, shit," the guy blurts. "It's the boss's psychic."

Alarm flashes over the other newcomers' faces.

Penny fires.

Two of the people fall immediately, while the others try to retaliate. Penny is already moving. She dodges left, firing three more shots, and three more of the demons tumble back, hitting the concrete and not rising again.

She grins, aiming at the last one alive. "Hi, there."

The guy is frozen. He's scrawny. Smaller than the others, with a ratty ponytail that probably would be blond if he washed it.

"I wouldn't try running if I were you," Penny advises.

"I don't need much. Just your palm print. Do you want to come with it?"

The man blanches at the implication.

"Alistair thought he was being clever, yeah?" the girl continues. "Hiding out in the building where he is now, like *that* was ever going to bother me. Installing biometric security there, rather than some key code or whatever I could see?" She chuckles. "But I don't *need* to see it; I saw you. He sent you to grab Arlene, but you help me get into where he's hiding instead. I don't think I need you alive for that, though, so how we go about it is up to you."

For a heartbeat, the guy hesitates. He manages an urgent nod. "Y-yeah, I'll help."

Penny gives him a cheery smile. "Good." She looks to Kyle while she tucks the gun away. "Ready? The cops will be here in forty-five seconds."

He keeps himself from scowling as he reaches out, taking her hand. With her other hand, she fishes a crystalline pendant from a side pocket of her backpack. Quickly, she loops the ribbon around her neck.

"Wait, now," Arlene stammers. "I-I don't need to be a part of this. You all just go on. I—"

"No," Penny snaps.

Arlene hesitates. "I'll meet you after—"

"*No!*"

Penny's shriek rings from the alley walls. Kyle suddenly wishes he hadn't taken her hand so quickly.

Arlene backs up a step.

"You *will* come. You *have* to." A twitching grin pulls at Penny's lip, the look in her eyes anything but sane. "You hurt Cait."

Arlene glances at him, like he has a goddamn clue what that means.

"I know you do," Penny continues, still grinning. "You hurt her. I can't see how or why, but I know it happens. And that matters. It's *important*. It makes this change. So you have to come." Her crazed expression vanishes into ice. "Or I kill you."

Arlene nods warily. "Okay. Sure. I'll come too."

Instantly, Penny beams. "Great!" She looks at Kyle.

He's made a deal with a psychopath.

But then, he knew that already.

Shadows blur around them. The gray fades, revealing the last place he would have expected Alistair to use for a hideout.

The old Corvinson Memorial Hospital lurks in front of them. A towering edifice of dark brick, the place has been closed ever since the main hospital moved to a newer, larger building over a decade ago. The location is theoretically slated to become a cancer treatment center, but renovations seem to have stalled.

Probably thanks to Alistair.

"Okay." Penny releases Kyle's hand and turns her attention on him, Arlene, and the Linden guy who's working hard to look useful. The girl grins like she's a tour guide. "Everybody stay *super* quiet, understand?"

"Why?" Arlene asks distrustfully.

"Alistair's here." Penny flashes another beaming smile. It looks strangely tight. "See? I promised you we'd get him."

The last is directed at Kyle. Or maybe Arlene. He can't tell, because he'd swear her grin is cracking.

Trepidation prickles through him. His instincts, the good ones that have kept him alive all these years, are yammering in the back of his mind, telling him this is a bad plan. Telling him to abandon this whole enterprise and just go, right now, get out.

His attention flicks to the building, to the girl who's grinning like a madman, and then down to her gun. If he walks away, he's worse off than when this started. Chances are, she'll take half his people with her. Chances are, they'll report his little coup to Lucretia, and then even *that* plan will be destroyed. Meanwhile, Penny wouldn't even need to get the shot off to kill him. There's probably nowhere he can run that she hasn't seen, or that she couldn't find him.

But she's still psychic. She's been right about everything thus far. So Alistair should be here. This should still work. And if Kyle is careful—and the gods know he's careful—he can still make this all turn out to his advantage.

Penny motions for the scrawny guy to go ahead of them. Without a word, the man walks toward a door on the side of the building. Kyle hangs back while the man presses his palm to a black box affixed beside the door.

A click sounds. The guy pulls the door open.

"Well?" Penny urges. "Go on."

When the scrawny guy doesn't move, she levels the gun at him. He walks inside.

Kyle trails them, scanning everything for traps as he goes.

"That way," Penny whispers. "Down to the left."

The man continues walking. The corridor is nearly black, but an intersecting hallway lies ahead of it. From there, Kyle can see gray light spilling from someplace to the right, and when they reach the turn, he spots the glass doors at the front of the building.

He wonders how many security measures surround that thing if this side door was the better path in.

They head deeper into the building. The hallway is

wider now, lined with old rags and buckets from various construction projects. Gritty dust and chunks of drywall coat the floor. Wires dangle from a square opening in the ceiling; remnants of where a panel light has been removed. Part of a wall is missing, open like someone had been halfway through making a new doorway. Past the gap, he can see a gurney shoved into a corner. Weathered posters with childish illustrations advise the best way to steer clear of germs, and what to do if someone stops breathing.

Penny makes an irritated noise. He glances back at her.

Her expression is tense. Angry. She twitches every few moments like something is poking at her.

Understanding sinks over him. She'd lived in a psychiatric hospital in Florida before the Houses found her. He knows; he researched her history as soon as possible after she showed up. The girl had been sentenced there by the court after she'd murdered her entire family.

And Alistair would know that…

Penny's hand adjusts on the gun like she's having trouble hanging onto it. "Faster," she snaps to the scrawny guy, her voice a heated whisper.

The man speeds up. They push past the double doors blocking the hall, finding nothing but more patient rooms and construction debris. No guards. No security measures. Not even a camera or a motion detector to let anyone know who's here.

This doesn't make sense.

Kyle's instincts clamor louder, making his heart pound. This has to be a trap. There's no logical way this *isn't* a trap. But then, wouldn't Penny have seen it? Of course she would. She's *psychic*, for pity's sake.

So why doesn't his gut buy that?

"There," Penny hisses. She gestures to one of the closed doors on the right.

Swallowing hard, the guy walks where she indicated. The man lets out a breath when he reaches the door and pushes it wide.

Nothing happens.

"H-hello, sir," the guy says while he walks into the room.

No one answers. No guards make a sound. Penny hurries after the man, her weapon raised. Kyle follows carefully, staying out of view of the doorway and bracing himself for the sound of gunfire.

"What?" Penny protests. "You're not—I don't—"

Kyle peers around the doorframe.

Alistair is sitting on a wingback chair, a cup of tea placed on the small table at his side and his hands folded in his lap. He doesn't say a word, watching while Penny gapes at him like she's just had the floor dropped out from under her. Like something is horrendously wrong. Kyle doesn't know what, but why—

A screen flickers to life on the wall.

"Hello, Penelope."

Kyle blinks. Alistair regards the girl from the screen. He's in a room identical to this one, with his own cup of tea nearby and his hands folded in his lap. Another flat-panel television is on the wall behind him, showing the same scene over again like a series of reflections in an infinity mirror.

The effect is surreal.

"Wha…" Penny stammers. "Wha…"

"Oh, don't be too upset, my dear," Alistair-on-the-screen says. "I merely used you against yourself. It's nothing to be cross about."

In quick glimpses, Kyle studies the man in the chair in front of him. He didn't catch it before, but the guy is trembling. It's difficult to see, yet now that Alistair is up on the television, the first man has started to look progressively more nervous by the second.

"What is this?" Kyle demands, trying to watch the screen and the guy in the chair at the same time.

"Ah, yes, you." Alistair's tone is dry. "The reported Volgert agent. Care to tell me your name, young man?"

Like hell. Kyle thanks the gods the man doesn't know it already.

"Very well. *This*, as you put it, is Penelope's vision— what she was willing to see of it. Not easy, was it, my dear? You didn't want to focus too hard on this part, beyond seeing my friend Oskar here." Alistair nods toward the camera as if to indicate the guy in front of them. "We had to go all the way to Sweden to find a body double of his caliber."

Kyle's brow climbs. What?

He looks quickly down the hallway. Trap. This is definitely a trap. And he's not the only one who knows it. In the corridor behind him, Arlene is backing toward the nearest line of shadow, her expression making it clear she's heard more than enough. The Linden lackey has plastered himself to the wall; he appears as if he'd run for the exit too, if not for the fact Kyle is standing in the doorway.

"I know you better than anyone else in the demon world, Penelope," Alistair says. "After all, I studied you meticulously while you were in my care. This power of yours is not infallible. You do not see everything, and yet you have a rather unfortunate tendency toward…shall we call it *unsubstantiated confidence*?" He chuckles. "You took a human from me. You briefly interfered with my ability to keep Cait in my custody. I will give you those triumphs, not that I suspect they have gained you much. Cait will be returned to me soon, and the human is of no consequence. Ultimately, my dear, your limited psychic power is your only *real* trick up your sleeve—and one for which I can more than easily compensate."

Kyle can't believe what he's hearing. The old man is belittling the very power he'd attempted to use to destroy his enemies only weeks before. And now he's talking about this cockamamie plan like it had been a foolproof strategy to—

Realization spreads over him. That's not what this is. Oh, it's still a trap, and leaving would be a great idea right about now, but the whole setup is ridiculous. A body double? A hospital to remind Penny of her former prison? Sure, Alistair studied her, but how in the hell had the old guy been sure those things would actually work?

He couldn't have. Maybe, anyway. The old man is smart, but a plan like this…it's ludicrous.

But what if Alistair was gambling, coming up with the best idea he could to stop the psychic hellbent on destroying him? What if he was desperate?

The thought would be comforting if Kyle wasn't standing in what feels like a mousetrap preparing to snap down.

He starts backing through the doorway, eyeing the room warily. On his metal folding chair, Oskar seems to tense further at the small motion. His gaze is twitching between Penny and Kyle, and his hands are slowly going white, as if it's also dawning on him how bad of an idea accepting this job had been.

Penny clears her throat. Kyle freezes.

"I *will* kill you, old man," the girl promises, her voice unsteady.

Alistair smiles. "No, you won't, my dear."

The screen goes black.

Kyle looks at Penny. She hasn't moved. He's not even sure she's breathing.

Time to go.

The Linden guy takes off first, bolting for the doorway.

Penny whirls. A wild spray of bullets hits the wall and the man alike. The Linden guy crumples to the floor at Kyle's feet.

She turns the gun toward him.

"Whoa!" Kyle protests.

She stares at him for a moment, but he'd swear it's not him she sees. Her blue eyes are glazed and far brighter than seems natural. He can't even begin to guess what's playing out behind them.

He just hopes it doesn't involve using that gun.

"I'm going to kill him," she whispers.

"Yeah," Kyle agrees. "You bet. Totally."

She nods jerkily, her face twitching at the words. "He… he thinks I'm just some—"

"He's scared of you," he risks interjecting. "Alistair made this whole plan because he's afraid you'll find him."

Penny's eyes seem to focus. She likes that idea, he can tell. "Yeah." A smile spasms over her face. "Yeah, you're right. He's scared I'll—"

The thud of footsteps comes from the hall, and she cuts off. Kyle looks over to see Arlene still in the hallway, now retreating quickly from the double doors.

He would've thought she shadow-crossed by now. But then…

Curses blur through his mind. If that were possible, the

people heading toward them would have done it too. There'd be no need for coming in through a door.

Damn this trap. And damn him for walking into it. He should have sent some of his people with Penny, rather than come here himself. His goal of not *entirely* losing control of this coup would pretty much count as an unequivocal failure if he's dead.

"Fourth-floor balcony." Penny pushes past him, the gun still in her hand.

They run for the end of the corridor. Arlene's flip-flops slap the tile floor loudly, and the shouts of their pursuers carry behind them. The stairwell door clangs against the wall when they run past it. He takes the steps two at a time, quickly outdistancing Penny and Arlene both.

The hell with this. With them. If he makes it out of this alive, he's done with that crackpot Pollyanna.

The fourth floor is empty when he reaches it. No construction debris, no equipment. The renovations haven't made it this far yet.

He scans the area fast, searching for access to the balcony.

Penny catches up to him and keeps running for a turn of the hallway. He races after her. He can hear Arlene behind him, breathless, her flip-flops making it easy to pick out her location.

Which means Alistair's people probably won't have any trouble finding her either.

A scowl twists his face. He could shoot her. It probably would just infuriate Penny, but it might be worth it if it gets him out of here.

He reaches for the gun tucked beneath his shirt.

Penny gives a victorious shriek, and his hand stills. She

shoves past a door at the end of the hall. Sunlight glares through the corridor.

Finally.

"Here!" Penny cries. "Hurry up!"

He tosses her a furious look and then grabs her hand. The pendant still swings from her neck, not that he gives a crap anymore about what shadow-crossing unprotected would do to her.

She said they'd get Alistair, not end up running for their lives because she couldn't stand to look too hard at a vision of a damn hospital.

Arlene bursts past the door. "You're not leaving me here."

"Then shadow-cross already," he snaps.

Her glare deepens. "Can't." The response looks like it's being dragged out of her. "Not enough energy left."

Oh, for fuck's sake…

"Kyle," Penny urges, shaking her hand in his grip like an impatient child.

He mutters a curse, grabs Arlene's wrist, and then drags them both over a sharp line of shadow cast by an adjacent wall. The balcony disappears. The narrow confines of a campus alleyway take its place.

Immediately, he drops both their hands. He's not safe yet. Leading Linden's people back to anywhere *near* his own properties is out of the question, but this place doesn't have any defenses around it.

Maybe throwing Arlene at them would slow them down.

He looks back to the woman, considering, only to find her glaring at him. "Don't even think about leaving me now, demon boy," she spits.

He ignores the threat, glancing at Penny.

She's staring at the space where they shadow-crossed as if she can see through it to Alistair himself.

Kyle backs toward the opening of the alleyway. Her gun is empty. Probably, anyway. And if he's quick—

"It's not over," Penny says.

He stops.

A tiny giggle leaves the girl, nothing remotely sane in the sound, and she turns. He wants to retreat at the crazed light in her eyes, but the deranged glow pins him as firmly as a needle through a bug.

"Oh, it's not even close," she promises. "Alistair thinks this is the only thing I saw? That I didn't have dozens of visions playing out besides this? That I've only got one trick up my sleeve? *One?*"

Her edgy laugh comes again, louder. Kyle's skin crawls.

Penny turns her focus to Arlene. Her smile spreads. "He has no *idea* what I'm capable of."

13

AMAR

"Yes, that's right. Fully furnished, for sale as of today." Amar waits for the confirmation from the real estate agent. "Thank you."

He hangs up the cell phone. In the stockroom at the back of Nasreen's store, he can hear Cait talking with Katsuro, finishing up the last of the pictures for her new ID. In only a few more minutes, they'll be ready to go.

It's not a pleasant idea. Leaving like this never is, no matter how many times he feels like he's done it before. New York after his father died. Several towns since, whenever the Houses annexed formerly neutral territory.

Home when he was a kid.

He pushes the memories away. If anything, he has leaving down to a science. It sounds like Katsuro does too. And regardless, it's necessary. Yes, it means relocating, stopping his college plans, and Cait's as well for the time being, which will probably impact his career aspirations afterward and hers too, but...

His mouth tightens. There isn't a choice. There never is where the Houses are concerned.

A small noise comes from behind him. He turns. Bianca is regarding him from several yards away, her fingers idly twisting through the vines of some plant he can't identify.

"Missouri."

The word is flat. Cold. He doesn't respond.

"You know I have, like, a *dozen* relocation plans in place by now, right?"

"I know."

She pauses. "Missouri."

"Yeah."

She looks away. For the longest time, she doesn't say a word. His attention slides to the other room. He can still hear Cait and Katsuro. It sounds like they're working on several backup IDs, in case the first one needs to be discarded. Probably a good plan.

"You're a good friend, Bianca," he says quietly. "You always have been."

Her face twitches coldly. She doesn't look back at him.

"You don't need to protect me from this."

A breath leaves her, a quiet scoff. "You think I care what you do?"

He's silent, weighing his own words. "I think you're loyal. It's one of the things I like best about you."

She makes an irritated sound, her shoulders shrugging the words away. "Don't get so emotional."

His lip twitches. "And I think you stayed in town these past few weeks for a reason."

"I had things to get in order."

He doesn't respond. The statement is bullshit; they both know it. She's had escape plans ready and waiting since before either of them moved to this city.

Seconds creep by.

"I'll never get you," she says finally. "You Legacies who…" She shakes her head. "You just can't see. You can't understand how much better it is, not getting caught up in all that…" She makes a disgusted noise. "The leverage you're giving other demons over you? The threat? Humans are vulnerable as hell, and you can't see how much better it is not to give in to all this emotional bullshit like they do?"

"I see it."

Her head turns toward him.

"I *saw* it. I understand. But this…Cait…what I feel…I couldn't stop it. I didn't want to." He pauses. "I still don't. Not with her."

Bianca is quiet again. A pensive expression passes over her face, almost rueful, maybe sad. "I left my new number with that irritating troll. Make sure you get it before you go."

"I will. Thank you."

Looking over, she meets his eyes. "You take care of yourself out there. I'd be…disappointed…if anything happened to you."

Something twists in his chest, pained. He's going to miss her. "You too."

She's still for a moment, as if torn by the urge to say something more, and then she nods, a quick motion, barely more than a jerk of her head. Without another word, she walks out the door.

He doesn't move. That went better than he expected, though really, there isn't anything to say. Bianca has to look out for herself. Staying near him, near Cait, keeps her in danger.

It's better like this, even if…

He pushes the sadness away. He'll see Bianca again. And he's not sorry for how he feels about Cait, about how his life and his priorities have changed. He can't apologize for that. And Bianca is a true friend, as close as any demon has ever come.

She didn't ask him to.

14

CAIT

"Few more minutes to laminate these, and we'll be done."

I nod while Katsuro takes the photos away. New pictures for my new life, wherever that ultimately ends up being. New names too, a main one and at least three backups, in case the Houses get their hands on any of the others.

I feel like I've fallen into a spy movie, except it's all too terrifying and real.

Making myself keep breathing, I turn away and head for the door out of the stockroom. Amar is in the main part of the shop. I want to know his plan for all of this. What new identities he might have as well.

"I'll never get you."

I come to a halt at the sound of Bianca's voice.

"You Legacies who…You just can't see. You can't understand how much better it is, not getting caught up in all that…" She makes a contemptuous noise, and my stomach twists. "The leverage you're giving other demons over you? The threat? Humans are vulnerable as hell, and you can't see how much better it is not to give in to all this emotional bullshit like they do?"

"I see it."

My mouth falls open a bit at Amar's response. What?

"I *saw* it. I understand. But this…Cait…what I feel…I couldn't stop it. I didn't want to. I still don't. Not with her."

A blush burns its way up my cheeks. Oh.

I shift my weight, unsure what to do. I'm eavesdropping. I shouldn't, because it's rude and because I wouldn't know what to say if Amar realized I heard.

But my insides feel quivery at his words.

Biting my lip, I retreat toward the office at the far end of the stockroom. I…I'll just wait for him there, and, um…

I stand in the middle of the office, at a loss for what to do with myself.

The stockroom door squeaks behind me. I look back over my shoulder.

Amar regards me from the other side of the room. "You okay?"

My mouth moves for a moment. "Y-yeah."

He gives me a curious look and walks toward me. "Cait?"

"I heard some of—" I nod toward the front of the shop. "I didn't mean to. I'm sorry. I just…"

"What did you hear?"

He doesn't sound upset. I shrug awkwardly, not meeting his eyes. Colors flare at the edge of my vision, but it's easier to ignore them, as if the ability is settling now, more in my control.

"How you, um…I don't know…feel?" He hadn't really said *how* he felt, I realize. And I don't know how to ask him. It's not like I want to pressure him to feel any certain way. "How you didn't want it to, um, stop?"

"Ah."

He steps closer until he's only inches from me. I can feel his warmth, smell that delicious earth-spice-*something* scent that's purely him. His hand lifts, brushing across my cheek, looping a strand of my hair over my ear, and then returning to gently draw my chin up toward him.

But then he pauses, watching me. "You all right?"

I manage a nod. "Yeah."

He bends down, slowly, carefully, and kisses me lightly, barely a touch of his lips to mine.

A small breath leaves me.

He hesitates again as if checking I'm still okay. I step closer to him, slipping my hands around his sides. The lights and colors at the edges of my sight try to flare brighter, but with some effort, I push them away. My breasts brush against his chest, a tiny sensation through my bra. "Mm," I murmur, pressing myself against him. "More."

A smile crosses his face, and his fingers slide into my hair, his mouth taking my own. He's still gentle, still cautious, even as his tongue tangles with mine and his other hand pulls me in closer, holding me carefully to him. My fingers dig into his back; I want more of him. More of this.

But he doesn't tighten his hold, doesn't bring me against him too strongly. He draws away a moment later, checking on me again, before laying kisses against my cheek, my jaw. I tilt my head to the side, giving him room as he traces a sensuous line of heat down my neck. His palm slides up between us, out of sight of the door, and takes my breast. A short gasp leaves me.

"You still okay?" he whispers.

"Yes," I breathe.

He kisses his way back up along my neck, my jaw, and lightly touches his lips to mine again before pulling back. His hand slips from my breast and comes up to cup my face. His thumb strays along my cheek, soft and slow. "Good."

My lips curl into a smile.

Voices carry from the front of the store. Ram and Nasreen. Maybe a few of the students. My smile falters as I glance toward the sound.

"We'll be all right, Cait," Amar says. "Your family will too."

I nod, trying to believe the words.

He bends slightly, meeting my eyes. "We'll just stick together, yeah?"

I nod again, more firmly. "Yeah."

His hand drops down, his fingers threading between mine. I take a deep breath.

"You ready?" he asks.

I start to say yes, when a new thought occurs to me. "Um…almost."

Reaching into my back pocket, I take out my cell. Amar gives me a questioning look.

"I…She hasn't answered my calls in, like, weeks. Ever. But I just have to try to warn her, you know?"

"Ruby," he says like he's filling in a blank.

I murmur an acknowledgment, but I'm already pressing the button to call her.

The phone clicks straight to voicemail, same as it has for weeks. The message informs me the mailbox is full.

I close my eyes and bite my lip. I can't do this. Leave town and not even warn my best friend. Lowering the phone, I shake my head and then type out a text, feeling like an idiot the whole time. Who sends a text about something like this? If I could have just *spoken* with her…

I press send and watch as the status doesn't change, just hovering as "Sending" without any sign the message ever arrived.

My eyes sting. For all I know, she got rid of her phone. Cut all ties to Corvinson. To the demons.

To me.

I sniffle briefly, tucking my cell away. Maybe I'm taking it too personally. Maybe she just hasn't turned on her phone in a while.

Looking up, I find Amar watching me, sympathy in his eyes. "Ready?" I ask him, my voice tight.

"Yeah."

I swipe a hand over my eyes quickly and nod. So that's it, then. New name. New life.

Time to go.

⸙

"When we get to the airport, you'll be traveling as Cayla Harrison, but only for this flight. After we land in Saint Louis, we'll start using the first of those other aliases we set up, understand?"

I nod, but my attention is only partly on Katsuro's words. Through the smoked window of the black SUV, more and more of the city is falling behind us with every block. The library where I worked. The places I went to school, even before college. Restaurants, shops, all of it, like snapshots falling away into memory. It's weird, I never really liked this town—it was a place to live, nothing more—but now I miss it.

We haven't even left yet, and I miss it.

My stomach quivers, and I pull my eyes from the window. Amar has taken the passenger seat ahead of me, and Ram is driving while Katsuro sits beside me. The vampire is still wearing his hooded coat, the thick fabric protecting him from the sun even more than the heavily darkened window at his side. We're not alone either; up ahead, another car carries more of Katsuro's people, while around us, Sorcha and the other bikers keep pace as a shield.

It's an unnerving reminder of how dangerous our escape actually is.

"Hey."

I look back to Katsuro.

"This is going to be all right, Cait," he promises. "We'll set you up somewhere safe, and hopefully we'll be able to bring your family there soon as well."

My stomach twists. I nod anyway.

"Now," he continues. "In terms of the flight, Amar will be seated next to you, and I'll be—"

I hear a shout from Ram, and then the crunch of metal fills the world. I'm slammed up against the door with images flashing by so quickly, they feel like a dream. The blur of the street, of cars, of a woman on the sidewalk with her mouth open in a cry of alarm. The SUV is spinning, tossed from its path like a toy while gravity pins me. I can't turn. Can't move. Flecks of something are pelting me. Glass. Fragments of glass like razor-edged stars.

Red paint, bright as a crayon, flashes across my vision. I try to scream.

We crash into the car next to us. Gravity can't make up its mind, tugging me between the spin and the impact, before giving up on both.

Popping sounds like firecrackers cut through the ringing in my ears. I start to turn, start to look toward Amar, and then something dark blocks the window. The door opens, and someone grabs me. Pulls at me. I shriek, the sound muffled instantly by a black cloth yanked over my head. My body is hefted from the seat and dragged from the vehicle.

Adrenaline floods me. Like hell this is happening. Not again.

Electricity surges over my body. My captor's hands vanish, and I plummet. Pain like a crimson explosion goes off in the darkness when I hit the ground, freezing me against my own will. I fight to make myself move, to grab at the hood over my head, and after a moment, I'm able to rip it away.

Sunlight blinds me. Blinking frantically, I scramble up, my palms scraping on broken glass and rough concrete. Two guys are on the ground beside me. The SUV is several yards away, pinned between a brown car and a red one. Amar is trying to escape the passenger seat, his eyes locked on me. Through the window, I can see Ram struggling, shoving at the driver's side door and the steering wheel alike.

"Get down!" Amar shouts at me.

Gunfire tears my focus from them. I race for cover behind a blue sedan while bullets strike the ground, the cars, the SUV where Amar is trapped.

My heart hits my throat, but he's okay from what I can see. They didn't hit him.

Yet.

My eyes dart around. Sorcha and the other bikers are pinned in the shelter of recessed storefronts across the street, but several of their companions lie in the road. I can't see them moving. The car with Katsuro's people is a mess of bullet holes. I don't know if anyone is still inside, still alive.

And as for Katsuro…

A dozen guys surround him, trapping him in the middle of the street. No one seems to be firing at him, but then, bullets don't do much good against vampires. The guys are carrying what look like cattle prods, though. Three more of their number lie on the ground, bleeding out in evidence of Katsuro's attempts to escape the group.

But the vampire is struggling. The sun is beating down on him. A burn already shows on the left side of his face, blackened and blistered from where sunlight must have touched his skin past his hood.

"Cait, run!" Amar yells. "Get out of here!"

I don't move. I won't leave them.

But I need help here.

A plan occurs to me, and it's terrible. I can't think too hard about it.

"Katsuro!" I shout.

The vampire looks toward me. Two of the guys nearest to me do too.

It's a big mistake.

Katsuro surges forward in a blur of motion. The two men can't bring the cattle prods up in time. The guys topple to the ground, and then the group is behind him.

But the rest recover after only a heartbeat. They run at the vampire. They're impossibly fast, and one of them bends quickly, snagging a weapon that looks like a crossbow from his fallen comrade. Lifting it swiftly, he takes aim at Katsuro.

Shivers course through me. I can see flashes of colors around the people ahead. The images and the memories, flickering like half-remembered dreams. There are so many that I don't know if this will work, but I brace myself, fighting with everything I have not to see Katsuro's history amid the flood.

The visions rush away from me. All of the attackers collapse, screaming, clawing at their faces in fear.

Katsuro is still standing.

A breath escapes me, and I'm relieved in spite of everything. I didn't hurt him. I controlled this.

Go me.

Bullets pelt the ground near the SUV, sending my heart clambering back up my throat. Katsuro starts toward me, and I motion to the SUV frantically. "Help Amar!"

He hesitates only for a second before he races for the vehicle.

My eyes skim over the street, the buildings, the rooftops. I think the bullets are coming from above us, but I can't tell where the shooters are hiding, and I'm guessing Amar can't either. But we can't attack blindly. I don't know how his abilities work exactly, but I'm pretty sure a random strike in the direction of the gunfire…yeah, that's probably going to kill innocent people too.

A string of cursing runs through my mind. How did these people find us? In all this town, how did they know we'd be *here* of all places?

I shove the thoughts aside. It doesn't matter. Katsuro's helping Amar, though, covering him while he escapes through the window and out over the hood of the car pinning his door closed. On the other side of him, Ram is shoving at the steering column. I hear metal groan and plastic snap. The driver's seat lurches backward.

"Cait!" Sorcha yells from across the street. "For gods' sakes, go! Get out of—"

Another burst of gunfire cuts her off, but it's not the same as before. I look over my shoulder as a slew of black-clad gunmen pours from an alleyway behind me. They're aiming at the rooftops. They're moving like a military assault team.

What the hell?

"Get behind us!" one of them shouts. It sounds like a woman. I can't see their faces—they're obscured by ski masks and goggles like the group is something out of a movie—but the nearest one motions for me to run beyond them while the rest fan out, scanning the rooftops and street as if they're searching for the next thing to shoot.

I look at Katsuro and Amar. They've escaped the SUV. Ram has too. He's running my way, staying low behind the cover of cars parked on the side of the road.

The three of them reach me. "Go!" Katsuro orders.

"Are they with you?" I ask.

He doesn't answer, gesturing for Ram to shield me. On the other side of the street, I can see Sorcha and the bikers eyeing us and the rooftops alike. They wait for a heartbeat, as if anticipating the next blast of gunfire.

And then they take off.

My breath catches. I can't take my eyes from them even as we bolt toward the alleyway. The people around me open fire, aiming at the rooftops, covering the bikers' escape. Sorcha swings over the cars between us while her companions surge past them, letting nothing slow them down. In only a moment, they're across the road and ducking into the shadows of the alley with us.

"Are you okay?" I call to Sorcha.

A spray of bullets follows the werewolves, striking the walls and sending chunks of red brick flying.

"We have to go!" The leader of the newcomers tugs

their mask away. It's a woman with brown hair and dark eyes. Colors and images tangle around her, nearly as overwhelming as the ones surrounding Katsuro. "Follow us. We can—"

Something flies through the air behind her. I only see a flash of silver like a bolt of lightning before she staggers, her eyes going wide.

Mine do too. A spike thrusts through her chest from behind. The colors around her evaporate like mist. Her skin begins to blacken, turning to burning embers and ash before my eyes.

Beyond the alleyway, people rush at us, cloaked and covered like vampires. They carry crossbows in their hands.

"Go!" The woman's voice is a ragged whisper. She falls, her body crumbling to dust.

Her own people rush at us. Someone grabs me. I stumble backward, sunlight and shadow flashing across my vision. But we don't shadow-cross. I see a doorway from the corner of my eye. The others flee through the opening.

The vampires are coming. Metal races at me, the spikes whistling through the air, borne by assailants who are only inches away.

And then the door slams, sealing me in darkness.

15

CAIT

Thuds shake the door, like metal cracking into the wood. I'm frozen in the pitch black, the vision of that woman dying emblazoned in my mind.

"Come on," someone urges. "This way."

"Cait." Amar is right next to me. I feel his hand take my back, bringing me close. "You all right?"

A shaky breath leaves me. "Yeah." I blink fast, struggling to regroup. "What the—Who are these people?"

"Volgert."

Alarmed, I look toward where I know he's standing.

"*Please*," one of the strangers insists. A thud from the door punctuates their words. "They'll be through in moments. We have someone downstairs who can assist in blocking anyone from tracking our escape, but we need to go."

I hear Ram growl. It's strangely comforting.

"Shadow-crossing, you mean," Katsuro says, his tone barbed.

Something strikes the door again.

"Please," the person urges.

"We can't stay here," Amar points out.

Silence follows the words.

"Agreed." Katsuro's voice is cold.

My hand finds Amar's arm when we start moving, and I grip him for balance as much as anything. I can't see in this darkness, but sound bounces back to me like the walls are close. The air is thick with the smell of dust and old cleaning solution. It makes me want to sneeze.

Another thud comes from behind me. A cracking sound too.

My eyes slide back toward the alleyway door, invisible in the darkness. Oh God…

"Stairs coming up," Amar whispers to me.

"Amar, the door—"

"I know."

I tighten my grip on his arm. A moment later, I feel the ground disappear beneath my next footstep, but Amar braces me. Together, we start down a stairway I can't see.

I'm not sure if it's the darkness or reality, but the steps seem to go on forever.

"Exit up ahead," Amar whispers.

I hear a click. Cooler air brushes over me, laden with moisture.

"Only a little farther," someone urges.

Amar's steps slow. "Where are you taking us?"

"There's a door to the right," the same person says, a touch of fear threading through their voice. "An old maintenance tunnel that leads between the buildings. We can buy more time to—"

The person cuts off with a muffled cry. A thud follows, and the sounds of a struggle.

Amar doesn't move.

"That wasn't an answer," Ram mutters.

Light flares in the dark, barely more than a flashlight aimed toward the wall, but it burns my eyes. We're standing in a basement. The walls are brick, and the floor is rough concrete. Pipes run along the ceiling, and water drips from them every few seconds, disappearing into drains on the floor.

But our rescuers are on the ground.

Ram glances over while one of the werewolf mercenaries sets the flashlight on the floor, casting sharp lines of shadow and light against the concrete. "Get out of here," the troll says to Katsuro and Amar, nodding toward the light.

Katsuro shakes his head. "I'm not leaving you, my friend."

Annoyance crosses Ram's face. "I'll meet you. Just—"

The door on the far end of the basement moves. "Truce, please!" cries a young woman's voice from beyond the opening.

No one responds. The door swings wider.

A dark-haired girl appears in the gap, and she's so incongruous to the basement around us that I can't help but stare. She's in a bedraggled maid's uniform, the outfit rumpled and stained like she's been wearing it for days. Colors and images tangle around her, oddly hesitant like even they are afraid of being seen. In her shaking hands, she clutches a white handkerchief like a flag of surrender.

"Please, Master Okoro," she says, her gaze locked on Amar. "Truce. On the life of my Mistress, I beg of you."

Ram growls, low and angry. The girl flinches away like she's expecting to be attacked.

"What is this?" Katsuro demands.

"No idea," Amar replies.

The girl wrings the white handkerchief between her hands. "Mistress Lucretia requests your presence. She, um…she needs your help, Master Okoro. You and—" She casts a quick look to me. Her eyes are red, I realize. Like Nasreen's. Like a djinn. "And her. That's why she sent us —the soldiers and me. We learned of the plan to ambush you, and we came to stop it. To help you. Mistress Lucretia needs you to see her, and she swears you have nothing to fear from acquiescing to her request. She ordered me to secure your safety and the safety of anyone traveling with you." The girl's gaze skirts toward Ram. "She didn't mention there would be a troll."

Katsuro grimaces.

"It doesn't matter," Ram tells him. "After five hundred years, you really think *these* demonic pissants are going to be the ones to bring me down?" He grins. There's ice in the expression. "I'll get out of here, I promise. The tunnels?" He looks to the girl.

She casts a worried glance toward the darkness at her back. "They lead to the other buildings, yes. I don't know if the others are aware of them, though—"

"It's good enough." Ram meets Katsuro's eyes again.

A crash reverberates above us.

"Please," the girl begs, looking to the ceiling like she can see our pursuers right through it. "I can block them so they'll stand no chance of following us, but we're running out of time."

Katsuro mutters vehemently in Japanese. "Go."

Ram nods and then runs for the maintenance tunnel door. Footsteps thud overhead.

"Master Okoro?" the girl urges.

Amar glances toward the ceiling for a heartbeat. "Okay."

Relief overwhelms the girl's fearful expression. "Thank you." She motions urgently. "With me, if you will, and bring the flashlight. I'll seal the door. Give your friend more time. But I beg of you, bring the Mistress's soldiers too. They don't deserve to be left for these assailants' revenge."

Amar nods to the mercenaries. They heft the black-clad people between them and hurry toward the exit. The girl retreats quickly, clearing a path for us all.

The door shuts behind us. I hear the girl speaking, her words making no sense, and I glance back. At the edge of the flashlight's glare, I can see her. She's holding her hands against the doorframe, her red eyes closed, and she's reciting something at a frantic pace.

Her words finish. "That should slow them." A worried expression flashes over her face, like she's not certain she trusts her own statement, and then she's moving again. "Set the light there, please."

One of the bikers puts down the flashlight. The girl hurries over, extending her hands over the device.

More strange words follow, and this time, an iridescent shimmer touches the flashlight's glare.

The sound of wood breaking comes from beyond the door. Shouts carry from the basement behind us.

"Go!" the girl urges in a terrified whisper. "Go now!"

Amar pulls me with him over the shadow's edge.

⌁

THE FIRST THING I SEE IS GOLDEN LIGHT GLARING IN MY EYES.

I blink, startled. We're in some kind of alcove with thick shadows behind us. Flickering candles stand in a glistening, wall-mounted candelabra nearby. Amar is at my side, and in only a moment, the shadows shift and the others are here too.

The red-eyed girl hurries past us. "Set the soldiers down here, please. Someone will be along to help them soon. If you'll follow me this way?"

"Where are we?" Katsuro demands.

"The Hotel Florencia."

I blink all over again. That's one of the oldest hotels in town, so old that Arlene's Chamber of Commerce buddies used to talk about trying to get it onto the National Register of Historic Places.

It's also fully on the other side of town from the basement we just left.

"Mistress reserved all of the top floor," the girl says. "The lower levels are guarded by—" She pauses oddly. "—by her elite forces. They're, um…We should be safe here."

That doesn't sound nearly as reassuring as she'd probably like.

"What's going on?" Amar asks as if he heard the weird tone to her voice too.

The girl looks back to him, worry in her red eyes. "Mistress will explain." She motions for us to come with her.

Amar glances at Sorcha and the others. "Stay behind me." He looks at me briefly, including me in the order.

We follow the girl down the hall. At the end, she pauses as if bracing herself. Magic shivers through me in response. This can't be good.

She pushes open the door. I see Amar freeze at the sight of what's inside.

"Hello, Amar."

The words are cultured but weak. Raspy. They sound as if they took all the energy of their speaker just to bring them into the world.

"What is this?" Amar demands.

He steps farther into the room. The shades are drawn, but the bedside lamp is on, casting the place in dim golden light. A woman sits beneath the blankets on the king-size bed. Pillows support her back while dark blankets cover her to the waist. She's pale to the point where her skin appears almost the same color as the white pillowcases, and her face is gaunt, inset with shadows.

Amar looks toward the girl in the maid outfit. Bent over the woman in the bed, she straightens the blankets lovingly while whispering something at a rapid pace. The woman nods when the maid finishes. "Thank you, Mira."

"What *happened*?" Amar presses.

The girl gives him an apologetic glance and then scurries to the corner without answering.

"Is this Cait?" The woman looks at me, and her lips curve into a smile. "But of course it is. My Josephine's daughter, like her mother reborn."

"Lucretia," Amar snaps.

I can't help but stare. Oh my God, this is her. The leader of Volgert. The one who made a deal with Amar.

She looks like she's dying.

Katsuro comes up beside me. "Answer his question."

"Now, Katsuro," Lucretia chides. "I would think saving you from certain death on a rooftop in Rome would have bought me *some* favor—or at least patience."

He's silent. She chuckles. "That little bit of altruism never did make you trust me." She glances my way. "Do come here, child."

I don't move.

Lucretia's brow shrugs equitably. "Very well. *This* is treason. Sabotage. And since it is swiftly becoming apparent that my physician's efforts will be unable to stop it… murder." She smooths the dark blankets with her pale hands. I can't help but see the shadows on them, like she's nothing but bones beneath a thin tissue of skin. "I trust you recall the minor situation at my manor several weeks back?"

"Yes," Amar replies flatly.

"Well, I don't suppose it's been a matter of some confusion, why my forces have not taken Alistair up on his little declaration of war after he so rudely destroyed my home?" Her smile turns acerbic. "Suffice it to say, we would have, but for that other niggling issue we discussed last time you and I met."

I glance between them. What the hell is she talking about?

"The coup," Amar translates.

Lucretia nods. "I'd say they've been rather more successful than I would have liked."

"What did they do?" he asks.

"The bullets with which Linden's forces shot me were witch-cursed, as we all knew. But the treatments to cure that poison, well…Someone has been interfering with them. No matter what I do, no matter which resource I seek out or use, the result has been the same. Or, rather, the lack of result. I grow sicker. My attempts to cure *that* have been equally unsuccessful; if anything, they have made the poison worse. And thus, I am left without anywhere to turn. But for Mira—" She nods to the maid. "—and a handful of others, every connection I possess has been systematically sabotaged. Meanwhile, Linden chips away at my forces left and right."

I eye her and Amar warily. "Why are you telling us this?"

Lucretia looks at me, her smile returning. "You even sound like her."

I shiver.

"I am telling you this for the same reason I sent out an assault team after my spies alerted me to an imminent attack on a random stretch of road in this town—one that, coincidentally turned out to be the precise location of your little convoy. I would like to barter a truce with you. With *all* of you, even the vestiges of the true Guardians, miraculously still alive and growing in power after nearly a millennium of exploring ever more inventive ways to get themselves killed."

"Why?" Amar demands.

Lucretia gives him a considering look. "Did you know what Cait was, back when you first took her under your wing? How far into this did you see?"

Amar doesn't speak.

"And what of you, Katsuro? I know you must have suspected it." She smiles. "Mira detected a flare of energy in the convergence, right at the moment of the attack today." She nods toward the maid. "It's taken her time to track it, isolate it, recognize it for what it is. But then, I suspect it's taken your own people time to do the same."

My skin crawls, and my eyes dart to the djinn girl huddling in the corner like she'd make herself six inches high if she could.

"We need each other, you all and I," Lucretia says. "Those assailants found your people for a reason, and that reason was not us. You have a leak in your organization, Katsuro. Perhaps more than one."

The words make me glance around, checking across the demons from the Guardians and Volgert alike. My weird, people-reading power doesn't tell me anyone is a spy, and the memories flickering around them…

Shuddering, I stop myself from looking too closely. I can't afford to get distracted here.

I can't afford to accidentally kill anyone, either.

"Not possible," Katsuro states coldly, his eyes locked on Lucretia.

"Truly? You say that after Rome? After Kyoto? After *Istanbul*?" Lucretia sounds amused. "Your precious Guardians have not been immune to betrayal over these many centuries, Katsuro. Surely, you can admit that. And as you well know, Linden and I are not the only ones interested in your newest member." She smiles at me. "They almost had you several weeks ago, didn't they, my dear? These impostors who've caused your vampire friend so much trouble over the years. I hear they found you in whatever rat-hole Katsuro was using as a hideout and they chased you all the way to a city park."

Her expression turns amused at our silence. "Those false Guardians resent you and your allies, Katsuro. They believe you interfere with their ability to redefine the memory of the Guardians in the bloody and fanatical way they would see fit. You know that. In addition, they would like nothing more than to claim a skill set like Cait's for their cause. As a new Legacy and someone who has lived as a human for so long, I imagine they see her as malleable. Capable of being forced to serve their whims." Her gaze runs over me, considering. "I rather think they would find they are wrong."

"Enough," Katsuro interjects. "You wish me to see those fools as responsible for the attack today when it would be just as simple to lay the blame with you."

Lucretia's hands make a small gesture, as if she would

shrug if she had more strength. "True. Except what would I gain by allowing your assailants to come within seconds of slaughtering you? How would I retain what loyalty I have left among my own people if I ordered them to *kill* each other for *show*?" She pauses, any humor fading. "I lost good people today, Katsuro. Members of my House who have served me faithfully for centuries. I would not sacrifice their lives so lightly."

He's silent.

"I sent my people to rescue you—to rescue all of you—because we do need each other. Linden practically has this wretched little city on lockdown, and you have a leak in your information stream." Her brow rises pointedly. "You'll require my help if you want to make it out of Corvinson alive."

"And what do you need?" Amar replies.

Lucretia seems to consider how to respond. "My people are in trouble. My House is in danger of falling. And as I said, short of Mira and a few precious others, every person whom I would trust to assist me in this has been kidnapped, tortured, and murdered in these past weeks. Only a few days ago, the last of my secret advisors disappeared—taken from me despite the fact that no one should have known her importance. Even those of my own House did not know I depended upon her advice. She was rediscovered yesterday, her body damaged by knives to the point it took hours to identify her. This has led me to one inescapable conclusion." Lucretia's mouth tightens. "One or both of my enemies are now in league with Alistair's psychic, and that psychic is responsible for all of this."

"But why us?" Amar's voice is guarded. He sounds as distrustful as I've ever heard him.

"Because…" Lucretia regards him thoughtfully. "I want you to save us."

I look at him, alarmed. Amar seems frozen.

"I am dying, Amar. My physicians are doing all they can, but I can see it in their eyes. They are failing." A hint of sadness flickers through her eyes. "I owe it to my people to plan for the safety and future of my House, no matter what happens to me."

"I won't be part of House Volgert, Lucretia," Amar protests incredulously.

"Not even to lead it?"

He stares at her.

"This isn't solely about your abilities," she continues. "Though I'll admit, the defense those offer definitely influences my consideration. But this is about trust. This is about the near-decade in which you could have betrayed or killed me, my people, or anyone else you chose to take down…and you didn't. This is about the years in which you *were* a member of my House, and how you only ever *voluntarily* used your powers to defend others, never to destroy them. Don't think I missed that little incident with the Chastain girl when you saved her from those Linden fools years ago. Your father was quite enraged about that."

Amar is silent.

"What would you say, Katsuro?" Lucretia persists. "Would you not be willing to form a truce with House Volgert if it were led by a man with whom you've *already* agreed to work? I highly doubt Amar has joined your Guardians—though, even if he has, how could his position as leader of Volgert be anything other than a benefit to you?" Her brow rises, questioning. "Could you not set aside centuries of distrust for the chance to assure peace and safety for your people?"

Katsuro studies her like he's never seen anything like her in his life. "Why are you doing this, Lucretia?"

She chuckles weakly. "There's one thing you never understood, not in all the years you've been struggling to undermine us. Ruling a House doesn't have to be about power. Not really. In the end, it can be about the loyalty of family. It can be about protecting those who take shelter in it, who swear their fidelity to it. You think I truly want a war with Linden because I simply like to fight? I want to secure the safety of my House and prevent it from being swallowed up in his own, and I will do *anything* to ensure that. You think my predecessors destroyed the Guardians because they wanted to rule the world for themselves? They overthrew the Guardians because they believed they could change the world and build something *better*, that's all." She gives him a tired smile. "Perhaps they were right."

Katsuro is visibly incredulous.

"You took my friend." I hear my own voice before I realize I've spoken. Swallowing hard, I press on. "You run the sets. You *kill* innocent people."

"Your kind arranges *all* of that," Katsuro snaps.

Her smile takes on a wry edge. "Then change it."

I let out a rough breath, speechless. I glance at Amar.

He appears thunderstruck.

Lucretia smooths the blankets on her lap again. "House Volgert is yours, Amar, if you will take it. Mira will assure the transition of power is witnessed, as will my elite guard —those who are left. They will spread the word among my holdings abroad. I trust, with your reputation, there will be little pushback against the transition of power." She pauses. "So what is your answer? Will you become the next leader of House Volgert?"

Amar doesn't speak. He doesn't even seem to breathe. His eyes are locked on her, and I can't hope to read what I see on his face.

"This could change everything." Katsuro's words are tight. He appears as tense as I've ever seen him.

I shake my head. "This has to be a trap."

Amar looks at me instantly, an urgent question in his dark eyes.

I flounder, realizing the implications of what I just said. "I-I don't mean…" I glance back to Lucretia, attempting to concentrate past my shock. "She's not…"

"She's telling the truth?" Amar asks softly.

My mouth works. This feels weird—no, it feels like *lunacy*, and it can't be this simple—but that's not the question he asked me. And for that, I know the answer. "Yeah, I…I think she is."

He drops his gaze from mine. I'm not sure what to do. There still has to be something wrong with this. For Lucretia to simply decide to hand leadership of her entire House over to the guy who has done everything in his power to stay out of it for so many years…

But maybe that's it.

Amar doesn't want this. Everyone else does. Kyle. Penny. Who knows how many others, waiting in the wings. But Amar…he's not interested in power. Not like that. He *has* power, but he doesn't use it the way others would.

He only makes sure the people around him stay safe.

A breath leaves me. This is madness.

"Cait."

I look up at Amar again, and in his eyes, I see a new question. One that sends chills running through me.

"You could protect her even more than before," Sorcha murmurs, so softly I can barely hear the words.

Amar glances at the werewolf. She ducks her head, a deferential and strangely animal-like motion, as if she doesn't want to cross a line with him.

"No," I protest. "This isn't about me. You can't—"

"This is about everyone," Katsuro interjects carefully.

I shake my head. "It's *about* Amar."

Katsuro's mouth tightens. "You'll run forever," he says to Amar. "The rest of your life, however long—or *short*—that might be. But the next leader of Volgert may not make any bargains with you. The balance that has kept you in safety thus far may not hold any longer."

Amar meets the vampire's gaze.

"A lifetime is a long time to have to run," Katsuro finishes quietly.

I look away. I can't believe this. This morning, we were trying to escape Volgert, Linden, *everyone*. And now...

Now someone could try to kill Amar like they're killing Lucretia. This will make him a target too. For Penny, Kyle, the other Houses, and *God*, Alistair...he won't be okay with this. Hell, he'll probably make it his life's mission to take Amar out.

But then...Alistair will probably do that anyway.

I look back to Lucretia. The balance, Katsuro said. The balance would be gone.

"Katsuro's right," I say quietly. My eyes find Amar again.

He's watching me. "House Volgert." His voice is tight. Controlled and yet I can hear the pain. I wonder if anyone else can.

"House Volgert," I whisper.

A scoff escapes him, soft and weighed down by more

brutal irony than any sound should be able to contain. For a long second, he drops his gaze to the ground, like a world only he can see is playing out in front of his eyes. And then he looks back up to Lucretia.

"Okay. I'll do it."

16

AMAR

Among all the twists and turns this day could have taken, he'd never for a moment imagined this one.

"—and if sir would please sign here as well?" The vampire arches an eyebrow at him.

He signs his name for what must be the thousandth time. Yet another piece of legal paperwork. Taking control of a House apparently requires copious amounts of them. There are financial matters, stock accounts, and properties in cities and countries he's fairly certain he would struggle to find on a map. In the space of a single day, he's been given ownership of them all. Even his father's holdings never came close to this.

His father's holdings never felt like signing his life away.

"And here as well."

The vampire places another paper on the conference room table. The man is one of an army of lawyers at Lucretia's—at *his*—disposal. Tight-lipped with features like dark leather stretched over sharp bone, the man's expression hasn't given a hint of his opinion on this transfer of power all day. No one has, which in itself feels like a commentary. The members of House Volgert aren't trusting him any more than he trusts them. They're sizing him up, weighing what this change could mean for their positions, for their own ambitions.

There will be assassination attempts in the coming days, he's sure. This is the weakest moment of power, this time before he's had a chance to secure the loyalty of anyone around him. Everything is up for grabs, and the leadership of this House most of all.

He reads through the document quickly. A mansion in Beijing this time. He writes his signature again.

"Excellent. Now, if sir does not need anything else, I will send these off to be filed in the House records vault. You will be provided copies as well, of course."

He nods.

The vampire leaves the conference room.

Amar closes his eyes, just briefly, just for a moment to ease the burning that's plagued him for all the hours this has taken. He listens carefully, though. The team of bodyguards around him is comprised partly of Guardians and partly of Volgert. Anything could happen in a moment of perceived weakness.

And he can't risk them seeing his true feelings on this day, besides.

No one has moved when he opens his eyes again a few heartbeats later. Taking a breath, he pushes to his feet. It has to be several hours past sunset by now. There are no windows in the hotel conference room to help him tell, but he knows it's getting late.

Bodyguards fall in around him while he leaves the room. The lobby is mostly empty, and darkness covers the street beyond the windows. Gold light from the chande-liers overhead spills across the maroon-and-cream tile, reflecting back from the flecks of metal embedded there. At the dark wood check-in counter, the concierge stares. Amar can feel the woman's gaze tracking him all the way to the elevator.

The bodyguard next to him presses the button to summon the elevator. "The Mistress—" The man hesitates. He doesn't know what to call Lucretia now. It's clear on his face.

"Yes?"

The man regroups, and the flash of relief on his face is abundant proof Amar's response was the right move. Forcing them to refer to Lucretia differently would only increase tension. Increase animosity.

It's all coming back. The politics. The machinations his father played at, just as much as everyone else.

Everything is strategic now, so much more than before.

"The Mistress has retired for the evening," the man says. "A suite upstairs has been prepared if…" Again the search for a word. "If you would like to do the same?"

He weighs his reply. He wants to find Cait and be sure she's safe. He wants to keep her nearby too, for this night, for longer. And all of him wants to sit down without the pressure of the watchful eyes of people who might try to kill him, their respective leader's orders be damned.

But for anyone among Volgert to know he cares about her…

"I wish to speak to Cait." He keeps his tone detached, but he glances at the Guardians more than the Volgert bodyguards.

"She is in a room on the top floor," one of the Guardians replies. "Your wolves are with her."

The words are a relief, though he gives no sign of the tension that leaves him. As bizarre as it seems, Sorcha and the other werewolf mercenaries might be the most trustworthy people in this building, if only for the fact they've maintained their contract despite the bribes Volgert and others offered them. It's not much, but it's more than whatever loyalty he could claim from the people surrounding him now—and that's without bringing into it Lucretia's accusation of a leak in Katsuro's organization.

His stomach turns. He needs to see for himself that Cait is safe.

The elevator car arrives. He enters and presses the button for the top floor. With the bodyguards around him, he waits in silence while the numbers on the old-fashioned dial climb. There's no way to keep the Volgert bodyguards from cluing in on his interest in Cait, he admits to himself, though if he's lucky, they'll draw the same conclusion as so many others have—that she's a resource to him, nothing more. Regardless, though, he can't send her away, not now.

For so many reasons.

He pushes the thought aside as the elevator slows. The door slides open, revealing the heavily wallpapered hallway and the candelabras of the upper floor. He glances both directions when he exits the elevator and catches sight of Cait curled into an armchair in the alcove at the end of the hall. A blanket covers her legs, protection against the air conditioning still running despite the late autumn season. Her dark hair is pulled around her shoulder, and her fingers are worrying at its ends. Her gaze is on the window and the night outside, ignoring the television playing images of a fire on the news. The light of the screen casts her features in a blue-white chiaroscuro.

His heart does a strange movement in his chest, as if it's growing and contracting all at once. So many reasons he can't send her away…

She glances from the window like something has caught her eye, and then turns farther as if following someone's gaze. One of the wolves, most likely. They probably heard the elevator as it left the ground floor. At the sight of him, though, she pushes the blanket aside and climbs quickly to her feet.

He motions for the bodyguards to hang back. To a person, they hesitate before taking up positions by the walls.

Cait eyes them warily when she comes closer. "Hey."

"Hello."

He's not sure what to say, how much to say.

And he's not sure how much longer he can keep this up.

"How are you doing?" Worry flickers in Cait's eyes.

"Fine," he lies. "You?"

"Eh, you know…" She trails off, her gaze darting to the bodyguards and away.

"Come with me?"

She nods. Sorcha and two other mercenaries materialize from the shadows behind her. The werewolves follow them down the hallway.

"Which room?" he asks the bodyguards.

One of the Volgert team leaves her post by the wall to lead them farther down the corridor, and one of the Guardians moves quickly to accompany her. The woman opens the door and strides into the room, checking it thoroughly and ignoring the Guardian who does the same, before she hands over the key.

"Have your people keep watch on the elevator and the

stairwell," he orders them both, knowing that like everything else, the words are political. The most trusted security would be placed at this door. The guards from Volgert would want that to be them; the Guardians would want the opposite. Both will take the mercenaries' placement there as an insult.

But it doesn't matter. He doesn't trust either group. And he's had enough of being watched for the day.

It's never going to end, the watching.

He shoves that thought down too. The Volgert woman nods, though he catches the side-eye she gives to Sorcha while she passes her on the way back to the elevator. For her part, Sorcha ignores her and the Guardian alike, merely bowing her head briefly to him before retreating to the opposite side of the hall. The other mercenaries do the same.

A breath leaves Amar when he shuts the door. For a moment, all he can do is press a hand to the wood as if it will keep out the world for so much longer than this night.

"Amar?"

He glances over his shoulder, his night vision finding Cait standing in the center of the dark room. The edges of her form are silvered by the trace of moonlight slipping past the thick brocade curtains. The space itself seems much like an apartment living room, albeit one from a century or more ago. A stiff armchair trimmed by wood and upholstered in jacquard fabric faces a roll-top writing desk. An equally stiff sofa waits against the opposite wall, framed by end tables that bear lamps with pale, stained-glass shades.

Reaching over, he flicks the light switch on the wall. Cait winces a bit when the buttery glow of the lamps flares to life.

"Are you okay?" she asks. "Really?"

He doesn't know what to say to her. *Confiding* in someone doesn't happen in his world. Trusting someone. Not with this.

Not with the way he feels like he's dying inside.

Cait crosses the room, her eyes never leaving him. Her hand moves toward him, and he tenses. She pauses.

"I don't want to hurt you," he says.

Confusion crosses her face briefly before understanding takes its place. "I can control it." The honesty he adores about her wins out. "I think."

Her hand reaches up, brushing his cheek. A breath escapes him.

"This isn't getting away from them, is it?" she says quietly. "Having a normal life?"

He turns his face aside, pain welling up like her words were a pickaxe to the wall he'd put between himself and those feelings today. Because he had to. It was the only way to survive.

It always is.

"I'm sorry," she says.

He shakes his head.

She moves nearer to him. Her other hand slips around his side. He wraps his arms around her, holding her close, feeling the warmth of her against his chest.

It helps. It always does.

"So now what?" she asks quietly.

He hesitates, unsure what to say. In his arms, he feels her growing tense.

"We leave town," he says. "As soon as possible."

She nods, the motion short, tight. "So will you, um... will you be somewhere I can still, you know, talk to you or..."

He pushes her back so he can see her face. "*We*, Cait. You and me."

"But don't you need to, like…" A question wanders somewhere in her voice. "You're in charge of these people now. Aren't there places you need to be and—"

"I *need* to be with you."

The words are firm. Desperate. They're more true than he knows how to admit.

He's going to lose his mind if he has to send her away and rule House Volgert alone.

Even if every ruler of a House has always been alone.

Releasing his grip on her shoulders, he steps past her, pacing farther into the room while he struggles to get a handle on himself. That's the problem, isn't it? No ruler of a House has friends, has loved ones, has anything that even *approaches* emotional connections. Not really. And with good reason. Everything and everyone in your life was a target when you ruled a House, not to mention being a perceived weakness as well. There was no way to keep the people you cared about safe, no matter how hard you tried or how many bodyguards you put around them.

Better to not care about anyone at all.

"Amar?"

He can't bring himself to look at her. This isn't solely his decision. She may not *want* to stay with him. Maybe that's where she's heading with this. He knows whatever he needs isn't the only thing that matters here, because today he's become a bigger target than before. Anywhere near him isn't going to be safe, not now, not ever. And her family is out there. Her best friend.

Her chance at a normal life.

The thought is like ice water seeping through his veins. She *could* still have a normal life. He'd done it, after all, at least for a while. And now he controls a House. Sorcha hadn't been completely wrong about what ruling Volgert would mean for Cait's safety. Once Linden and Penny are dealt with, he could make sure no one would ever threaten her again. Maybe that's what she—

"I need you too."

Her words pull his eyes back to her like nothing else could.

"We're safer together." She gives him a questioning look. "Right?"

His heart aches. It's a strange feeling.

And he doesn't know what to say. People will try to hurt her. Hurt her for a thousand reasons that have everything and nothing to do with him. And that's not even bringing into it what she can do.

He's being an idiot. A selfish idiot.

"Cait—"

She comes toward him again. "We're safer together." There's no question this time. "And if you don't want me to go—" She seems to see something in his expression, something that only makes her tone more certain. "Then I'm not leaving you."

The truth pushes at him. "I never want you to go."

A tiny smile breaks past the solemn look on her beautiful face. She reaches out, and he brings her back to him. He slips an arm around her and takes her cheek carefully, watching for any sign she's having trouble controlling her abilities.

But there's nothing. Just her, like he remembers. Like he's been longing for, craving for so much more than just this night. Guiding her closer, he brushes her lips gently with his own. A short breath leaves her, followed by a hungry noise. Her grip tightens on him, keeping him near.

He digs his fingers into her, needing her, craving her, and he kisses her again, deeper and longer than before.

The room begins to fade, taking the day and everything in it. The world becomes the taste of her lips. The warm, sweet scent of her skin. The way her soft hair falls against his arms. He can feel himself growing so hard for her.

She breaks from him, breathless. "Can you…" She appears to struggle for words, but her body speaks for her, crushing her against him, grinding on him almost desperately. "I just…I want…I need to feel you after everything that…Please." She looks to the bedroom behind her, past the open door, and relief surges through him when he realizes what she's asking.

But there's still her new ability to consider. "Will you be okay?" he asks her.

She gives a quick nod. "Mm-hmm." Her hazel eyes rise to his, pleading. "Do you think we could—"

"God, yes."

His lips capture hers again, and then he's lifting her. Carrying her into the bedroom and kicking the door shut blindly behind him. Her legs are wrapped around him, so reminiscent of the first time he was with her. The memory fills him with desire. With peace. So many people in his past, but none of them—not a single person in all his life—have come close to what he feels when he's with her.

He lowers her to the bed. Her eyes meet his, hunger in her gaze. Desperation too, like she craves this as much as he does. He wastes no time. Reaching for the closure of her jeans, he unfastens them and draws them from her. She sits up after they're gone, tugging her shirt over her head as if she can't wait to have it off. He takes the opportunity to pull his own clothes away. His shirt passes over his head, the fabric obscuring his view for only the moment it takes her to remove her bra.

His gaze roams over her breasts, round and soft and beautiful. But the view can only last for a moment. He wants her now.

She strips off her underwear and reaches for him, her own desire clear.

He retrieves a condom packet from his wallet before his pants and underwear join hers on the ground. And then he's climbing over her, the soft mattress giving beneath his knees, the silken comforter cool on his warm hands. He kisses her as she lies back on the bed, and he slides one hand up her side to embrace her breast. She pushes herself toward him, her fingers clutching his sides, his back.

"Please," she begs when his lips briefly leave her own.

Her hand moves down, finding his cock. Her grip moves on him, her thumb playing at his tip, and his breath catches at the sensation, his pulse flying higher and thudding in his veins.

She grins. He mirrors the expression.

"I want you," she whispers. "Please."

He nods. "Same."

Rocking back onto his knees for a moment, he rips open the packet in his hand and rolls the condom on with a speed born of adrenaline as much as practice. The material is thin, so thin, but the thought races through his head all the same.

What would it be like without this between them?

He bashes the question down as fast as he can. Impossibilities don't matter. They need to protect each other. Now. Forever. He's a demon, but he's not invulnerable. Neither is she. They can't be like that with each other.

And this is enough.

He lowers himself over her, guiding his cock to the soft layers of her pussy. His tip slips against the wetness between her legs, and desire drives every other thought from his mind. He wants to kiss her, taste her, touch every inch of her body.

She lifts her hips, eager for him, giving him more access to her.

God, yes.

He pushes inside her, a blinding thrill running through his veins to feel her tightness around him. He needed this. Her. Sex has always been food, but this is something else entirely. Overwhelming. Desperate. Frantic. He can't even give it a name.

His lips claim hers. His hand shifts around, raking up through her hair to hold her to him while he thrusts into her again, again, again.

Her breaths come faster, and he moves to kiss her neck, her shoulders, giving her a chance for air.

"God," she gasps. "Amar…"

Pleasure surges through him, brought about by so much more than what he's doing with her. The sound of his name on her lips is always incredible, but never more so than now. He wants to drive her to screaming it, the werewolves and the guards and the whole universe be damned. He wants to fill his world with the sounds of her pleasure, with the beautiful smell of her skin, of sex, with the gasp of her breaths as he drives into her.

Because his world died today, and only this makes him feel like he might still be alive.

He shifts around, and she understands in only a moment. Rolling, he ends up beneath her. His eyes fasten on her body moving atop his own, on her breasts rising and falling so quickly. Moisture builds between them. He slides his hands up her sides, over her amazing curves and breasts, before returning to her hips and thrusting himself deeper into her over and over again. She tilts her head back, closing her eyes, a choked cry leaving her.

It's beautiful. Intoxicating. He wants to show her all he knows, all he's learned, and use it to let her feel every ounce of what her beautiful body can do. He wants to take hours to make her scream with pleasure again and again, but he needs this too. He can't wait. He grips her harder, hitting her as deep inside as he can, driving himself into her with all he has.

Her body tenses. Clenches tight around him. She cries out a second time, louder, and he watches as the orgasm overtakes her, shivering and surging through her. He doesn't stop moving even when she collapses against him. Even when she comes back to Earth enough to roll with him, roll beneath him again and let the soft blankets engulf her.

Warmth surges through his body from something so much more than sex. Than desire.

It's something else entirely…

He grips the bed rail above her head, using it to brace himself with every thrust. His mouth finds her neck, her shoulder, anything of her he can reach, and the scent of her fills his head. The day disappears, drowned in her, lost in her, washed away utterly by her.

She clutches his back, his hips, like she wants to pull all of him into her body. Her nails dig into his skin, and a rough sound escapes him, a groan or growl, he can't tell. He feels her softness clenching around him again. Sweat slicks her skin beneath his palm. Her scent is like a drug, and he wants it all. Her hips rock into him, deepening his thrusts, and she makes a pleading noise like even that is not enough. Her hands tighten on him.

Gasping, she comes again. She hangs onto him, her body stiffening as pleasure rockets through her. He thrusts harder, desperate to keep it going for both their sakes. Pressure begins to build higher in him, in his cock, in his body, tensing his back and legs. He wants to continue, wants relief now, wants to make this last forever if only to forget everything that—

His orgasm overtakes the last shreds of his control. A cry escapes him, muffled by the pillows, but loud all the same. His body moves on desperate autopilot, still thrusting inside her, wringing himself out into her while pleasure blurs the world. And he's not dead. Never dead.

Not with Cait.

The orgasm fades. The room and the bed reassert themselves as real. His breaths come quick and don't bring in enough air. He pushes away from the mattress to look down at her.

"I love you."

The words leave him before his mind can catch up, before instincts from a decade of survival can have any say in stopping him. And they're true.

They're deadly.

And still true.

But she doesn't answer. Her mouth moves, her eyes wide, but she's silent, and the warmth inside him begins to shrivel.

He knows this feeling. Learned it well in his father's world.

Fear.

He made a mistake, saying this. Admitting this. He doesn't know what she's feeling, what she's thinking after everything they've been through today, and those simple words leave him more vulnerable than he's ever been. But he rules a House now, and to a neutral demon like she is, that makes him an enemy—or a threat at the very least. Never mind that he now leads the very House that tried to kill her friend. Maybe she—

"I love you too."

His world stops.

Her hand lifts, touching his cheek. Are those tears in her eyes? She smiles, so tentatively, so overcome by something that looks like happiness, but he can't tell.

"I love you, Amar. I—"

He kisses her, frantically, desperately. She laughs against his lips, a deep sort of relief in the sound, and a chuckle rises from him too.

She loves him.

Cait *loves* him.

He has no idea what to do with himself now.

Heart racing, he draws back, his mind reeling. Old habits for survival try to make themselves known, but they feel as out of place now as he does.

And she smiles again. "Thank you."

Confusion hits him. "For what?"

"For telling me."

He doesn't know what to say.

She brushes his cheek with her soft fingertips, tracing the curves and planes of his face like she's memorizing them. He leans into her touch, closing his eyes. He needs this too. As much as the sex, as much as the release.

He needs her touch like it's made of magic that could take this life away.

"How are you, Amar?" she asks softly. "Honestly?"

He hesitates. "I don't know."

She's silent. He moves off of her, removing the condom and then lying back at her side. She props herself up on an elbow, watching him.

Time slips past, the pleasure of his orgasm fading and leaving peace in its wake. He sighs. "I wanted to go to school. Get a job, you know? And now…"

"I know."

A new feeling moves through him at the simple words. It seems like comfort.

"But…after this is over, maybe you could find someone you trust who'd want this instead?" she suggests.

He pauses. He hadn't thought about that. Doesn't know who it could be, either, considering short of Cait, Bianca, Rafael, and Brett—neutrals, each of them—he doesn't exactly trust anyone in the entire demon world. But it's still an idea. "Yeah."

She shifts closer. He pulls her into his arms while she rests her head against his shoulder. Her leg wraps over his own, and a smile crosses his face. He loves it when she does that.

"I'm with you, you know that?" she says quietly. "I promise I'm not leaving. Not if you don't want me to."

He closes his eyes briefly and kisses her head. "I don't."

She nestles in against him. "Sleep then, yeah? Maybe it'll seem…" She searches for a term. "Less terrible in the morning."

He nods. Maybe it will.

If only because she's here.

1 7

———————

KYLE

THE DOOR TO THE MAKESHIFT BEDROOM IN THE BARN OPENS, and he can't help but feel a small surge of relief. She hadn't been too loud, thankfully. But the knowledge that some succubus was feeding behind the plywood walls had still been distracting, and he needs to concentrate if he's going to survive the debacle that his coup has become. For that matter, Penny's next stage of her plan is bound to be more complicated than the teenage psycho predicts, no matter how much she promises it'll pay off.

It's not like he hasn't heard her bullshit before. And of course she could be lying—hell, she probably is. But it didn't take much, after getting back here, for him to realize he didn't have a choice. He's gotten his hands on a crazy bitch who could find him anywhere in the world. One who ostensibly is carrying on like she's on his side. One whom everyone else wants, which means that even if he's stuck on the bucking bronco of crazy, at least no one else gets to ride.

So he's giving her a little more rope, one last time, to

prove she's worth all he went through to get his hands on the stupid bitch.

And he hopes like hell he's not hanging himself with it.

"Better?" Penny asks when Arlene walks in.

Arlene affords her a mildly condescending smile.

He leans over, checking past the open doorway and noting the silence from the next room. "You kill him?"

The woman's expression turns biting. "I was hungry."

He shakes his head. Great. Another body to clean up. He should start a damn service.

Scowling, he returns his attention to the tablet screen in front of him. This wouldn't be easy. Winslow Manor might look abandoned, but his recognizance teams say it's surrounded by enough defensive magic to stop a full-on assault by all of Volgert itself—and it has guards and security stations, besides. Admittedly, his forces are already in place, their vans parked deep in the forest around their ultimate destination. The Touched are there as well, brought by Penny's order and not his own—a fact that he *swears* he'll make her pay for eventually. The lunatic horde is all locked inside heavily reinforced vans stationed around the entire location. His people are watching them —waiting for what, the gods only know.

He certainly doesn't. But scouts posted on the perimeter report no unusual movement at the target. It's past midnight now and has been for several hours, so the darkness will help as well. He hasn't got a clue what the little teenage psycho intends to do about any of it, but he has escape plans involving everything from calling in emergency assistance from the local forest service to blowing up the damn manor house. Once the three of them show up and all hell breaks loose, though, even shadow-crossing wouldn't keep their egress from being—

"Kyle?"

Annoyance surges at the interruption. He looks up from the tablet, glaring at Penny before he can stop himself.

She blinks at his expression. "What's with that face?"

He wrestles his irritation down. "Nothing."

"Okay, well, we're ready to go."

"I don't have this ironed out yet."

She scoffs. "Oh come on, silly. It's *me*. We'll be fine."

He manages to control his reaction this time, despite how much he wants to comment on the pure idiocy of her incredibly liberal definition of *fine*. Sure, she'd bounced back like a deranged rubber ball from their near death at Linden's hands. Hell, she carried on like Alistair's ruse at the hospital hadn't even happened.

But she's certifiable, and he knows his life depends upon making sure he never lets himself get screwed over by her again.

He sets the tablet aside. He'll make it out of this alive no matter what. If there's one area in the world he excels in, it's survival. And he'll make all this pay off too.

Somehow.

"Of course," he says, extending a hand to her.

She wraps her fingers around his. The barn vanishes. A small clearing appears around them, ringed with deep shadows and plenty of places for Alistair's security to hide.

Such as twenty feet in front of him.

Kyle tenses, but Penny's already moving. Her gun swings up, and she fires, the shot muffled by the silencer she's acquired at some point. He doesn't bother to wonder where she got it. Probably one of his people, same as ever. He makes a mental note to thank them for giving the crazy bitch an accessory that makes her even *more* dangerous than she was already.

The security guard collapses into the dead leaves and doesn't move again.

Penny lets out a small giggle and tucks the gun into her butterfly-covered backpack. She looks to him and Arlene. "Ready to go?"

Without waiting for a response, she trots across the small moonlit clearing and then deeper into the forest. Scanning the woods around them, he walks after her and Arlene. He still has no idea why the woman is even with them. Penny simply swears she'll be useful.

"They'll be looking for that one." The idiot girl doesn't even bother to keep her voice down. "But we have a few seconds until that happens." She grins. "More than enough time."

Kyle makes no comment.

They continue through the undergrowth, branches swiping their legs and leaves rustling underfoot. Penny ignores any pretense at silence, swaying back and forth with her arms out from her sides like she's dancing. A ten-foot-tall fence topped by barbed wire interrupts her only briefly; a pair of wire cutters from her pink backpack make short work of its chain links.

And then she's off into the woods, dancing again.

Kyle slips past the gap in the fence and stalks after her, his attention flicking across the trees, the bushes. Alistair's people could be anywhere, even without bringing shadow-crossing into the equation. And yet here she was, spinning through the forest like a damn—

She stops.

Grinning back at him and Arlene, she holds up a finger and points. His eyes follow the gesture. A tiny camera perches in the trees ahead, barely distinguishable in the darkness even to his heightened night vision. Its lens is aimed straight at them.

He bites back a curse. Did that little bitch just lead him into a—

Penny turns back to the camera and waves.

"What are you *doing*?" he hisses. "They'll—"

"Oh, Kyle, you silly." Penny starts walking again. "Don't you trust me?"

He stares after her while Arlene follows, grim determination on the woman's face like she's continuing onward despite every better instinct she owns.

He knows the feeling.

His head shakes. No, of course he doesn't trust her. What kind of moronic question is that?

But then, what choice is there? Alistair's seen him, back at the hospital. These cameras connected to the-gods-knew-where have all seen him now too. His anonymity has been as good as dead for days, if not weeks, and anywhere he goes, the Houses will hunt him for information on this deranged girl.

And she has to know that. She's not stupid. Psychotic as a clown from hell, but not stupid.

She's perfectly aware that he's trapped.

His teeth grind. He walks after the lunatic, his eyes scanning the trees for more cameras and finding them. One in the maple to his right, another thirty feet to his left. His scouts reported seeing the things, but he'd assumed that his *psychic* would not only be able to avoid them, but that she'd *want* to as well.

More the fool, him.

The edge of the forest comes into view.

And the air around him begins to crackle.

He retreats fast. "Son of a—"

It's too late. The security system has already been triggered. Guards rush from the house. A dozen of them, some holding guns, others knives or crossbows. Still more have electricity flaring around their hands in every color of the rainbow.

And against that is him, a middle-aged succubus, and a psychic who *should* have said something before he set off the damn alarm.

That bitch.

It *is* a trap.

His feet turn, starting to carry him away from this indescribable mistake. He's still in the shadows of the trees, whereas the guards are in the open beneath the bright moonlight. They haven't seen him. Not on anything more than the cameras, anyway.

"Kyle," Penny warns. He ignores her. "Wait."

Her gun swings up, aimed at him. He stops. This was all an *epic* mistake. Idiocy of the highest level. What the hell had he been—

"Arlene?" Penny prompts.

His eyes flick to the woman.

Arlene's mouth tightens. "Yeah." She bites off the word. "Sure."

She draws a breath. Releases it in a huff.

And nothing else happens. Kyle looks between them. Delusional, the both of them. They're—

He feels weird.

His eyes dart around. It's like a high-pitched ringing in his ears, barely on the edge of hearing. Like one of his teeth has gone numb. Like any number of constant sensations he hadn't even noticed before, all of which are suddenly missing.

A possibility occurs to him. He lifts his hand, trying to summon up the magic under his skin.

Mist sputters from his palm like the last coughs of exhaust from a dying engine.

His eyes go wide. What the *fuck*?

Penny grins at him. "Told you she'd be useful." She glances to one side. "Arlene?"

"Yeah, yeah," the woman mutters.

Kyle looks between them, confused.

And then Arlene makes a swatting motion with her hand, and all hell breaks loose.

The air in front of him turns to lightning, the charge crawling upward and outward like it's met an invisible wall. Crackling and snapping in a myriad of colors, the electricity spreads across the magical defense in the space of a few heartbeats, growing larger, climbing through the air until it covers the manor and all its surrounding area in a massive, electrical dome.

But the impression lasts only a moment.

The dome of electricity slams downward. The ground shudders, and he sees the guards collapse like puppets with cut strings. A blast of wind rocks him and the trees alike, as if all the air in the clearing ahead has been driven out.

Arlene exhales and inhales raggedly, sagging like she's just run ten miles while standing still.

Kyle stares at the guards, at the manor, at all of it. Nothing moves. "What…in the *hell*—"

Penny giggles. "Fun, right?"

He can't take his eyes off Arlene.

"Coming?" Penny prompts.

He takes one step forward, followed by another. The air doesn't change. The magical defense is gone. A burnt line glowing with embers marks the trees and grass, a perfect arc across where the barrier must have once been.

But the air past the burning line feels strange. Charged, somehow. He can't explain it. The feeling is almost like the world doesn't quite line up right in this place. Like when he stepped past the remnants of the defenses, everything around him shifted just a tad off-kilter, even if it looks normal to his eyes.

It occurs to him to wonder if the magical shield Arlene just destroyed had another purpose. Maybe it wasn't only meant to keep people out.

Maybe it was meant to keep something *in*.

"Kyle?" Penny is becoming petulant. He continues onward, cautious and slow. She giggles at her success in getting him to move and then scampers on ahead.

One of the guards groans when they come closer.

Kyle freezes. They're not dead. He thought they'd be—

A muffled gunshot makes him flinch. Merrily, Penny trots between the guards, firing once at each like a kid playing some mad game in a park.

In a moment, Kyle, Arlene, and Penny are the only ones in the clearing still alive.

Penny continues across the overgrown lawn.

Kyle balks. This is lunacy. He can't leave, but staying has to be suicide.

"What about security in the manor?" he tries. "Are they—"

"Security," Penny says the word like it's a pathetic joke as she swaps out the clip in the gun and shoves a new one into place. "Trust me, Kyle." She grins. "Nothing's getting away from us this time."

18

CAIT

I open my eyes, and for a moment, all I can do is smile.

Because he's here. Amar is here.

And he loves me.

I turn my head in the darkness, careful not to make the blankets rustle. His arm is draped over my side, and his body spooned around mine, the warmth of his chest pressed up against my back. It's still a while until sunrise, and I don't know why I've suddenly woken up, but I don't care.

Amar *loves* me.

I never thought it'd affect me like this, hearing those words from him. It's like a glow inside me. Like a light in a room I hadn't even known existed, now suddenly visible. Like an impossibility made manifest and Christmas rolled all into one. I'd been desperate earlier, desperate simply to feel him with me—in me—after sleeping with someone else for the first time. I'd needed the man I loved, grounding me back in who I was, what I wanted in my life, even if he didn't feel the same way.

But *this*…

I find his eyes in the darkness. He's already awake.

He doesn't look pleased.

Confusion flickers through me. I open my mouth, only to have him place a finger across my lips. "Shh," he whispers.

He slips from beneath the sheets we'd pulled over ourselves earlier. With his eyes on the door on the far side of the room, he takes his clothes from the ground and draws them on quickly.

Icy trepidation spreads through me, washing away the comfort and warmth. Moving as carefully as I can to avoid making any sound, I climb from the bed too. In the darkness, I manage to track my clothes back to where I remember tossing them, and in only a few moments, I'm dressed again.

Amar takes my hand. Keeping me behind him, he leads me out of the bedroom.

A knock comes on the hotel suite's front door. We freeze halfway across the living room.

I look to Amar, confused. Why would someone *knock* if they wanted to hurt us?

Amar takes a short breath and continues across the room, still making sure I'm behind him. At the door, he pauses briefly and then pulls it open.

I wince at the golden light coming from the hall lamps. I don't recognize the woman waiting there. A Volgert bodyguard, maybe. The Guardians would almost certainly look more familiar by now. A few people I remember from among the mercenaries stand by the far wall of the corridor. Sorcha is nowhere to be seen, though I would figure even a werewolf needs sleep.

"Yes?" Amar says.

The woman's gaze flicks to me for all of an eye blink. I can't tell what she thinks of seeing me here. "Possible trouble, sir. That vampire, Hisakawa Katsuro, is demanding to speak with you. He has a woman with him who insists—" Her attention returns to me, more pointed this time. "—insists your evening companion requires their assistance immediately."

My blood goes cold.

"Where?" Amar asks.

"Down in the—"

A ding comes from the elevator, and my attention snaps toward it.

Katsuro strides into the hallway, Nasreen on his heels. A trio of middle-aged guards hurries after them, looking flustered and more than a little peeved.

"I'm sorry, sir," one of the guards starts. "These *people* would not—"

"What is it?" Amar demands of Katsuro immediately. "What's going on?"

"Is it my dad?" I blurt.

Nasreen shakes her head. "Your father is fine. We—" She looks at the Volgert guards, cutting her words short.

Amar jerks his chin at the bodyguards. "Leave us."

They hesitate.

"*Now.*" Amar's voice is as cold as ice. He glances at the mercenaries. "You too."

They all go, retreating to opposite ends of the corridor like two sides of a parting sea.

Nasreen draws a breath. "We have a problem. The convergence, it's…" She pauses like she's trying to choose her words carefully

"What?" My hand clenches tight on Amar's.

"It's more affected by you than we thought. Did you see the news last night?"

I blink at her, baffled. "Yeah, but…"

Memory plays back. The local news I'd barely been watching. The story they'd reported.

No…

"There was a fire on campus," Nasreen says, putting words to the dread that's suddenly punched me in the gut. But it's impossible. I'd seen that there was a fire at the computer science building, yeah, and sure, that's my department, but—

"Not long before that," Nasreen continues, "there was a fire at a restaurant called Goa Café. Katsuro says you ordered takeout from there a week ago. You told your Guardian bodyguards it was your favorite place on campus." She pauses. "A server was killed."

My mouth moves for a moment before I can find words. "Pradeep. The owner. Was he—"

Nasreen shakes her head. "A young man who'd started there several days before."

My stomach roils, and not just with horror. Relief is there too, cold and wrong like a laugh at a funeral. I can't help it, though. Pradeep, that sweet old man who owned the café, who tried to defend me when some guys came after me over how I'd accidentally hurt their friend…he isn't dead.

But someone else is.

"But…" I flounder. "A fire there doesn't mean it's connected to…"

"There was also another fire several weeks back, on the same evening Amar was shot and Penny escaped. We didn't think anything of it, because it didn't seem connected to the events at that time, but given these other fires now and their proximity to significant uses of your abilities…" Nasreen looks grim.

I blink at the ground, reeling. Significant uses of my abilities, she said. Like the night I changed Penny back from being Touched when Amar couldn't. Like the night I escaped Alistair's people.

Like the ambush yesterday.

Nausea climbs my throat.

"Where was that fire?" Amar asks.

"A bar. The Silver Bullet. We haven't ascertained any link to Cait, but—"

"Oh my God." My hand clamps over my mouth as if to trap my horror inside. This isn't *possible*. It just isn't—

"Cait?" Amar prompts.

"M-my dad. He, uh…" I drag down a ragged breath. "Arlene told me once that was where he and my birth mom…"

I trail off. This isn't possible. This is *insane*.

But I remember now. I saw that on the news too, back at the veterinary clinic where Katsuro's people helped Amar after Penny shot him. I'd just been so distracted by worry over whether Amar was going to die that I hadn't even registered the significance of the fire's location.

"I'm doing this?" I look up at Nasreen. "My power? Me? I'm causing fires that kill—"

"It's not *you*," Katsuro cuts in.

I stare at him like he's thrown me a lifeline, but I'm not sure if it's actually a snake.

One that might bite and kill me. "But she said—"

"We think it's the convergence *reacting* to you, Cait," Nasreen says firmly. "Not that you're causing people to die."

Like that's better.

I wrap my arms around my middle. A few minutes ago, I would have sworn it was warm in here. Now I'm so cold, I'm shaking.

"But what does that mean?" Amar demands. "The convergence is connected to her? *Stalking* her?"

I can tell already that Nasreen doesn't know, not for certain. It's clear in her expression. "There's no precedent for this," she says. "The psychic who foresaw the convergence only knew that powerful demons would appear at the same time. She said nothing of what appears to be happening with Cait. But I have my people looking into it. Martin especially. He's incredibly gifted and has an affinity for energy magic." She gives a breathless chuckle like her words only scratch the surface of the truth. "I have him attempting to unravel this as we speak."

"So…what do I do?" I ask. "How do I—"

"The only thing we can think to do right now is get you out of town, same as before," Nasreen says. "The convergence is here. Why it is so focused on you, we're not certain, but if you're elsewhere—anywhere, really, far enough from the convergence here—there's a chance you'll be safer and everything in this town will be as well."

Katsuro nods. "We need to—"

Pain stabs through my midsection. I gasp, staggering. My back hits the wall.

"Cait?" Amar starts toward me.

I open my mouth, but no words make it out. Instead, the pain gets worse. Excruciating, like someone's yanking my insides around. Like someone's taken a knife to my core. I choke on a cry while my hands grasp my stomach. I'm almost shocked at the fact there's no blood.

What the—

The thought disintegrates as my vision swirls. My legs

buckle. Amar grabs me when I crumple. I flounder, desperate to stop myself from seeing his memories.

But there's nothing. Colors that turn to ash and blow away like they're caught in a windstorm. Past them, I can see Amar holding me. The ceiling is too far away, and the walls are all wrong. I think I'm on the ground. I see his mouth moving, calling to me, and then he turns. His shout cuts through the rushing in my ears.

"Get a doctor!"

Darkness swirls around me. My world feels numb, like the air has become thick cotton engulfing me, and yet my body hurts so much.

What's…

Katsuro's here. Sorcha's beyond him now, her hair disheveled and her jacket askew. She looks like she's ready to kill something if only somebody will give her a target. And then the world shifts when Amar lifts me.

Why is this…

My vision stutters and fragments like shattered glass. Everything becomes snapshots. The long corridor. A golden candelabra lighting the damask wallpaper. Nasreen at the elevator, her cell phone clutched to her ear. An open doorway. The bedroom. Our bedroom for one night, where Amar told me he loved me.

Where I'm dying.

The mattress gives under me when Amar lays me down. His arms slip from beneath me.

My hand flails out, catching him, silently begging him. Don't leave me. Don't—

The pain vanishes.

I lurch upright, gasping as if I've been drowning and I've just found air. My heart pounds, and everything feels too sharp, too real. For a moment, I stare around, my body thrumming with residual shock and adrenaline.

"Cait?"

I look toward Amar. My hand is still clutching his arm. "What…" I rasp. "What the *hell* was—"

The door to the hotel suite opens. Nasreen rushes in, a scrawny kid with oversized glasses scurrying after her. "Is she—"

Nasreen cuts off. Not taking her eyes from me, she motions to the kid, who sets to digging random objects from the pockets of his oversized coat. Confused, I watch him place them around the bed, moving with deliberate and yet vaguely frantic speed.

"What…" I start.

The kid mutters something. Light flares around me.

Even the tingle I'd thought was residual alarm fades from my body. Suddenly, I just feel strange. I can't put my finger on it for a moment, and then it clicks.

Normal. More normal than I think I've felt in weeks.

"Somebody want to explain this?" I beg.

"Is she safe?" Katsuro asks Nasreen.

"Hey!" I demand.

Katsuro glances at me, looking edgy as hell. It sends chills through me.

"Martin?" Nasreen calls.

"It'll hold." The boy nods but then seems to reconsider. "For the moment, at least."

I stare at him. *This* is Martin? The one who's supposed to be figuring this out?

He looks like he's *twelve*.

"What the hell just happened?" Amar aims the question at Nasreen and Martin, but his eyes dart to me with every other breath like he's scared that horrible pain will start up again. He hasn't moved to take his arm from me, either.

"Are you still hurting?" Nasreen asks me.

I shake my head. "No, but—" I falter. "Really, what happened?"

She lets out a breath. "What we were just discussing, I believe."

I'm lost.

"The convergence. It would appear that, in addition to you affecting it, the convergence can also have an effect on you."

She glances at Martin, who's muttering over another assortment of knickknacks he dumped in the corner. By the door, the Volgert guards watch him like they can't decide if they should stop him or retreat.

"My people tell me they detected a change in the energy of the convergence only seconds before I called them just now," Nasreen continues. "A…depression, if you will. As if something deadened the convergence, if only for a moment, which is wholly dissimilar to anything we've seen thus far in response to you. But they can find no explanation for it. Nothing natural, at least." She casts a brief look at Martin as if checking the truth of her words. The boy is still mumbling and staring at the assortment in front of him like the bits and bobs are speaking to him. "It appears someone else has found a way to affect the convergence too."

I tremble. Oh God.

Arlene.

"Where?" Amar asks shortly.

"Martin and the others are working on that," Nasreen says. "This protective spell should help buffer Cait against any repeat events, and my people should be able to determine the location—" Her phone buzzes. She smiles, but there's only grimness in the expression. "Right about now."

She walks a few steps away from me and lifts the phone to her ear. I watch her go.

"Cait."

I glance back at the sound of Amar's voice.

He places his other hand atop mine where I hold his arm. "Are you okay?"

I nod. "I think so."

Nasreen hangs up and turns back to us. "How familiar are you with Winslow Manor?"

It's a heartbeat before I can place the name. "Wait, that's still there? I thought the city was going to tear it down."

"Apparently not."

"What is this place?" Katsuro asks.

"It's a massive old house in the woods outside town," I say. "Kids used to go there when I was younger to, you know, drink or do drugs or whatever. A few years back, a staircase collapsed and a girl ended up in the hospital, so I heard the city was going to bulldoze the whole thing."

I exhale. I haven't thought of Winslow Manor in years. I'd only been once with Ruby, back in high school. It'd been one of those places that seemed fascinating and tempting when it was forbidden to me as a social loser, but once I got there, it was just a big house. Creepy, sure. The local kids had countless stories about the former occupants. It'd been owned by a rich old woman who murdered her entire family and lived for years with their corpses, or it'd been owned by a banker who went mad in the last economic crash and started filling the walls with dead animals as a food stockpile. Story was that whomever the owners had been, their ghosts haunted the place, but in reality, no one actually knew much about whoever lived there before.

God, I wonder if the ghosts are real.

"I know the place," Amar says. He releases my hand, heading for the door.

"Wait." I start to follow him, only to hesitate when I realize it'll take me beyond the boundary of the objects surrounding me. "Amar, I'm coming with you."

He turns back, his incredulity obvious.

"Cait," Katsuro starts. "You need to stay—"

"Who do we know who can affect the convergence?" I don't look away from Amar. "That everyone *thought* could affect the convergence?"

"What?" Nasreen interjects, alarmed. "Who are you talking about?"

"How does that matter?" Amar counters.

"It matters because I can distract her," I say. "She loves to gloat. If she sees how she's hurting me…"

Amar stares at me like I've lost my mind. And maybe I have, but right now, I don't care. I need to do this. She hurt my dad. Me. Now she's doing it again.

And with some massive magical power that could destabilize everything and set fires and kill innocent people.

Chills run through my skin.

"Are we talking about your stepmother?" Katsuro hazards. "The one Amar told me was a succubus? Went into hiding because of the Houses?"

I nod, not taking my eyes from Amar.

"We don't have time for this," Amar argues to me. "This *hurts* you, Cait. What if next time it kills you?"

Another shudder courses through me. I try to give no sign. "I can help, Amar."

"It's too much of a risk," Katsuro says. "Your stepmother is undoubtedly *not* alone. Whether she's allied herself with Alistair, Penny, or another force, she—"

"Sorcha will be with me." I glance at the woman. Her expression makes it clear her presence was never a question. "The other wolves too. But I'm telling you, if Arlene sees me there, you'll stand a better chance. She's a sadistic bitch. If she sees that she's hurting me—"

"You're not going there to be cannon fodder for her!" Amar protests.

"I'll be careful. I won't—"

"Cait's right."

I turn at the sound of Martin's voice, surprised.

"I-I mean, not about the cannon fodder thing," the kid stammers. "I don't agree about that at all, but..." He exhales. "A-about the convergence...yeah. She needs to be there."

"Why?" Amar demands.

Nasreen gapes at her student. "Martin, the closer she is to this—"

"I-I-I know it's a risk, but..." He pushes his glasses up a bit higher on his nose in a nervous gesture. "You asked me to study this. Track it, remember? And...and this place..."

"It's connected," Nasreen fills in, barely asking.

"Very. And not just because of this...this *depression*. Someone's been drawing the energy of the convergence toward this location. Slowly, yeah, and it's hard to notice if you're not looking right at it, but the change is there. Now it *might* be this Arlene person, but given what just happened..." Martin's hand gestures toward the objects in front of him and then pauses, like he realizes he's pointing at something we can't see. "The draw is like a subtle shift in the threads of a cloth. Like a warping, but too consistent to be totally natural. And what just hurt Cait…it was like somebody hurling a *cannonball* onto that fabric. But I don't think these two forces are working together. I mean, maybe they are. Maybe this was a test or something, but it doesn't really matter anyway. Someone's trying to take control over the energy of the convergence, and Cait's connected to that energy. She…she increases it. This *whatever*-it-is decreases it." He gives us an uncomfortable look. "Cait might be the only one who could offset this. That could slow down whoever this is, or stop them from taking control of the power of the convergence fully."

I stare at him. Stopping Arlene is one thing, but this…

"He's right," Nasreen says quietly.

"*No,*" Katsuro replies immediately. "This is too much of a risk. We have no evidence that Cait's involvement will do anything but hurt her."

"Don't we?" Nasreen counters. "Whoever is doing this to the convergence, they appear to be trying to dampen it. Cait has the exact opposite effect. With her and this other force there—"

"That could kill her!" Amar snaps.

"That could be explosive," Katsuro adds.

Nasreen eyes them both. "Or it could be our last chance to gain control of this situation before someone else does."

Katsuro looks away.

"What about these defenses?" Amar motions to the objects around me. "She can't bring those with her."

"It, uh, it seems to have paused for the moment," Martin says nervously. "The more damaging effects, anyway."

"If we move quickly," Nasreen adds, "we may reach this place before the disruption has the opportunity to start up again."

Amar scoffs. "That's not good enough. She could—"

I get up from the bed, leaving the circle of objects. Amar steps toward me immediately, alarmed, but I hold up my hand to stop him.

The tingling feeling starts again, but not quite as strong as before. I just feel…tense, like a bowstring.

"I'm fine," I say.

I can tell Amar doesn't believe me.

"I'm going."

"Cait—" Amar begins.

Gritting my teeth, I cast a glance at Sorcha and then head for the door. It doesn't matter. None of this matters. I'm going to handle this. Stop this.

Arlene's done enough damage in my life.

19

KYLE

IN THE YEARS BEFORE HIS SUCCUBUS MOTHER CLAIMED HIM from the deadbeat, drug addict, waste of space that had been his biological father, Kyle had seen his fair share of decrepit locations. From crack dens to halfway houses, he'd survived more rat-infested hell holes by the time he was ten than most people see in their lifetimes.

But this might just beat them all. Three stories of overgrown mess, complete with shattered windows that gape like open wounds, the house looks like a decaying corpse. Mold clings to the building like a second skin, steadily devouring the amateur graffiti scrawled along the stone walls while bushes claw at the house as if they want to do the world a favor and swallow the structure whole.

Penny pays no attention to any of it.

Kyle's eyes dart to the tiny cameras perched on the ledge surrounding the second story. In the moonlight, he can just make out the wisps of smoke rising from the devices, though the sparks of futile electricity also make it clear the things are dead. Whatever Arlene did, it killed the technological security too.

Ahead of him, the teenage lunatic trots up to the arched entryway and the enormous wood door it holds, ignoring the fact that guns exist and that Linden might have more security inside. Without waiting for him or Arlene, she pushes the door wide.

He braces himself, but nothing happens. The long foyer ahead of him appears empty, at least of demon or human life. Nature has made its way in, however, scattering dead leaves across the cracked tile and chewing dark gashes into the water-damaged wallpaper. Vandals have too, leaving their own detritus of empty beer cans and cigarette stubs. A trail of wires hangs from a mount on the ceiling; the previous home of a chandelier, perhaps, though now the fixture is gone. Open archways on either side farther down the hall give access to more of the massive house, while a broad and broken stairway waits at the end of the foyer, flanked by rotting wood banisters and climbing up into shadows his demon eyes can scarcely penetrate.

A small clattering sound comes from beyond one of the arches. His attention snaps toward the noise.

Penny gives a tiny giggle. Without taking her eyes from the archway, she pulls her gun from her bag and skips down the hall. He follows while Arlene trails after them. Grinning widely, Penny swings around the archway, aiming the weapon ahead of her.

"Please!" comes a pleading cry.

The girl doesn't shoot. Peeking his head around the entrance, Kyle catches sight of a brown-haired man kneeling on the floor, his gun on the ground ahead of him and his hands raised defensively. The room around him is an abandoned mess of splintered floorboards and moldy wallpaper. A hole in the ceiling shows only darkness, while across the space, broken shelves clutter the base of what seems to be a bookcase built into the wall. The man on the ground barely spares Kyle a glance; his pleading gaze is locked on Penny.

"Please," the man continues. "I surrender. I—"

Penny giggles again and swings the gun around fast, aiming behind her without looking. Two shots snap out, loud as firecrackers, and Kyle spins in time to see another man, gun in hand, tumble to the floor.

With a furious noise, the first guy grabs for his weapon, only to freeze when Penny's gun whips around again.

"Did he tell you that trick would work?" the lunatic girl asks. "Or is Alistair such a coward that he just left you here to figure it out on your own?"

The man doesn't respond.

Penny scoffs. "Oh, please."

She fires the gun. Kyle grimaces, looking away while blood splatters the rotting floorboards and the man falls limp to the ground.

A knife clatters from the dead man's grip, dropping from one hand as if the guy had been trying to hide it in preparation to throw.

"They really don't understand the word *psychic*, do they?" Penny's grin returns. "Come on. It's here. I know it."

She starts off down the hall.

Kyle stares after her. "*It?*"

She doesn't respond, peering through the next archway.

He strides after her. "Penny. What do you mean, *it…*"

His words trail off when he sees the room. A glossy flat-screen television hangs on one wall, utterly incongruous. A small table and a wingback chair sit below it, bizarrely untouched considering the graffiti and destruction throughout the rest of the building, but that's not what gives him pause. He recognizes it. The scene, the angle.

Alistair had been here, sitting *right* here, when he spoke to them over video in the hospital.

Kyle's hand adjusts on his gun. The old man *was* here, which means he might still be here, and that was all kinds of bad. He wasn't going to get trapped by Penny's incompetence again.

He catches sight of motion beyond one of the windows, and he hurries toward the glass, careful to stick to the side where he'll be shielded by wood and plaster, and hidden from view by the darkness that hangs thick on the room. The three of them got in here too easily. This might be a trap too.

Or a nightmare.

The blood rushes from his hands and feet, freezing them instantly when he sees the scene outside. Two dozen people form a protective wall ahead of almost a half dozen more, and he recognizes some of them. Cait. That damn vampire. A collection of werewolf mercenaries he'd tried and failed to hire weeks ago. Amar.

Lucretia's elite guard.

Short breaths jab into his lungs in hot bursts. He feels like the ground is wavering. The soldiers move from the forest, scanning the terrain like the military-grade team they are, while that pathetic weakling Cait and all her little bodyguards follow them. But when they reach the fallen Linden henchmen, one of the Volgert soldiers glances back.

A choked gasp leaves Kyle at Amar's nod.

Amar controls them. He's *in* control of them. Lucretia's elite soldiers, her personal bodyguard, and he—

Another soldier speaks to him, and Amar motions toward the side of the manor at the words. A dozen of the soldiers split off, heading where Amar dictated.

It's not possible. That insufferable prick of a Legacy wasn't even *part* of House Volgert, and yet here he was, in charge of bodyguards who only the leader of Volgert could…

No.

Under control, Penny said. She had Lucretia under…control…

He hears the blood rushing in his ears. He can barely hear the stupid bitch behind him saying his name.

"Kyle, come *on*," Penny calls from the opposite side of the room, not careful at all. Not caring that his entire coup has officially, finally, *totally* gone up in flames, costing him his one chance to take out the vampire queen and instead handing leadership of his House—*his* House, dammit; it was always going to be his!—over to *that*.

But then, Penny had to have known. She's *psychic.*

Lightning tangles beneath his skin, coursing through every limb in his body, snapping and snarling with his rage. He turns back, expecting a gun pointed his way, expecting that damned knowing expression to be on her face right before she shoots him to stop him from killing her. Because he can't hide this. Smother this like he's smothered so much else. That bitch is going to *die* this time.

But she's gone. Penny. Arlene too, not that he cares. He's standing alone in the room, and when he glances at the window again, already he can see Amar and the Volgert guard moving for the front door.

An inarticulate snarl breaks free of his control. He runs for the hallway and catches sight of Penny's pink dress just as she disappears around the turn of the massive stairs.

Fine. He'll kill her on the second floor.

But he'll be smart about it.

A slower breath makes its way into his chest. He *is* smart. Smarter than her and damn well smarter than that fool Amar. He can still make something out of this.

He climbs the stairs after her.

"It's here," he hears Penny say when he reaches the landing. "It's *here.*"

She's running down the hallway, hopscotching past the gaping holes in the hardwood floor while she flits between the graffiti-covered doors lining the corridor, pushing open one after the other. In the darkness, she has to be blind as a bat, yet she still stares into the rooms like they're personally betraying her.

His fist clenches, his skin burning with the urge to blast her into the oblivion she deserves. He stalks after her.

"It's *here.*" She speeds past another corner and beyond his reach. The massive building is comprised of two wings, the west and the east mirroring each other with the enormous stairway in the middle. Each wing is a loop. The hallway is lined with doors on either side and stretches around a core of interior rooms. He can't see anything of value inside. Moonlight pierces some of the exterior-facing rooms, though, glowing on collections of rusted springs and struts that probably had once been furniture.

He fantasizes about impaling her on them and then keeps moving, tracking her voice up the stairs to the third floor.

"It's…" Penny is gasping now, the crazed light in her eyes more frantic than he's seen. She's rounding the last corner of the wing now, heading back toward him and nearing the main stairwell again. He thinks he can hear voices coming from the first floor.

He lets the energy build in his fingers. He'll have one shot. Maybe less, if he takes too long.

"It's…" Penny spins in a circle, not seeing him, the idiot who let her drag him along like a stupid puppy to do her whims. "It's got to be…"

"What about this one?" Arlene offers casually, like she couldn't care less. Kyle's concentration fractures. He glances over to see the woman point at a stretch of wall several yards behind her.

Penny whirls, staring between the woman and the wall. "Huh?"

"This door?" Arlene gestures to the wallpaper again.

Great. He thought Penny was the only one who was nuts here.

But the girl just grins. "Oh, that sneaky, *sneaky* little…" She jogs back toward the blank stretch of rotting wallpaper, leering at it like it's a Christmas present she wants to stab.

Wariness prickles in his veins. What's this?

And then the girl turns, locking her bright blue eyes on him. Whoops, his instincts chime, too late. Too damn—

"Don't worry, Kyle," Penny says. "Only a few more minutes, and you'll have Volgert for the asking."

He stares at her.

"Or did you think I'd forgotten you?" She grins and takes out her cell phone. "Let them out," she tells the person on the other end and then tucks the phone away again.

Understanding filters through to him. Oh…oh, *shit*.

Suddenly, he's glad they're on the third floor.

Penny feels along the wall, but there's nothing there. A stretch of water-stained wallpaper that might once have been patterned in flowers. A broken molding of wood that looks like it met a thousand too many termites.

And a door that she pulls open because it's always been there. Dark, narrow, made of rotting wood. He can't figure out how he didn't see it before.

Unless…

Trap. His instincts change their message, clanging with the alarm that's kept him alive time and time again. Trap, trap, trap.

But he's the only one who hears it. The only one who cares, because then that crazy bitch whirls back to him. "Not long now. Four minutes. Maybe five."

"Until what?" Arlene presses.

Penny's grin could light a football stadium. "Until Cait dies."

"You told me you can't see her," Kyle says.

Arlene looks between him and the crazy girl, the relish in her eyes dimming back toward her customary caginess.

"Well…" Penny allows. "No. I can't see *her*. But I can see things around her, and that—" She giggles. "Oh, that's enough."

Without another word, she scampers up the shadow-choked slit of a staircase, leaving the two of them to follow.

"Caitlin is mine."

He looks to Arlene. The woman's beady eyes are like gimlets.

"I get to kill her," Arlene insists. "I get to rip her little Legacy heart out, do you understand? *Me.* After what that brat took from me, after what she put me through for over twenty years…" She looks ready to gut Kyle if he argues with her.

Which is ridiculous. Like he cares who kills Cait? But why the hell would he make a deal with a freak succubus when there's nothing he wants in—

"And I'll stay out of your way with the other one." Arlene's eyes flick to the stairwell before snapping back to him. "Maybe see if I can't help you out a bit. Deal?" Her eyebrow cocks, waiting.

Ah. Well, now that's different. Useful, even. And *long* overdue.

His lip twitches. "Deal."

Arlene nods once.

Hiding a grin of his own, he trails Penny up the stairs.

20

CAIT

G ATHERING AN ARMY APPARENTLY DOESN'T TAKE AS LONG AS I thought it would.

Even if it's only a small one.

Nervousness tangles in my stomach like a choking vine while I stand in the middle of the hotel conference room, eyeing the collection of demons around me. Katsuro's people on the left and behind me, Volgert forces to the right and up front. Sorcha's people are closer. I think Amar trusts them more, if only because he's paying them, so he has a better idea of where their loyalties lie. Plus, there is Lucretia's insistence that Katsuro's people have spies among them to consider…

My skin pebbles with anxiety. It hadn't felt like she was lying, but that didn't mean she couldn't be wrong.

Hopefully.

I pull my focus back to the Volgert group. Some of them don't look as pale as vampires, and they don't move quite like werewolves, making me think they might be incubi or succubi or maybe djinn—or something I've never heard of altogether. A few of them are heading over to pull out the accordion wall that could divide the large space around us into two smaller conference rooms. With the lights off on one side, it'll create a line of shadow pretty much everyone around me could easily cross.

I wonder what the hotel staff will think when they come inside the room only to find that the large group who walked in here is nowhere to be seen.

I wonder what'll happen when we reach the manor.

My stomach starts to do flips.

Amar comes over. "Ready?"

I make myself nod. "Much as I'll ever be."

He echoes the motion and then takes my hand. I grip his palm tightly, anchored by the solidity that is him. We follow the others to the accordion wall and into the dark shadows beyond it.

The conference room vanishes, and a forest takes its place. We keep moving forward, leaving the patch of moonlight and striding into the shadows beneath the trees. I can't see much: dark tree trunks, black undergrowth, and tiny swatches of stars between the dense branches overhead. But whenever someone moves to where I can distinguish their form from the shadows, flares of color spring to life around their shape.

It's useful, I'm sure. But distracting and potentially destructive too. I try to ignore the memories as best I can. I need to stay focused.

Moonlight begins to thin the shadows ahead. We continue onward, and I see a large clearing coming into view. At its center stands the manor. Three stories with an attic, towering among the trees. Formed of bricks and rough-hewn stonework, the building looks like, despite the obvious decay, it's still determined to stand until the end of time, nature and kids and vandalism be damned. Windows gape emptily, some with the glass still intact, many without, and overgrown grass and weeds choke the space around it. I can't see any ghosts, but that doesn't mean much.

Ghosts are the least of my worries right now.

The foremost guard reaches the edge of the clearing and holds up a hand. Word comes back in whispers: the magical defense has fallen. They think there are bodies in the yard too. I see Amar glance at me. I keep my focus on the manor. My skin has started to crawl, but not because the information basically guarantees Arlene or whoever is helping her is already here. It's something else. Something…odd.

We start walking again. The others around me are tense. But for my footsteps and the occasional rustle of grass around Amar, I can't hear anyone, though. It's not comforting, but like the ghosts, it's not the main issue, either.

There's something wrong with this building. With this place.

With me.

My breaths are shortening, like the air is too hard to breathe. Like I don't *want* to breathe it. I feel weird every time I do. My pulse is pounding in my ears now, hard and deafening. My eyes catch on a charcoal line scoring the tree trunks and grass, an arc larger than the house, like something was burned into oblivion right at this spot. A few embers still glimmer in the dark.

We're moving forward again. Amar sends a few guards to the sides of the manor in a whisper I can't hear. Grass rustles around my feet, too loud. I feel like my head isn't attached to my body. Like I'm floating. Not here. Not there.

Not anywhere. Just…adrift. And yet so very concentrated, as if my entire being is drawing toward a single spot, even if I have no idea what or where it is.

"Cait."

Amar's whisper snaps me back to reality. I'm in my body, in this place. Demons surround me, and the manor is only a few yards away. In that timeless moment, I've crossed the entire clearing like reality bent itself around me.

I swallow hard. What the hell?

"You okay?" he asks.

I don't know how to answer. "Something's wrong here. Just…feels weird."

He watches me for a moment, weighing options.

"I'm not leaving," I say.

He frowns, but he doesn't argue. "Then stay behind me."

I nod and start to take a step back. My eyes register the bodies several yards away.

My gorge rises. They've been shot, just once but straight through the heart from the look of it. The blood on their chests is still wet.

Oh God.

I get behind Amar without a word. The Volgert people start forward again, heading to the thick wooden doors. I pull my attention from the bodies, locking it on the manor. Graffiti covers the front entrance, and carvings in the wood have all but obscured what must have been ornate scroll-work once upon a time. Now the door looks like it's been nearly devoured by a bunch of teenage termites.

One of the bodyguards pushes the door wide, staying clear of the opening. Nothing happens. With careful, prac-ticed movements, they slip around the frame and disappear into the shadows. Others follow, and a few moments later, the word comes back. All clear.

I don't trust them. How could it be? I know Arlene or someone has to be here. The bodies—

The werewolves' eyes snap to the forest behind us. Katsuro and the other vampires do the same. They stare at the woods like the trees have come to life and all of hell is bearing down toward us.

But I can't pick up on anything. The woods are silent. The whole world is, in a way too unnerving to be natural.

And suddenly, I hear it. The howling. The chittering. It's off in the distance like a nightmare on the horizon, and I can't see its source. But it gets louder. Becomes a crashing, a tearing, a screaming from inside the woods. It's closing in. It's surrounding us on all sides.

"Shadow-cross!" Amar orders the others. "Now!"

He grabs my hand, drawing me with him toward the side of the house and the line of shadow cast by the moonlight there.

One of the Volgert guards ahead of us races across the line of shadow, but he doesn't disappear. He doesn't even move. For only a heartbeat, he freezes like a snapshot before I see him turn his head toward us, his eyes going wide.

His head keeps turning. Too far, too sharp. His bones snap—wet, popping sounds, like twigs inside meat that begin to grind on each other—as his body bends. Contorts. Twists impossibly until it wrings from him a strangled scream. He starts to contract then, drawing in like he's being suctioned into nothingness. I can't do anything but stare.

Amar pulls me away, hides my face with his arm, but the image is burned into my mind. The man's screams become distorted, as if they're being drawn away too. Holding me tightly, Amar retreats. I stumble along with him.

"Get inside the manor," he says to the others, his voice tight. "Barricade the—"

I look up when he cuts off.

I wish I hadn't.

A horde rushes from the woods. No other word describes it. Zombies flash through my mind, along with every horror movie I've ever seen. Stumbling, staggering, and shoving over top of one another, the mob of people surges toward us like the forest has unleashed a flood. Their hands claw at the air; their mouths gape wide. Their clothes are stained, rusted brown in broad smears like old blood. I swear they are people, but they look insane. Screaming, rabid, and insane.

Touched.

"In the house!" Amar shouts.

The howls grow louder. More desperate, but successful, and I recognize that sound. I heard it before we saved Ruby, when she thought we were going to feed her the mist. Over a hundred throats let out that cry now, and it makes my legs want to become jelly with horror.

I scramble up the broad stone stairs. The open door to the manor looms ahead of me like a black void, but I don't care. I race inside, throwing a frantic look over my shoulder while the others stream past me. Outside, the horde is coming closer, closer, closer.

The demons slam the door shut. Others move fast to drag anything they can find in front of it. There isn't much. The broken hull of a bookcase. A three-legged chair. Vandals have long since made off with anything remotely heavy or useful.

Leaving us nothing.

"Guard the windows," Katsuro orders. "Anything you can—"

Something crashes into the door. I think it's people. Howls of frustration, of desperate hunger, come from beyond the heavy wood.

I look around. The hallway is a shamble of old beer cans, moldy curtains dragged in from god knows where, and walls with holes punched through. The rotted boards show past holes in the water-stained floral wallpaper, jagged like broken teeth. Wires trail from a ring of molding up above, marking where a lamp must once have been.

Useless. All of it, useless.

"Go to the back," Amar says to the others. "Rear door or a window. Whatever you find. Head for the forest."

Another thud comes from the door behind me. I hear wood cracking. What do the Touched do to you, once they grab you? What *can* they do?

From the faces of the demons around me, I'm guessing it isn't good. At the set, the Touched had been kept in cages that could stop a rhinoceros. In fights, they were surrounded by demons with cattle prods while they tore each other apart with their bare hands. Maybe there was something to that. Maybe Ruby was holding back when she grabbed Amar's arm, or Penny was when she grabbed mine. Maybe they hadn't wanted to damage their food source.

But they'd been alone, not surrounded by an equally rabid horde that would fight over us.

Maybe now the Touched would try to tear us apart, if only to get to us first.

Sorcha rushes toward me. "Back hallway, now."

I nod, stumbling away from the door. A hall is behind

me, past the stairs, black and gaping like everything else in this horrible place. I can't tell what's beyond it, where another exit from this place even is. We stayed in the main rooms when I came here with Ruby, years ago. Exploring wasn't big on our to-do list, considering the floors could give way.

And then the front door does.

Splintered wood scatters across the entryway floor. The heavy door flies wide. The Touched pour through the opening, tumbling in like a flood made of humans. At the head of the tide, some of the Touched go down, stumbling or staggering from the push of the others behind them. But the torrent continues on, more Touched scrambling over them, crushing them into the grit and broken tile.

And they're fast. God, they're so fast. How in the hell did I never know the Touched were *this* fast? They charge toward us, and I feel like all their eyes are fastened on me. On Amar. On any incubus and succubus in the room. I know it's crazy, but I'd swear they're staring right at us, like a nightmare I can't escape.

The monsters are coming for me.

Glass crashes in the rooms on either side of me. I hear shouts, growls. More Touched pour in from the parlors, and in only a moment, they're between Amar and me. Sorcha grabs my arm, dragging me back and swiping a hand at a Touched that has come close. The man falls back, bloodied gashes on his chest.

The demons closest to the horde brace themselves, snarling, but instantly, I have the answer to my question. The Touched fly at them. They tear at them. Blunt teeth and fingernails aren't the same as fangs or claws, but it doesn't matter. Cannibals don't care. The Touched rip into the demons like they're shredding through a wall, barely even looking at their victims, barely even registering whatever damage the demons manage to inflict.

And they're still looking at Amar and me.

Horror spreads through me, deep and cold, freezing my bones. I'm not crazy.

I'm dinner.

"Go!" Katsuro shouts.

I lose sight of him as the horde of Touched sweeps past him.

"Sorcha!" I hear Amar yell. "Get Cait out of here!"

Wait, *what*?

I stagger as Sorcha drags me into the hallway, her claws digging into my arm. The mob races after us, snarling, hungry. But I'm not leaving. I won't leave—

The Touched charging toward me topple like they're dominos. I catch sight of Amar beyond them, feel the breath of cold that I know comes with his power, and I see the pained, desperate look in his eyes.

Sorcha hauls me around a turn of the corridor, and I lose him.

"Wait!" I cry. "We can't just leave—"

"Yes, we can."

"Sorcha!"

"Cait." She hauls me around another turn. "We need to stay out of his way."

Her voice is flat. Cold. I look to her, my feet stumbling to keep up with her rapid pace. "But—"

Sorcha glances at me, her eyes gleaming like an animal's, and even in the darkness, I know I won't win. Not without hurting her.

She has her orders.

Horror crushes my chest as we wind through the halls. I won't leave Amar. I can't. But the corridor is a shadowy pit around me, and I can't see any way back to help Amar. Moonlight pierces the darkness from underneath the closed doors around me, but Sorcha doesn't slow. Even I can hear the glass breaking in those rooms, hear the Touched howling while they scramble through the windows. They'll be on us at any second. Those thin doors won't hold.

A crash comes from up ahead. Shouts too. Sorcha slams to a halt, and I do the same.

Oh God.

The doors behind me split. Moonlight glows on the hands scrabbling at the wood, at the handle, at anything they can reach.

Sorcha curses. The Touched pour around the turn behind her, several demons fleeing ahead of them, blocking our path.

We're trapped.

"Run!" Sorcha takes off with me in tow, retreating down the hall, and I don't know where she's going. There's no way out of here. "At the turn, keep going strai—"

She cuts off with a cry. My arm flares with pain when her clawed hand rips away. I look back.

The doors are open and the moonlight is enough. I can see them pouring down the hallway, tumbling over each other to reach me. But I can't find Sorcha. I hear an inhuman snarl amid the howls, hear cries of pain I hope come from the Touched and not her.

And then they're on me.

Hands grab at my arm, my hair, taking my feet from under me. Memories flare like firecrackers across my vision as I crash to the ground, and I shove the colors back, driving them away from me with all my strength.

Screams follow. I scramble back to my feet and run for all I'm worth, racing around the turn of the hall before I risk casting a glance over my shoulder.

More lights. More colors. One of the Touched is right on top of me, ahead of the rest. His face is a rictus of rage, his mouth agape, and his eyes and hair are wild. Bloodstains mar his striped polo shirt and ripped khakis. Dark moisture drips from his hands and teeth. With a viselike grip, he snags my arm and spins me around, slowing me down.

I shove the nightmarish kaleidoscope of memories back at him. His eyes fly wide. The crazed look fades. Fear crosses his face, and pain and confusion too, filling his expression for all of a heartbeat, as if he's only a lost child. But a moment later, he begins screaming again, collapsing to the ground and clawing at his own skin like I've thrown acid on him.

That wasn't…Ruby had looked like that when I…

I can't finish the thought. More Touched are racing after me. The turn creates a bottleneck, slowing them, but it won't work for long. Already they're rounding the corner, scrambling over each other in an effort to reach me faster.

But I can see the colors. Flares and flashes that blur until they become a rainbow-colored mist. Images blur too, but if I let them in just enough, if I push them back just like this, if I'm *careful*…

The nearest Touched staggers. Her eyes go wide with fear, with horror.

I fight to stop myself from hurting her, from letting *whatever* the hell it is I'm doing press in on her farther.

She doesn't fall.

I gasp, turning my eyes to the next closest. Images rush at me and then back to their owner, fast as thought, fast as lightning under control. The man gasps too, like he's just been woken from a nightmare, and I pull back, not pushing any harder.

And I don't stop. I can't stop. More are coming; a never-ending flood. More images fly to me and away, faster, faster. But something is changing. Something feels strange, like a tingling spreading up through my feet, up through my limbs. Like I can feel the colors now, not just see them. Like they're rushing into my veins from the very ground beneath my feet.

I'm not running anymore. I'm not sure when I stopped. Now I'm moving forward, and the Touched are retreating. But they're not the Touched anymore. They're just people. Dozens of them. I'm taking in the memories and returning them as fast as my eyes can move. I walk onward, and the people pull back, parting like a sea. Energy thrums through me, carrying me like I'm riding a tide. I stretch out my palms, and I swear I can feel it surging up from the ground beneath my feet. My limbs tingle while I pass through the flood of people, turning them to human as I go.

Sorcha is ahead of me.

I blink, holding myself back from pushing memories at her. She's become a wolf now, enormous and terrifying. Blood streaks her fur, but I can't tell if it's hers. I somehow doubt it. Bodies surround her like a barricade. She lets out a snarling sort of bark at the sight of me. I wonder if it's my imagination that I hear a surprised question in the sound.

But images flash through my mind when I see her. A forest. Other wolves, racing with me between the trees and bushes. My brothers, young and carefree. Then a house. A fire. Two people inside. My parents, screaming. They can't get out. I can't reach them.

The memories fade like smoke. But I don't fall. I don't get lost this time. Instead, I keep walking, pacing past her, changing the Touched still clamoring to get to her. She jogs after me in wolf form. I come upon the other demons, the ones I'd seen racing toward us before the Touched filled the hall. They've formed a cluster, each with their back to the other, but blood drips from countless wounds as if in testimony to the fact they'd been doomed. At the sight of me, the group freezes in mid-defense, confusion taking the place of terror on their faces.

And soon, there are no Touched left. At least not here.

The demons stare at me, but I barely notice. Magic pours up through me, still. I turn, heading for the main room. The former Touched—sane and oh-so-human now— part ahead of me. They're watching Sorcha, the massive wolf with blood on her fur at my side. They're watching me and the others too, fear in their eyes at the sight of us.

Demons, all.

Discomfort tugs at me while I near the main room. I'm not just a demon. I'm not *only* a demon. I'm human too, and I—

A crash comes from beyond the turn of the hall.

Adrenaline shoots through me, fracturing the strange sensation of magic rushing up from beneath my feet. "Amar!" I shout.

A cry of pain carries down the corridor. It sounds like it comes from a guy.

It sounds horribly familiar.

Fear shreds the last of the tingling coursing through my veins. I take off, barreling through the hallway toward the main room. The door is gone, and the large foyer is a slaughterhouse. One of Katsuro's people is on the ground in the doorway. The Touched are rushing over him, past him into the corridor, heading straight for me.

Sorcha yelps behind me like she's shouting a warning.

It's too late. I see the Touched start to collapse. I catch a glimpse of Amar beyond them.

And ice hits me like a wall.

Everything goes cold. My breath is gone like the world is suddenly empty of air. My eyes lock on Amar, and I see the moment he sees me. The pained and gritted determination disappears from his face, transforming to shock, to denial.

To unbridled horror.

His mouth moves, screaming no.

I start to fall. The world tips. The corridor around me blurs, and suddenly—

"Don't," Ruby says.

I'm in our high school bathroom, years ago, when the world was a hell of a different kind. The smell of industrial cleaner stings my eyes and nose, and cold porcelain chills my wrist where it rests on the edge of the sink. Overhead, the utilitarian lights glare down, relentless and merciless as an artificial sun.

Gently, Ruby puts her hand over the little pocket knife clutched in my trembling fist, and from the corner of my eye, I can see our reflections in the scuffed mirror, like a movie playing out about how to intercede with a suicidal person. But there's real compassion in her eyes.

"Whatever it is," she says, "please don't let it kill you."

A charge runs through me, coursing in a wave from deep inside my body and out through my limbs. And my foot steps backward fast, bracing me before I fall. The rotted ceiling snaps into focus, and air rushes into my lungs. My body quivers like every muscle has suddenly woken up from being numb.

"Cait!" Amar's hands grab me as if to catch me. He appears terrified and sounds it too.

I blink. Let out a breath. Take in another. "Yeah?"

He stares at me.

I straighten, looking around. I almost wish I hadn't. The room is a nightmare, utterly overwhelming. Most of the Touched are dead. So many others too. A few demons have the remaining Touched pinned down, though it's taking a number of them just to hold the survivors to the ground. I see Katsuro, alive and staring at me like he's never seen anything like me before in all his life. Many of the demons are staring at me too.

Shivering, I pull my attention back to Amar. "Are you okay?"

Amar appears dumbstruck. "You...you aren't..." His hands run up and down my arms like he's trying to convince himself I'm really here. I can feel him shaking.

"I, um, I need to..." An explanation fails me, mostly because I don't have one. I step past him, past the dead Touched on the ground, seeking the others. Any of them still alive.

It's even easier to change them back than before.

A breath leaves me. The last of the Touched stop struggling, and the demons freeze when their deranged adversaries suddenly panic, shrieking with fear and trying to shield themselves from the demons for the first time. And just like that, the fight is over.

I look back at Amar.

He's still staring, but his attention is torn now between me and the former Touched in the hall. They're taking shelter in the shadows like they're lost, like they can't figure out how they ended up in this hellish place. Their eyes scan across the destruction and death in the main room with terror. I can hear a few of them crying.

"What…what is the meaning of this?" A hefty guy in a ragged dress shirt pushes past the others. His voice trembles despite his attempt at taking charge. "Who are you people?"

I don't know how to begin to answer that.

"Go." Amar motions to several of the demons. "Get them out of here. Safely."

One of the demons nods. She strides past, and I don't think it's my imagination that she gives me a wide berth. "It's okay," I hear her say. "If you'll all please head…um… back down the hall here."

"You should go too," Amar says to me, his voice rough. "I'll send a few of the guards with you, have them take you back to the hotel."

He looks like he wants to beg me to go.

I shake my head. "No. I can help you."

And I need to know what's here. What this is.

All of it.

Amar's mouth moves, but no words come out.

"Where do we go from here?" Katsuro asks.

I glance over to find that he's addressed the question to me.

Like I know where to go.

I look around, at a loss. "I don't—" My attention goes to the stairs.

There's nowhere else. And something about it feels… right, like the weird atmosphere of this place is more *concentrated* in that direction.

My skin crawls. I don't want to go up there.

I remember the guy who tried to shadow-cross. The

places around town that have been catching fire, and the young man who died because of it. God only knows what saving the Touched around me has done to the city.

And that doesn't even bring into it the weird feeling still tingling in the air around me.

I exhale slowly, trying to stay calm. I *really* don't want to go up there.

I'm not sure whether whatever is in this place is going to give me much of a choice.

Katsuro seems to read the fact I can't take my eyes from the path to the upper floors. "Right." The vampire strides toward the stairway. "Let's get this over with, then."

21

CAIT

I CLIMB THE STEPS INTO THE DARKNESS, EXPECTING ARLENE TO jump out at me at any moment. I feel like I'm a kid again, like I'm ten years old and sneaking to my bedroom after yet another night of hiding from my stepmother, hoping she won't wake up to punish me.

Of course, now I have magic that could kill her.

I take a quick breath. I don't want that. I want this to stop, not to kill anyone.

She might not give me another option.

Struggling to push the thoughts aside, I continue after Katsuro up the last of the steps. He left some of his people behind us, guarding the rear, while the rest surround us like the watchful guards I know they are. It's dark on the second floor, though strangely not as bad as on the first. Windows are few and far between, but many of them are broken, letting in moonlight as much as they've already let in nature. Dead leaves, driven by the wind, cluster in corners, and open doorways reveal rooms that only occasionally have furniture or, in some cases, floors. The ancient wallpaper has peeled away, dripping with condensation and mildew, and revealing holes in the boards and drywall. The smell of dust and mold makes my nose itch. The last thing I need to do is sneeze and draw attention from someone hiding up ahead.

Not that there seems to be anybody.

I peer into yet another doorway. There's no one. We're nearly halfway around the entire second floor, and yet I haven't seen a single trace of—

My eyes twitch to a window, and I stop. There are people outside on the edge of the forest. They aren't moving closer; they're just watching this place. "Katsuro," I whisper.

He glances back and then follows my gaze. "Linden."

"You sure?"

Katsuro nods. "I recognize a few. Don't worry, *this* I expected. If they come closer, my people downstairs will handle them."

He continues on. It takes me a moment before I can follow.

I hope he's right.

My eyes dart around while I trail him past the next turn. Like the one before, there's nothing here. Just empty rooms with rotting floors that sag all too easily under my feet. My vision has adjusted to the darkness as best it can, but everything is still a mess of leaves and wallpaper and gray shadows broken up by moonlight.

And that's it. We circle the remainder of the second floor, disturbing moths and spiders and nothing beyond that, before we head for the third.

It's possible they left, I tell myself. Maybe Arlene and whomever she's with couldn't find anything here too.

Maybe this is a trap.

I file the thought under "Not Helpful" and try to focus. Why would Linden have that first group of guards outside if there isn't anything to protect? And then there is whatever blocked shadow-crossing to consider, because that isn't remotely normal, nor something that should be happening if nothing is here. I think it's still blocking us, too. Maybe even getting worse. The air feels charged, like I'm standing at ground zero of an impending lightning strike.

Arlene has to be here somewhere.

I keep going. The third floor is a worse wreck than the one below. The windows were covered up, once upon a time, and most of the boards have survived the ravages of teenagers and vandals better than those on the lower levels. Parts of the floor have collapsed, though, leaving holes that my eyes can barely pick out in the moonlight. Amar guides me around them. I hear wind through the gaps in the wall, carrying through the house in whispers, and scuttling noises greet our approach, hinting at rats. Spiderwebs trail around us, already broken in places.

Someone else *has* to have been here. But where did they go?

I glance around in confusion. We've searched everywhere, but there's no one. Nothing. No sound, no trace, no—

My hand reaches out, touching the wall all on its own. But there isn't a wall. There's a door, and a handle too.

I blink at it in the moonlight. I had no idea that was there. Why did I reach out to—

My skin crawls. Something is *so* wrong in this place.

"Hey," I hiss to the others. They turn, and I can feel their confusion more than see it in the darkness.

"What?" Amar whispers back.

"The door."

Silence. "What?"

He can't see it.

My discomfort grows. So wrong…so *very* wrong here.

But my hand turns the handle anyway. I need to know.

I ease the door open. Dusty air brushes past me, carrying strange scents. Mold and mildew, but something else too. Something I *know* shouldn't be here, but I can't place the smell.

A dark stairwell waits behind the door, leading upward. Voices carry down the steps, indistinct. I recognize one of them. I'd know her voice anywhere, considering it's been harassing and insulting and criticizing me for the better part of twenty years. But beyond even that, there's something else.

I start up the steps.

"Cait!" Amar whispers, furious.

I can't stop. It's up here. Something is up here.

The answer.

I don't even know the question. I didn't even know there *was* a question, not until now. I just *know* I need to be up there, to see this, to understand what this is, because whatever it is, it's here.

On a normal day, that thought wouldn't be comforting. But on a normal day, I'd also be running for the hills.

The voices grow louder.

"—how much longer? They'll be coming."

Rage twists through me. Kyle.

"Who cares about them?" Penny. Oh God, it's Penny. Arlene found the psychic. Or the psychic found her. And that…that is *so* bad.

She probably knows we're here.

My heart is racing. I feel like I can't breathe. It's not just Penny, though. The air is getting stranger. Tingling still, and with that same odd smell, but stronger.

The steps don't creak under my feet, though I'd swear they should. Cobwebs infest this place, clinging to the walls like a second layer of wallpaper, but they don't stick to me when I pass. The door above me is open a crack, spilling a silvery sort of glow down the weathered, splintered stairway. It looks like moonlight, but wrong somehow.

Like everything else.

"It's coming, you silly!" Penny continues. "It's *coming*!"

That really can't be good.

It also feels true.

I creep up the last of the steps. I feel as if something is calling to me now. Like singing, but beyond the range of normal hearing.

I should leave.

I can't.

My hand moves on its own again, pushing open the door. I hear Amar behind me, whispering my name desperately, and I know he's coming closer. Following me. But I'm unable to stop. I take the final step and enter the room.

The door delivers me to the corner of the room, and the windows on the far wall make the source of the moonlight clear. The ceiling is a hole-ridden wreck, adding to the glow. Penny is in a corner, her hands pressed to the aged wood of the walls like she's expecting it to do something. Kyle is in the center of the space. Something about his body language gives me the impression he'd rather be anywhere else.

And Arlene is looking out a window on the other end of the room.

"It's coming any *second*!" Penny whirls. "It's—"

She catches sight of me, and her eyes go wide like I'm one of the ghosts this house supposedly contains. "You... You're *dead*!"

Arlene turns from the window. Behind me, I hear others come in. My peripheral vision confirms it's Amar and Katsuro, along with Sorcha and several of the Guardians.

The air feels like it's made of pure electricity. Something is *so* wrong...

Penny's eyes go from me to Amar and back, her mouth gaping like a fish. "No!" She stomps her foot like a furious child. "*No*! I saw him do it! In a dozen futures, a *hundred*! He killed you! He hit you with his power, and you died in his—"

Light erupts in the center of the room, bursting into existence only a few feet from where Kyle stands. For a heartbeat, it looks like a glowing ball of white fire, searing my eyes, hovering at chest height above the floor, and then it swirls outward. Upward. It flies apart and becomes a spinning ring of silver flames with something more in its center.

A vortex. My eyes feel like they're being dragged through the distance there, into the rainbow of lights that whirl like a carnival ride gone insane. The depth never seems to end, and my mind can't make sense of the sight. It tugs at me like all of oblivion has opened up in the room, like all of oblivion waits for me. If I stare for any longer, I'm going to go mad.

Crying out, I rip my gaze away.

No one has moved.

I don't think they can.

A ragged breath escapes me, so loud in the strange silence. Kyle is frozen, one foot above the ground like he is stumbling back from the vortex. Amar is reaching for me, his hand in the air only inches from my shoulder. Likewise, Katsuro seems caught mid-motion to his people, and Penny's face is a rictus of confused and thwarted rage.

Arlene still has her eyes on me.

Warily, I step closer. She's not blinking, not breathing, as paralyzed as the rest. I'm the only one in the room who isn't.

My eyes twitch to the vortex. What the hell?

Arlene charges at me.

I stumble back, but she's already striking out. I see the green flash, the electricity coming right at me, and I can't get out of the way.

The blast curves in the air, drawn toward the vortex like a magnet, burning past my face. I can feel its heat, and then it disappears into the swirling, kaleidoscopic void.

Which grows larger.

I gasp, but Arlene is still coming. I try to strike out at her.

Same result. Purple lightning whips away into the maelstrom, making it grow. The vortex is almost on top of us now.

It wants me to come inside.

I retreat, bumping into Kyle, who wobbles like I've run into a plastic mannequin. But my feet slip as if the ground is sludge. I can't move away from the vortex. The convergence is there. I need to go toward it. And something else...something...

Arlene slams into me. I tumble backward onto the rough wooden floor.

"You spoiled little bitch!" Arlene shrieks. "You ruined my life!"

I try to scramble away, but I'm not fast enough. She crashes down on top of me, and her hands wrap around my throat. My fingers claw at them, at her face, at anything in reach, but she barely even flinches. I can see colors flaring around her, still muted and strange. I can't get enough of a grasp on them to shove them back at her. To save myself.

"I had everything!" Her hands tighten. Blood pounds in my head, in my ears. "Everything!"

My hand flails out, trying to find a weapon, anything, but the room is empty. The vortex swirls behind her. She pins me down, squeezing my neck tighter, tighter. My legs kick, useless and slowing. I can't escape.

I'm going to be killed by my evil stepmother.

"You'll pay," she snarls. "Right here, right now. You're going to pay for every single insufferable second I had to keep you alive all these years, and for everything you took when you walked into my house and brought this world back down on my head! Do you hear me?"

My hands aren't moving right anymore. They're prying at her fingers, but they keep slipping.

"And after this, I'm going after your dear daddy too, understand? That old bastard's finally going to die, and it'll be *all your fault*."

No. Please God, no.

Light and darkness splatter and dance across my vision, but I can still see her grin. "No way I'm letting some human run around, knowing what I am."

My mouth is moving, fighting for air, fighting to scream. My body feels distant, heavy, like a big thing of clay I can't seem to operate. My entire world is drawing down, becoming small and trapped inside my own head.

But hot.

White-hot.

Blinding.

"He's dead," Arlene whispers in my ear. "Bloody dead, just like your mother. And it's all because of *you*."

My world explodes. Arlene's hands disappear from my throat. Blood rushes out from my head, and I choke, my own hand grabbing where hers had been as if to protect myself. My vision clears fast, too fast, and I see her fly backward, through the air, into Kyle.

Into the vortex.

I scramble to my feet, coughing and staring. Arlene collides with Kyle, and he topples with her, the two of them falling, falling, down and away. And around them, the vortex begins to change. Pulse. Throb and flash like it's suddenly unstable. The swirling magic begins to contract, spiraling in tighter and tighter while the edges flare as if they want to set fire to everything close by. I try to move back, but I can't. The pull is still there, trapping me and yet pouring into me, *through* me. It wants me to go forward. To follow them down into oblivion because it needs me there. My foot slips forward on the wood-slat floor while my eyes lock on the impossible distance, unable to look away, watching as my stepmother and the bastard who hurt my best friend tumble forever into an ever-shrinking infinity.

But then infinity changes too. Kyle and Arlene are gone, and I see something else in the distance. A city of skyscrapers, flashing before my eyes like it's been there the whole time and I just hadn't registered it. And then an alley with strange graffiti on the walls in brilliant colors.

And then a desert stretching out beneath a sunrise, saguaro cacti standing tall in the rocks and sand.

And an old woman.

I flinch. The desert stills behind her like someone slowed down a movie, the sand and sunrise holding place at the edge of eternity, except she's not in it. Standing ramrod straight, she's poised amid the vortex of light and color, her long silver hair stirring as if in a faint breeze. She turns her head and meets my eyes over the impossible distance.

Her lips curl into a cold smile. "There you are."

The vortex collapses.

I stumble back, gasping. I hear growing shouts of alarm around me, rising like the world is being brought back up to speed after being put on pause.

Which is exactly what it looks like.

I look around fast. The magic is gone. My stepmother and Kyle too. Where they had been, only empty air remains. The strange smell is fading too. I recognize it now. Creosote bushes in the desert after a rain. I remember that from Arizona when Ruby and I visited her family, years ago. But meanwhile, the others are starting to move, slow like they're pushing through air that has become molasses.

Oh God, this is creepy. And yet—

It's the only chance I'm going to get. I rush at Penny.

Time returns.

"—arms!" Penny shrieks.

Her bright blue eyes go wide with alarm. I grab her, shoving her backward into the wall as hard as I can and holding her there.

She gapes at me. "How did you—"

Her fist swings at me. I snag her wrist, pinning it.

"What *are* you?" She yanks at my grip and then swings

at me again with her free hand. I struggle to grab it too without letting her go. *"What are you!"*

"Help me!" I yell to the others.

Katsuro appears at my side, grabbing the girl too. Penny flails, unable to break the vampire's hold while he pulls her from the wall and hands her off to his people.

"Do it," he orders.

One of his people produces a syringe from a pocket of their cargo pants. They jab the needle into Penny's neck.

The girl shrieks, but her struggles begin to slow. She doesn't take her eyes off me. "What are you?" Her head begins to loll, her voice growing weaker. "What *are* you?"

I wish I knew.

They carry her from the room.

"Cait," Amar says, coming up next to me. "Are you all right?"

I don't know what to say. I nod.

"Is it gone?" Katsuro asks. From the corner of my eye, I see him watching me, checking.

I nod again. "I think so."

"And your stepmother?"

I swallow hard. My throat hurts. There are almost certain to be bruises.

Probably not as many as there should be.

Shivers creep through my skin. "Gone too. And Kyle."

Silence follows. "Gone where?" Katsuro presses. "How?"

I blink, suddenly wondering what they'd seen. What they'd been able—no, that's not the right word. Somehow, I know it's not the right word. What they'd been *allowed* to see. The light and then…

This is getting to be too much.

"I…" Floundering, I shake my head. "She, uh…"

"Later," Amar interjects. He puts a hand on my shoulder, careful, gentle.

I make a short noise of agreement. Yeah, later. Or never. Or…I don't know when.

My eyes creep back to the space where the vortex had been.

There you are.

I bolt from the room.

2 2

CAIT

SUNRISE HAS PASSED IN THE TIME WE'VE BEEN IN THE ATTIC, but it doesn't matter. The magic of the vortex—of the *convergence*—is fading from this place, and suddenly, shadow-crossing works again.

Alistair's people appearing in the hallway are enough of a clue.

The Volgert guards and Katsuro's Guardians make quick work of them, though, the advantage of numbers and enough adrenaline to last us all a lifetime shifting the odds decisively in our favor. And then we're gone, back to the hotel, security measures around the place allowing us through and blocking anyone from following.

Or so Amar tells me.

Hours later, when everyone alive is accounted for and all the wounds have been bandaged, I'm sitting in the hotel dining area, watching the late-afternoon sun cast gold light on the carpet. A mug of coffee and an uneaten sandwich are going cold on the dark wood tabletop in front of me. Sorcha lounges at a table nearby, her leather jacket slung over the back of the chair beside her. A Celtic knot tattoo glistens on her upper arm, the intertwined loops of a tree and its roots seeming formed out of an ink that shines like bronze in the sunlight. She doesn't look my way while she casually sips her own coffee, her attention on anyone who would dare to come into the room. Not that there are many people who still seem to be staying here—I think Volgert's forces quietly encouraged them out.

It's awfully quiet for a hotel, really.

Katsuro's people are taking care of Penny, locking her in a secure location Nasreen had prepared. They aren't going to kill her, Katsuro said, though I'm not sure they shouldn't. She tried to murder Amar. Me. If she gets free, she'll almost certainly try again.

It's grisly, thinking like that. When did I become so cold?

When did I realize I had to be?

I shift on the mauve fabric of the chair, uncomfortable with my own thoughts. Sorcha glances over, her eyebrow twitching up in silent question. I shake my head. "Nothing."

She goes back to watching the door.

I'm not sure what we're going to do now that Penny is captured. The convergence seems to be fading too. I feel more normal with every passing moment, like a thunderstorm is rolling onward, its damage now come and gone. Martin and Nasreen are watching it, but I almost don't need their report.

I know it's leaving. I don't know why, but it is.

Linden is still around here, though, and Alistair won't be too inclined to simply leave us alone, especially now that Amar has taken charge of Volgert. Corvinson isn't safe. Life can't get back to normal, as much as I wish it could. And meanwhile, the question remains of where we can go.

Amar comes around the corner, a trio of bodyguards trailing him. That's going to be a common sight too, I realize. Bodyguards.

A few weeks ago, we were just college students.

Discomfort twists in my chest. I try to ignore it. "Hey."

"Hey. You doing okay?"

I nod, more or less telling the truth. I'm alive. I didn't fall into the swirling vortex that swallowed Kyle and my stepmother. I didn't get killed by a horde of Touched— most of whom have been delivered to police stations around the city, in the hope the bad guys can be sorted from the good, and the innocent can go home. On the whole, I figure that's close enough to claim okay.

Details notwithstanding.

"You?" I ask.

"Yeah." Amar comes farther into the room, stopping the guards from following him with a brief motion. He's a natural at this, I think. I wonder if he would think that's a good thing. "Listen, whenever you're ready, there are some, uh—" He looks almost embarrassed. "—properties we could take a look at. Maybe figure out where to go from here?"

"Yeah, sure."

He hesitates. "It's not forever. Just until we can—"

"I know."

Amar nods. "Okay, then—"

My phone buzzes. I blink, jarred by the sudden sound, before tugging the cell from my pocket and glancing at the number on the screen.

I don't recognize it. With a wary look at Amar, I swipe the icon to accept the call.

"Cait?"

I freeze. Ruby. Oh my God, it's actually Ruby. She—

"Cait, are you there?" She sounds breathless, like she's been running. I hear traffic in the background. Commotion like a city street. Where is she?

"Y-yeah, I'm here." I don't know what to say. "Are you okay?"

A scoff leaves her. Answer enough. My heart starts to pound for a whole different reason. "What's wrong?" I ask.

The noise from the other end becomes muffled. She's talking to someone. A guy from the sound of it. I can't make out their words, and I don't recognize his voice.

"Ruby?"

"Yeah, I'm here. Cait, listen, I know it's asking a lot, but can you come to Arizona as soon as possible? Amar too?"

Oh, this can't be good. Not good on more levels than I can *name*.

City. Desert. The smell of creosote after the rain…

I shove the thoughts aside fast. There's no question, at least where I'm concerned. "I'm on the next flight. What's going on?"

She makes a relieved noise, but there's an edge to it too. "I need your help. Both of you. We have a problem."

The Demon Guardians Series will continue!

To make sure you hear about the next release, join my New Release List at skyemalone.com/mailinglist. You'll receive an email notification on release day.

ABOUT THE AUTHOR

Skye Malone writes action-packed fantasy and paranormal romance. A fan of magical books since childhood, they adore stories that pit ordinary characters against extraordinary odds and reveal the strength within. Abandoned buildings are their passion, along with old castles and deep, dark parts of the forest where anything is possible. A graduate of the University of Illinois with a degree in English literature, Skye lives in the USA Midwest with a retired racing greyhound and a three-legged mutt.

amazon.com/author/skyemalone

bookbub.com/authors/skye-malone

facebook.com/authorskyemalone

goodreads.com/skyemalone

instagram.com/authorskyemalone

twitter.com/Skye_Malone

ACKNOWLEDGMENTS

Whenever I write an acknowledgments section in a book, I am always afraid I'm going to leave someone out.

As I often do, I'll lead off by thanking my family because, in all honesty, without them none of this would be possible. My mother and my sister keep me grounded, and their love gets me through every day.

I also, as always, want to thank my friend Robin Augsburg for her help with grammar questions (and, sometimes, grammar debates), and for how her humor, support, and friendship keep me going. Thank you, Robin.

Thanks as well go to my friend and fellow author Sara Whitney for beta-reading, brainstorming, and for all her great support.

For her insightful sensitivity read and all her input, many thanks go to Veronica of Salt & Sage. My gratitude also goes to Erin Olds, owner of Salt & Sage, for coordinating communications, scheduling, and for being an absolute pleasure to work with.

Thank you to my Facebook reader group for their suggestions and help with my various questions.

And last but absolutely *not* least, thank you to *you* for buying this book, for reading this book, for hopefully leaving a review if you liked this book, and for making this wonderful author career possible. You have my deepest gratitude.

www.ingramcontent.com/pod-product-compliance
Lightning Source LLC
Chambersburg PA
CBHW050828190726
48286CB00007B/2008